VELORIO

VELORIO

A Novel

XAVIER NAVARRO AQUINO

HarperVia

An Imprint of HarperCollins*Publishers*

HarperCollins books may be purchased for educational, business, or sales promotional use. For information, please email the Special Markets Department at SPsales@harpercollins.com.

FIRST HARPERVIA EDITION PUBLISHED IN 2022

Designed by Bonni Leon-Berman

Library of Congress Cataloging-in-Publication Data has been applied for.

ISBN 978-0-06-307137-7

22 23 24 25 26   LSC   10 9 8 7 6 5 4 3 2 1

For the thousands lost

and the unaccounted

The fear and dread of you

shall rest on every animal of the earth,

and on every bird of the air,

on everything that creeps on the ground,

and on all the fish of the sea;

into your hand they are delivered.

GENESIS 9:2 (NRSV)

ONE

CAMILA

It wasn't until after I dug out her body that I learned to love my sister, Marisol. You'd think it strange, to see destruction as a way to learn her, to grow with her and our people, but that's how it went. It started with the mudslide that came through and busted my bedroom window. As huracán María raged outside, Marisol slept with all our dreams.

No one can tell you how much pressure is outside during a huracán. In the rain clouds unstitched, the wind breezing, and the storm, a large squeeze in your entrails and a hum so loud, you begin to forget. Those howls sing in tiresome anger. You feel your ears pop. "Las turbinas de un avión," is what Mami chanted throughout the night. And I felt our house tremble like I believed God was fuming. We all did. Mami held on to us after the lights went. Mami felt the ground shake from under our feet and walked with Marisol and me, hand in hand, to the bathroom. There we curled under the wooden vanity and she prayed, "Dios will be here. He will."

"But what if he's not?" Marisol asked.

"He will!" I snapped back.

That was all I could say or needed to say. She tugged on my dress at first, then moved her fingers away from mine and left us there.

"Marisol!"

"Ya, Mami. I'm going to sleep."

"So, sleep here, nena."

But she didn't listen. She went to my bedroom and shut the door and that was it.

UTUADO WAS BEAUTIFUL. A town that reached heaven, at least downtown where the church is. We lived way up; me, Marisol, Mami, and the neighbors. It was a beautiful place, the town center perched on a hill with a plaza central and all the shops run by friends. They sold yarn for knitters and there were cafeterías where you could get bacalao and tostones every day and as much as you like. Mari and me played there often when Mami ran errands. She spent a lot of days with el licenciado Cabán. She said she needed a lawyer a lot back in those days when Papi was still around. I didn't like Cabán much. He always looked at Marisol funny, with hunger in his eyes even though she didn't have anything to eat. This was before Papi finally disappeared. After Papi, I was happy because we didn't need men like him in our lives. That's what Mari used to say too. She was all sorts of maniática, with that quick and sharp temper which often collided with Mami. But that never bothered me since she loved me in her own way. She was pretty and unafraid. She liked to race me down the thin roads of our barrio, always sprinting down the jagged hillside where the bamboos twisted toward the river crest and the only visible shade of green was a constant fire. Mari wasn't perfect. She needed things her way. Don Papo, our neighbor, used to joke that her manic episodes were her way of becoming a woman. He'd eye her from his butaca as he rocked back and forth, his hands clasping down at his crotch. An absent stare and deep brown eyes that wanted to penetrate us. His aged white skin like a cow's hide would slick in sweat. He called me la fea because I was so big for a twelve-

4

year-old. My arms thick as palm trees. I was strong. I could lift Marisol up so high she reached the clouds. She told me that it didn't matter what children said about me, Don Papo was the vicious type. Whenever we walked by his front porch back from school, Marisol always tried to rush me past his gaze, said to never go outside alone, never turn your back to that viejo sucio. I try to remember as much as I can, but I keep hearing wind and seeing night.

The sea is out there somewhere in the darkness, behind all that used to be green, those tree spines and jagged caves. It takes a lot to get here, the roads narrow as you drive up from Arecibo and I imagine now it is harder to reach us. Energy comes and goes on normal days, so you can guess what mean weather can do. I call it that, even though everyone calls it gasoline and power. But I like Energy because it means more and it's all the same. The people that brought the Energy my entire life warned that if something were to happen to the roads, the Energy would be difficult to repair because we were so far and high on the mountain. That made me chuckle because Energy is something that's never consistent. It's fragile. Some of us bought these portable electricity sources, but I hated them because when they were on, they sounded like lawnmowers, and if the Energy was gone for more than a day, the night was filled with a buzz so loud it was hard to think or sleep. I'm sure the coquíes hated them too because they weren't able to sing to each other.

We all thought we were ready for María. Mami made sure to prep all the food and batteries and clothes. She had her machete sharpened. She was sure the trees around us would snap and fall everywhere, and she'd be the one to clean it all up. As the big night approached and María started making her mess,

Mami sent me to the backyard as soon as the lights went to get the lime green kerosene lamp and machete. The lamp sat in the wooden shack that Mari and me helped build. We looked all over the sides of the mountain for wood the day we decided to build it and Mari always made me carry all the wood. She said I was the strong one even though she's the eldest.

The machete was pierced into a wooden stump. I liked going out into the night because the air felt clean and the stars cast a large net above. I watched as the stars moved and the trees shuddered with the wind and I saw long stacks of smoke rising over the mountain's silhouette as if a giant was ascending into the sky.

I grabbed Mami's things and rushed back and yelled to them that there was something dark climbing our way.

"Mami, two long clouds are out there, and they keep moving toward us."

Mami walked over to the kitchen window and pushed the curtain. "That's smoke, Cami. Don't worry about it. They must be burning something en la plaza."

"But it's moving toward us," I said.

"Estúpida, that's the wind." Marisol said and rolled her eyes.

"Mami . . ." I said. I wanted to cry.

"Leave her alone, Marisol." She turned to me and put her big hands over my head. "Cami, it won't come this way. Don't worry about it, mija. Now, you two come. Let's go to my room."

Mami wanted to sing us both a lullaby, which I always liked but Marisol hated. As María came and turned everything dark, Mami made us crawl into bed with her that night to sing. She started by first humming the words to "Lamento borincano" before shifting to La Lupe. La Lupe was Mami's favorite. I liked La Lupe because her words sounded determined as though she were always angry at someone. They sounded like she needed to sing her songs, or she wouldn't be able to live happily. Mami growled the same way, grunting when she reached for the highest notes. The whole house shook and the flames on the devotionals flickered. That was the power of her voice and she tried to tell us that La Lupe was the person to listen to if we were sad because she gave you powers through her songs. Marisol hated La Lupe, but I liked her.

So Mami started grunting and growling and her dark skin was fire and shadow in the darkness. I curled up next to Mami as she orchestrated the notes with her hands. The wind started picking up outside. Marisol sat on the edge of Mami's bed and picked at her toes with a nail clipper. Her curly black hair fell down her back and she looked beautiful, as if she were a still bronze statue. But as Mami kept singing, Marisol grew impatient.

"Ya, Ma! It's loud outside and now loud in here. I'm tired of those same songs again and again."

Mami didn't listen and kept singing. She winked at me as she continued to move her hands and it made me smile because I knew that Mami was there protecting us with a spell.

"Okay, Ma," Marisol said getting up from the bed and walking toward the door. And Mami stopped midsong.

"Marisol! Come back here. I'm not done."

"It's really hard trying not to freak out and you're over here acting like this is a game."

"A game? Who said anything about a game, Marisol?"

"Forget it, Ma. I'm going to la sala."

"Marisol, ¡quédate aquí! It's safer here."

"It's like death and church in here. I'm going. I need quiet."

"Marisol! I'm not telling you again."

"Ya, Ma!"

Marisol opened the door and a shudder came into the room and the hairs on my back rose and it felt cold. Mami moved out of bed and grabbed Marisol by her thin arms and forced her back inside. She then slammed the door and sat on the bed next to one of her devotionals.

"Ma!"

"Ya, Marisol! Ya! It's safer if we stay together."

The wind started thumping on the windows and the trees outside were alive, screeching and howling louder and louder. I started to miss Mami's singing.

Mami's room was damp and cold and I knew Mari hated being there because she felt everything in there was judging her. Mami's religious things, her many bibles, some bound in leather inscribed with our names, el padre nuestro framed nicely in gold over her night table, crucifixes on the walls, and devotionals. She'd light them every night before bed. Some were lined on the nightstand and others on the wooden dresser. She had a few more in the bathroom behind the toilet seat. I smiled at those because it was like Mami needed help doing her business.

Those devotionals surrounded Mami and I think they made her feel safe and closer to God. Mami was that way. She even tried teaching me how to make rosaries once, but I never got the rhythm because my fingers are sausages. Mari would've been good at it if she had wanted to learn. She had those nice delicate hands, thin and long. I really liked her hands.

Now, I CARRY her with me. It started with me taking a piece of her. The tip of her pinky. The one that stuck out from the

8

mud. I cut it from her hand with a shard of window glass. Only because Mami told me that she is no longer with us. That we would have to wait for the people to come collect her. Mami was too busy seeing me off, trying to nudge me away from all the dead satos washed up by María's currents. Mami never checked up on Marisol so I knew that it was okay.

I never saw Mami cry. When Marisol disappeared into my bedroom, Mami simply went to the window and watched God deconstruct the landscape, María serving as his contractor. She stopped praying but I knew she still believed, so I guess that's why I wanted to perform a resurrection.

A week after María left, Mami spent most of the day counting our water containers, checking to see if we had access to the river to collect what little liquid we could to flush the toilets. She started whacking away with a machete at the web of branches that kept us, for some time, trapped on our end of the street. Her broad black shoulders flexed with every stroke she landed, her short hair disfigured, and her mouth open and breathing heavy. She then started to ration out the little trash bags we had so as to not waste them. She said the mountain of filth would start collecting and we'd need every one of those bags because the garbage people were not coming. Not anymore.

The only time Mami seemed to show any emotion was when I used the toilet. I peed and flushed and Mami stormed into the bathroom with a broomstick and swatted my feet.

"¡Eso no se hace! Do not ever waste water like that again."

"Ma," I started to cry. "I'm tired of the smell. I don't want to keep going on top . . ."

"¡Cállate, Camila! If you flush again without letting more days pass, you will go outside."

So I did. For some time, I took to peeing in the darkness. I tried to wait until I desperately needed to do it, found a spot where two giant palm trees snapped in the middle and served as a natural barrier from the seeing world. Nothing but the quiet moon shining its light helping me avoid making a mess.

After the storm, there was no water in the colmado and I needed to find Marisol some hydration for her lungs and for her wounds. Even though Mami said not to talk to her, to leave her alone, I figured she needed water. Or food. Or something. I think Mami was afraid because we were only prepared to keep hold for two weeks, hoping that aid would come all the way into the forests, to us in Utuado. Mami started losing faith as time passed and that's when I started to worry.

The roads were swept off the mountain and the river camped out in la plaza. All that water around us but none of it drinkable. This was before people got desperate. Some said they started collecting whatever was around. They started by setting all those dead things on fire just to taste something.

When Mami left me alone at night, I'd creep back into my room where a wall of crystalized mud trapped poor Marisol. I'd open the door and see a sweeping brown river frozen in a wave. I worked to chip away at it, every piece of her showing as I jabbed into the petrified guck. Slowly. Excavating Marisol back to life.

During the daytime, I would walk around with Marisol's pinky in my dress pocket and after a while it started to stink. I missed her.

Just after the huracán, like all people, I wanted to return to a normal state. So, I took care to clean Marisol as best I could. It took a little time but when I finally freed her, I dressed her with her favorite pair of jeans. They had a sharp tear on the knee that I thought looked distinguished. I found her nice blue blouse that had a smudge of dried blood on its neckline. Of course, Mami was busy with the machete. She soon moved away from our house and started on the bridge that connected us to el barrio. I knew she was trying to clear a path to God. To ask him if he was planning on getting back to work anytime soon.

"Marisol, we need your help. I need you to wake up so you can help Mami and the town." I shook her after putting clothes on her dusty body. I asked her to take me with her. Wherever she had gone, so far and free from all the water and mud. I asked if she was willing to see through her closed eyes one more time, to try and leave all the green shades I imagined were in heaven. How the shine from the breaking waves in the ocean still captured the sun. That no matter how terrible the island looked, someday, it would all heal.

But Marisol just smiled, her eyes shut from the world.

"Okay, Mari. Okay." I combed her hair with my fingers and imagined how nice she would look with the sun against her skin. Her hand with the missing pinky was a little smelly so I rushed to the shed and teased out some gardening gloves. I went back to her and shoved them on.

"You need fresh air. You are starting to pick up that smell that the satos got after being out and still for so long."

I imagined Mari happy in her new home and I made up conversations thinking how Mami would react if I told her about Mari's new home. Mami would probably object, but that's how I saw us all, talking to walls that didn't respond.

"She is a part of the dirt now and the mountain is us, the mountain is our people. It's all a part of the mountain, the ground, the sky, the sea," Mami said.

"The sky floats, Mami. It belongs to heaven." I said.

"Okay, Camila. But the sky would not exist if the mountain wasn't there. It would then be called something else. Without the earth, the sky isn't the sky."

"And the sea?"

"The sea, Cami. The sea is water and we are all water. But this is our mountain, this is our home. When you are lost, you search for the mountain. When you are lost, you never forget you're home."

"I don't understand, Mami."

"That's okay, Cami. That's okay."

DUSK WAS FALLING over the hillsides and I heard Mami return to our house. I dragged Marisol out from my bedroom and into her quiet den. Mami would never think to look for Marisol there. Must've been, to her, a special place because she didn't even want me in there rummaging through all of Marisol's things. The stillness of all her objects, all the drawers from her dresser begging to be held by familiar hands, all the hangers where her clothes hung longing to be dragged down their metal spine.

Mami had managed to steal a transistor radio from Don Papo and that's where she began to live. At night all that could be heard throughout our house was the barking of Francisco Ojeda passing judgment, and Mami curled up next to his voice on our dining room table, her broad shoulders hiding her face. She listened intently as if she was listening to the songs of a church choir. Trying to understand their celestial glow and pick out the answers that would solve anything. The candlelight that hit her body only gave her a growing shadow that seemed to drape the entire house.

I heard her speak to herself, "When are they coming? ¿Cuándo? Dios mío, where are you?"

I knew then what we needed to do. Marisol and me needed to make it to la plaza, we needed to trek through all the mess and reach the center of town, to find the people and meet them. They spoke of FEMA, of the National Guard, of the Army. The people that would return things back to how they were.

As Mami started to drift into sleep, I rushed back to Marisol. I put her on my shoulders like my school backpack and we set off. She wasn't as heavy as I thought she would be and the night was dry and quiet. All the wind of our island must've left with María. That's why it was so hot after María went far away. For so many days, everyone thought all the dust in the air and the dead sun that dully shone overhead meant God would soon be returning to Earth to pick up his favorites and take them back home to heaven. I thought so too. Maybe that's why Marisol was no longer here. She probably didn't want to leave that place and return to all of this.

I knew I had to be careful because all the light was gone. The governor mandated a curfew. Mami overheard it on the radio and applauded him for it. "It's better to stay safe. To lock ourselves away from all the maleantes that are out on the roads."

"But how will anything ever get fixed, Ma?"

"The police are out there working."

"But they have their own houses to worry about."

"Yes. That's true. That's why Rosselló requires us to be back in our homes. It's for everyone's own good."

I had told her that I heard Yesenia—a cranky older girl-friend of mine—say that they were stealing the life.

"What life?" Mami asked.

"The life of everyone. The trucks. The ones that are carrying all the energy."

"El diesel?"

"I guess."

Mami paused and could only look toward my bedroom. It was as if she were trying to speak to God again through Marisol.

MARISOL AND I moved through the darkness. I wanted to find a place to leave her for the night. I knew I wouldn't be able to see well and that it would be dangerous to tiptoe my way down the cracks and fissures in all the roads. Not to mention the inflated river. If the police people found me, I wondered if they'd take Marisol from me, or try to hide her death from the official numbers being reported to the old government. Mami told me Tío knew of makeshift gravesites. That there were so many stranded bodies drowned by the force of water pillaging houses. And because all the phone lines were destroyed, the alcaldes of all the towns and cities on the island could not justify their dead to Rosselló. I knew that in order to keep my Marisol away from all that, she needed the fresh air, the moon or the burning sun, anything to keep her here with us, however small a piece of her I could trap in this world.

As very young girls, we often played tag and escondite and there was a favorite cave of ours we often used. It was carved into the side of a white coral mountain, where for some mystical reason, tall grass and shrubs refused to grow. We began telling stories to each other every night before bed about the cave. The stories we made up were terrible. Things to keep us awake and scared. Those games felt serious, so we did anything to win. I never liked climbing rock after rock just to catch Marisol fleeing from me. So the stories became more frightening. Such things as how all the older boys would take little girls against their wishes and make them bleed. That Don Papo would be seated on his butaca right at the mouth of the cave, under its long yellow teeth. We'd joke that he'd soon enough turn to stone there, rocking back and forth in his usual rhythm all while he watched the boys as they performed the ritual. Papo, with that same intense desire he watched us with. Every day. How his hands clutched his crotch, his eyes dead and heavy.

We moved along, inching our way toward the cave. Marisol started to gain weight and I needed to catch my breath. Soon enough we reached the gravel road that diverged from the main street, the path that took us to the cave entrance.

I grew tired. There was a fallen ceiba tree serving as a barricade between the gravel and the asphalt. The ceiba's long roots lifted from the ground, a drawn curtain exposing the heart of the earth. I wedged us between its gray roots and sat her on the red dirt while I caught my breath. There, Marisol could wait. She could wait until the stars stopped shimmering and our island returned to the ocean bed. Her jeans were now stained with dirt. A red so familiar.

There was a time when Marisol had a jevito named Ezekiel. And he was older. Much older than me or Marisol. Mami had tried her best to warn us about the types that would linger around schoolyards. I watched them together just before the two of us walked back home. He'd drive up in his rusty Civic and wait at the school entrance for Marisol. She'd tell me to stay in the cafeteria while she caught up with Ezekiel.

I questioned her about Ezekiel, and she snarled back at me to "let it be."

"He's going to take you to the cave and perform the ritual," I'd say.

"Qué graciosita. The only ritual he'll perform is the one where they take him to the hospital."

"But Mari . . ."

"Cami, enough." She put her arm over my shoulder and kissed my cheek. "And don't go telling Mami about any of it."

"Okay."

I SAT NEXT to her and put my hand on her knee. Her head fell to my shoulder and it was just the two of us again, sleeping in the backyard watching the cucubanos light up the darkness with green specs of light, flickering until they died.

We got up and kept trekking the gravel road. The darkness would occasionally leave as the clouds revealed the moon. While I marched, I felt her long curly hair whip against my shoulders; her head slumped to its side. I thought of all the things we could now do together, now that she was away from her muddy prison. Now she could be a spirit overseeing Utuado.

When I reached the cave with Marisol, I sat her on a stone that resembled a stool, next to a rustic rock with a cemí hieroglyph carved onto its face. A rock from the before times when Taínos used the caves as shields to outlast the huracanes. Marisol could live there and the cemí would bear good omens to her and a safe passage between our two worlds.

"Okay, Mari. I will leave you here. Wait for me until I can return and take you to la plaza."

Marisol's body twitched and bent over the ancient rock, her head slumped down, and her hair danced and twisted.

"This is the place of our ancestors, Mari. Don't worry. I'll come back for you."

Her hands fell to her sides and she tumbled from her stool onto the dirty ground. The gardening gloves I placed to hide her stink loosened and detached, her hands were now exposed. I hesitated to help her up because I knew she was angry, that she might be maniática again and thought maybe all I should do was leave her there without saying goodbye.

WHEN I RETURNED to our house, Mami was pacing in the living room. I walked into that dark space and she froze.

"Dónde carajo were you, Camila?"

"I was seeing the river, Ma."

"The river?" She crossed her arms and looked away, patting her toes against the tile floor. The clicking sound echoed in the silence.

"It looked scary, Ma. All swollen and moving against the moon."

"The river!?"

She stomped toward me and grabbed me by my ear.

"¡Que sea la última vez, Mari!"

"What?"

"Cami!" She corrected herself. "¡Que sea la última vez, Cami! If I tell you to stay here because it's dangerous out there, you listen."

"Okay, Ma." I tried to jerk my head away from her grip. "Okay!"

She let me go and disappeared into the kitchen. She brought back her transistor radio and set it on the couch and turned it on. I stood there waiting for her to cool off. Ojeda began again with his yelling. Kept saying how all the towns en el campo were completely wiped out. I thought it funny because we were still here. Waiting.

Ojeda started an hour segment on his radio show where he'd dedicate that time to reading names of those who were lucky enough to call and check themselves in as "safe."

He'd read their names out: José Gabriel Hernández, Yarizel Guzmán, Adien Medina, Carlos López López, Ninoshka Díaz. I couldn't help but hear those names and think only about all the people that were unable to call in. And there was Mami, curled up again next to the radio, next to Ojeda. How she must've wanted desperately for him to comfort her, to tell her that people were on their way. That Rosselló would ride in with God and all his chariots and personally come to deliver us.

"Tomorrow we are going down to the Shell. We need to fill up the candungos with gasoline. The car is low on gas," she said.

"But why? Have you been using it? There's no way out of Utuado. All the roads are gone and . . ."

"Cállate, Camila. I've been looking for help. Everything's closed or the lines are impossible." She paused. "But we need to try."

She patted her hair down. She looked exhausted and her eyes, in that dark living room, were like two black blotches of paint.

"We are getting up early, Cami. At four in the morning we walk to the Shell."

"But what about curfew? It doesn't end until six."

"Stop it, Camila."

And then she finally broke, she started sobbing.

"There aren't enough trucks. There aren't enough drivers. There isn't enough . . ."

I could only make out in those words that there wasn't enough diesel for power.

"The energy?" I asked.

"Yes, hija, the energy. That energy is important to keep everything working."

"Can it bring things back to life?"

"Ay, mija. Just forget it. I'll figure this out. No te preocupes."

"No, Ma. I'll go too. I'll go with you tomorrow."

MAMI AND I walked early the next morning toward the Shell. I carried our candungo like a newborn puppy, embracing its red plastic skin with my thick arms. Mami didn't say a thing to me. Occasionally she would pet my back and gently press me forward. I felt an urgency in her. One that she tried hard to contain within herself, so deep down it was splitting her in two.

When we made it atop the road, atop the hill that overlooked the barrio, the Shell station was swarmed with metal—a line of cars wrapped around the station and disappeared long into the stretch of road, so far away you could no longer see the multicolor in the darkness. I think it reached la plaza miles away. I knew it reached God. There were so many people, too, camping with umbrellas ready for the sun, and all their candungos swarmed and dotted their feet like red periods.

"Ma, what are we going to do?"

"Get in line."

"But we'll never make it. They'll run out."

It was four hours. Ma would check her wristwatch every hour to keep time. She must've been tallying the score, ready to take it to God as evidence of his disappearance.

The row of cars that were lined next to us only moved every twenty or thirty minutes, so they weren't going much faster than us. In that waiting, I wished to bring up Marisol. To tell Mami that Marisol was now free and that we didn't need the people to come take her away. I wanted to yell out to her, "I found her a new home, Mami!" and watch as she gushed with joy. But I knew she wouldn't appreciate what I had done. How difficult it was to resurrect our Mari and bring her back to life. Mami needed Marisol in that room. It kept her waiting for all the promised people to arrive in their camouflage, in their uniformed trucks with the entire lost aide.

"I can see the pumps, Cami." Mami jumped out of the line to get a better look. By now the morning sun was bright and heavy. We managed to catch the shadow of the mountain, so we weren't suffocating under the sun. But behind us, people wore their sweaty faces with frustration. Those that came prepared opened their plastic umbrellas and we all began to look as wilted as a field of flowers harvested and left to die on top of the boiling road.

"But we are still so far, Ma."

"As long as we make it, it won't matter."

A skinny man with a gray baseball cap was peddling his chrome bicycle up to the row of cars next to us. Boils and puss scarred his face, but he seemed nice. He smiled and spoke to the passengers of the parked cars. He would stop at each window and say something I couldn't quite make out.

"Ma, el viejo."

"I see him, Cami."

She started cracking her knuckles as the skinny man peddled toward us. The people in front got mouthy and I knew what he was telling them.

By the time he reached us, Mami didn't even ask what we already knew.

"When is the next one coming in?" She finally said to the viejo.

The man slowed to a stop and sighed before he spoke.

"No sabemos. It could come later today or tomorrow. Since we can't communicate, we don't know when." He stopped speaking directly at Mami and began addressing everyone, even those in their cars. "You can stay here and wait, maybe leave your car and come check on it from time to time."

"¡Sí, claro!" A man in a purple Explorer shouted and he wiggled out of his spot and sped off.

Mami now looked too tired to stand. I told her I'd stay in line and wait for the energy. She didn't fight me and started off back home.

The energy didn't come until past curfew. The owners of the Shell almost shut it down but the police who were parked at the pumps let them continue for a few more hours. According to Mami, they had to start staking out gas stations because of all the thieves. As I filled my candungo, I was feeling happy because soon I would get to visit Marisol.

There was so much noise near la plaza. All the generators that used energy to power homes droned into the night and I was glad Mami didn't live too close to all those people.

I RETURNED TO the cave and found Marisol still in one piece. I carried the red candungo full of energy and placed it next to her. I picked her up and pressed her cheek against my lips and almost threw up my insides, so I jumped back from where she sat. She was a touch darker and greener. Her face was bloated, and her smell was hard to digest. There were trails of red ants lining her limbs and other white things, like grains of rice, collecting and wriggling in her sores. The missing pinky finger looked like it was gnawed down to its bone. She was messy but still in one piece.

"The people have finally come to fix things, Mari." I tried approaching her but she wasn't happy. Her eyes were bulging out from their sockets and she was crying. Like Mami. Like everyone these days.

"I saw them in town. They said they would get started on the energy soon. That food and water were more important, so they are setting that up first. Little camps where people go to get something to eat."

Marisol looked at me with her plum eyes, those bruised ugly things, and kept crying.

"I know that, Mari. I know that there's never enough to go around." I started pacing in front of her. "And you don't have to remind me to take care of Ma. You're not there! She can't go get the food. She doesn't want to leave Ojeda and her radio."

I stomped away from her. I became angry.

"I'm doing my best, Mari. I'm doing my best!" I yelled.

Her swollen body fell from the stool and thumped to the ground. I ran up to her and held her. She no longer smelled rancid to me. I had to take her out to the sun. To la plaza. The dampness of that cave was killing her, the darkness was blinding her sight.

I knew she could still hear me so I fed her slowly. I took the candungo of energy and poured some into her mouth. It was the fuel she needed to spark back to life, and we set off, her ugly body hanging off my back.

As we walked, the smell followed, and we passed the lines and lines of people waiting for the energy to come in on those metal trucks, I knew they looked at me and they whispered to each other about how smelly and bloated Marisol looked. But no one stopped us. The smell didn't bother me.

I walked her to the center of la plaza, to La Iglesia Parroquia San Miguel Arcangel, the old church in the center of town, to see God in person and speak as close to his ear as possible. All the people below were still fighting over which ration of water belonged to them, people were still lined up at the Shell gas station looking for energy, some had been waiting for days, inching closer to it, and their faces spoke of sadness.

None of that mattered to me and Marisol. I took her ugly beautiful brown body and we snuck through the pried gate of the churchyard, Marisol so brown, so green and stiff. We climbed the sidewalls with the same determination we had when we trekked to the cave for the first time together. We made our way up between the two short bell towers and climbed higher and closer to God. We were never supposed to be there, but no one was watching, and there I showed Marisol how the big people decorated all the houses without roofs. As if planting blue fields so wide, the ocean and sky met us there and we all became a soft blue blanket. They put up those blue tarps suspended over all the abandoned homes almost as if to tell us "we are coming," or "we will be back." But they never returned.

I saw us all suffering in Utuado and I imagined everyone on our entire island suffered too. All of us wishing for something different, how we straddled onto hope, how we walked as though we were ghosts. And all that was to come, all that we dreamed through, toward something new, felt necessary.

BAYFISH

There are no tales to justify our death so I can only speak of terrors. In the night, I heard us sing as a collection. First it was Banto. Then Urayoán. Then Cheo. We got to mind that we'd create a new fire for the world after the calamity hit Puertorro. It was called a calamity, but Ura saw himself as a prophet. He saw the opportunity. Something to start fresh.

Banto came to me as he always did, with his round legs and stubs for arms. He knocked on the door of my outpost, a modest and simple shed I built with a hatchet. It was just under el puente of our barrio in Florencia. I liked my shed because it was wedged under the shoulders of that concrete. No matter how hard the wind blew, no matter how large and mean she got, my place was going nowhere.

After a week had passed, after her rage syphoned all the living environment around us, Banto came over and said we were all mobilizing, coming together because Ura had a plan for some great society in the mountains. It would start with stealing some of the trucks carrying the gasoline and diesel.

"Oye, pescao. We got word. Things will get going near the center of Florencia, Ura knows where they're off to," he said, knocking on my door.

"I'm going fishing with the mongers, Banto. The fish have to be everywhere."

"It's not a request, Bayfish. Ura insists—"

"So? We'll go after."

I tied my laces. My shoes are gigantic because my feet are

wide and long. Banto and Ura tried giving me shit for that, but it would never stick because I moved in on Banto and his pudgy figure. He was the easy one to shit over and once we started up on him, that was the end.

"Look, mano. Ura's not going to like that. I'm not taking the hit on this one. I don't want it. It's on you, okay?"

"I want to check up on Cheo and Jorge, cabrón."

"Ura's going to be mad."

WE STARTED OUT. My outpost banked near the river but just high enough from its crest that even when she brought in the worst rip current from the mountain, it didn't faze my home. All she left was garbage washed up by rain and water, huge dunes of rusted metal, synthetics, and tires that littered the ground like their own plastic stream. The wind clipped at us, which was odd. After she left our shores, it was as if she had exhaled and taken all her gusts with her on her journey into the Atlantic, so it surprised Banto and me to feel any wind outside.

Our barrio sat on an uneven hill that steeped into the large river. Below we saw houses with cars speared into fences like olives on toothpicks. Shacks used to line the banks. They were painted with murals so bright they glowed. And some were re-purposed into chinchorros. Every Thursday night you'd catch most of the viejos bellacos drinking and playing dominoes. Whenever there was a capicu, the loser would have to take two shots of chichaíto. But if someone won with a chuchaso, the players would leap into a frenzy and force a palo down the loser's throat. Double zeros, papi, that's how you get it in.

You'd hear the clattering of the dominoes echo into every alley even the zinc rooftops rung from all the noise.

Now, there were only the skeleton husks from the shacks. There were no roofs. There were no doors. Many houses had their windows torn right out, concrete and all. It was frightening to see the electric cables webbing the roads and the walls of those abandoned places. The black cables wrapped everything. Some even sparked with electricity. Most people evacuated before she hit. Went off to el Coliseo Clemente for refuge. Or the Robin Morales public school. I knew the mongers wouldn't leave. Those that chose to stay said it was their home. That no matter how hard she hit, we would be there to rebuild.

I always met with the mongers to catch my share for the week. To keep me healthy and up on my nutrients. Banto managed well. His mother was one of those gentle types, always cooking after she got home. She complained to Banto that he was fat. Much too fat and needed to run the hills. I'd joke that he'd soon roll down the hills before running. She tried and tried, nagging him whenever she got a chance, all the while serving him a tower of arroz con salchicha. And he ate every grain. In his sadness, he'd eat everything he could find and go back for seconds, thirds, and then dessert. Most of us around these parts were slender and thin. Maybe ugly and malnourished, but never pudgy. And poor Banto, he'd look at me with those big brown eyes of his feeling sorry that he couldn't control the urge, and I sympathized. His own madre molded him with her sweets and guilt.

I much liked my routine with the mongers, and whenever Banto invited me to eat at his place, I passed because the food never tasted real. Everyone thought it so tasty. But me? I wanted it fresh from the stream, still wet from the catch.

"This is so stupid, pescao," Banto said as we walked. "We shouldn't be going fishing now of all things."

"You going to feed me, cabrón? Are you?"

"No, but—"

"Pues cállate la boca."

"Look, pescao. Not trying to keep you from all that. But you know how Ura gets."

"Then he'll answer to me, cabrón. It won't take long."

THE RAIN HAD come to a still drizzle, a constant tap that left everything in a wet mist. There was an odd smell in the air, a caked dampness that resembled wet feathers. At first, I thought it was the trash that might have spilled onto every corner.

I pushed through the escombros. Banto could only stare. He stopped walking and gazed into the expanse. The color had left the horizon. All the trees were naked from green and everything looked sharp and jagged.

"Diache, she's impressive. How everything looks burned. How she bent all to her will," I said, trying to tame the silence.

"There's still the whiplash from her tail that might hit us, pescao."

"She's moved way past us, Banto."

"You never know if there's more. Like an earthquake. An aftershock."

"That's not how it works, cabrón."

"You don't know!" he said. His face spoke of sadness and somehow, he looked like he was about to cry.

"Is Banto cagao en sus panties? You need to call tu mamá?
Maybe to feed you some cookies and cream?"

"Not now, pescao."

"You are! You are terrified!"

"Ya, Bayfish!"

He made to strike me, but I dodged him and slapped him
over his head.

"Mamao. You aren't fast enough to catch me."

"At least I don't look like a rotting shrimp."

"Cuidao, bicho." I puffed up to his face and shoved him. He
fell backward and spit on the ground.

"Mala mía, pescao. I didn't mean it. Perdón."

I turned and kept walking to the mongers. In our barrio,
whispers told of my past. Of how my mother came to have me.
The only thing certain was that she deserted me by the river. It
must've been what she wanted, the rising tide to drift me away
so deep into the sewers that I'd drown with all the garbage
from Florencia. I wanted to call it lies. As soon as I was old
enough to understand words, I refused to listen to anyone that
talked that kind of shit. I knew I looked like a shrimp with skin
roughed with green boils and hair on my body, but some called
it distinctive. Like dark plates of armor. Yet people knew not
to push past the shrimp references.

When I was older, Ura found me begging for change on the
streets. He offered me a space and introduced me to Banto.
Ura helped me build my outpost. In the beginning, he'd bring
me the leftovers from Banto's house. I was grateful, of course.
I no longer needed to peddle. It wasn't until he introduced me
to the fish mongers that I learned I liked fresh fish, or that I
liked most of my food clean and uncooked. But even now I still
think it was Ura who saved me.

The wind started again and Banto got scared and started trembling.

"Bayfish. This is so stupid. We shouldn't be going fishing."

"Are you going to feed me then, cabrón? Are you?"

"No, but—"

"Pues, cállate la boca."

"Bayfish, Mamá can give you some food when she gets back."

"Back from what, cabrón? Do you even know where she is?"

"No, but—"

"Pues, cállate."

WE ARRIVED AT el cruce, a subtle two-path divide. One path was lined with a string of houses painted in the colors of our flag. Each boxed house was grouped so close together they looked like a long snake that led to the mouth of the river. There, you'd find the dock where the mongers hung out. The other path went down a long corridor of tilting bamboos and connected to the main road out onto the highway.

But the paint that used to light the rows of houses in their technicolor was faded and smeared with some yellow hue. And the bamboo path was nonexistent. There was no road in the mountain of debris.

"That color, Bayfish."

"That's the color of leaves, Banto."

"Of leaves? You mean tree leaves?"

"Sí, cabrón."

"Dios mío. We should head to Ura, pescao. If we get her tail, we'll be the new paint."

"Shut up with that tail shit. There is no tail. She's long gone."

"You don't know that, Bayfish."

"I do know that."

"No, you don't. How could you? There is no way for us to know anything with the news and power out. What if she stalled just north and we receive whiplash? What if by God she is pushed back down to us? What if——"

"¡Ya, Banto, ya! We are almost there. Let's finish here and I'll explain later how huracanes work because you're too stupid to understand."

"There's no way to walk in this mess, pescao. If we get stuck trying to push through and more water and wind comes, we are done."

"¡Ya, cabrón! I am going to the mongers. Keep talking, cabrón. Keep talking."

"But, Bayfish."

"You can stay here if you're too scared. The mongers are still here. I'm going to meet them."

"You can't possibly know that."

"Cabrón, I do know."

"They must've gotten——"

"¡Ya!"

I punched into his ribs something evil. He winced and started to tear up trying to catch his breath and only his puffing could be heard in the silence. I felt bad. After seeing him struggle, he looked helpless and pathetic.

"Perdón, Banto. Perdón."

THE DOCK WAS only two miles away but it took us hours to walk through the mess. The remains of the houses stopped and as we came up to the dock, all that was left were two wooden stubs poking out of the river. The river roared and seized in a thick brown muck. It moved so fast you'd think it just discovered the mouth of the ocean. The mongers usually tied their boats next to the abandoned industrial water storage tanks. They'd been abandoned for decades and the mongers set up their fish shops just outside the fenced enclosing and sold their stock. When business was plentiful, the shacks were lined multicolor, brimming with the yellow eyes and scaled red bodies of the chillo, the smooth tender cuts of the dorado, and tin buckets full of live crabs ready to be boiled. On good days, they'd even prepare some cooked samples. Local anglers passed by wanting to purchase their homemade señuelos used for leisure fishing. Cheo and Jorge built a reputation for making the best lures, claimed their bright rainbow poppers or plumillas brought in a bountiful morning catch.

But none of their boats remained. I left Banto alone and went ahead.

"Bayfish!" he yelled out to me, but I kept going. I reached the ladder near the white industrial tanks that would lead me down a long concrete corridor where the mongers lived.

"Cheo!" I yelled. "Cheo! Any of you here?"

"Pescao!" a voice responded. It was Cheo. An older man in his midforties who fancied himself a bona fide poet. His skin was the color of dark bark. His arms were thick, and he was short with a beer gut. He only had hair on the sides of his head. I went over and hugged him.

"I was afraid you slept through María. Had to make sure, tú sabes."

"I did. Slept through el ojo. She took her sweet time passing through, mano. The slowest I've ever seen. Ni siquiera Hugo. And he was mean too."

"¿Y Georges?"

"Pal carajo con Georges. That thing's a cutie compared to this. You seen how it looks out there right?"

"Yeah, I saw." I turned and scanned his home. "Cheo, where are the others? Jorge came by earlier this week and said the fish were flowing."

"They took off long before she hit, mano. Headed to Bayamón and Toa Baja to stay with family. They should be ok."

"But I just saw him, Cheo. When did he leave?"

"No sé, mijo. It's been some time now. Maybe before she made landfall."

"And you let them take off like that? Hombre, ¿estás loco?"

"They tried talking me into going, pescao."

"Then why didn't you?"

"I wasn't leaving. This is my home. If it goes, I go with it."

"Bueno, I think the worst has passed."

"I hope so, mijo, I hope so."

I moved a milk crate from the side of the wall and sat down. Cheo's space was much like my own. It was humble with only a simple kitchenette and a cot to sleep on. Most of the mongers used the local bars for bathrooms and they'd shower in the river.

"You have any bait, Cheo?" I said to him.

"Sí . . ."

"Where at?"

"Bayfish, you really going out?"

"I need food, Cheo. I'm hungry."

"It's bad out there."

"Chico, it's alright. Just a little messy. Nothing that won't get fixed up in a couple of weeks."

"No, Bayfish. The people . . ."

He stopped himself and turned around. He didn't say any more.

"What about it? Cheo?"

"The bait's in the refrigerator out back. The town has been using it to store things. What's left of the town, anyways. We keeping it running on generators as long as they last. Not sure how much time we have, but we'll keep it running until we run out. It's working now. That's all that matters."

"Okay," I stood up and started making my way out. "Mira, Cheo. Ura has an idea to get things running up again. I'll be back and tell you the details. Says it's going to be big. Says it's going to solve everything."

"No, pescao. I have to stay here until the rest come back. Besides, you know I don't get along con ese cabrón."

"Cheo. Just hear me out when we get back. You're coming. Relájate. Don't fight it. I'm going out to catch. I'll meet with Ura and figure out what he has planned. Then I'm coming back here, and we'll go together."

"Bayfish . . ."

"Ya, Cheo. You're not staying here alone."

I patted his shoulder and went out through the side into a muddy pasture between the rusted and abandoned industrial tankers. The mongers had a large walk-in refrigerator where they kept their fish and supplies. I got to the fridge, picked out a toolbox with the bait, and made my way back to Banto.

Banto was leaning against one of the light posts next to the river. He was consumed by the raging water, its brown melody humming throughout the air.

"Okay, Banto. Let's do this."

"Bayfish, how are they?"

"Now you care, cabrón?"

"How are they?" he repeated.

"Cheo is fine. We coming back to get him after we find out what the hell Ura has planned."

"And the others?"

"Cheo says they're fine. They went to Toa Baja and Bayamón."

"They went where?"

"Toa Baja and Bayamón."

"Toa Baja? Bayfish . . ."

"Yeah?"

He didn't say anything. He turned away and started walking upstream. His silence felt different, as if he were keeping God's secrets. I pressed him but he wouldn't tell me more, so I just left it.

Banto and I looked for the best spot to fish. We looked where the river was the least angry, where we could cast our rods without worrying if the currents quickened, or if the ground beneath us was too brittle to support our weight. We climbed the steps of abandoned homes and verandahs absent from people and their conversations. We looked for the best possible spot. We searched for all the fish that the mongers promised, we scanned with our eyes to see if there were any washed up on the sidewalks, we dug inside cabinets, under the covers of bedsheets, underneath drenched sofas heavy with the weight of water, in refrigerators abandoned with weeks supplies of food, now, gone to waste because there was no power. We searched and Banto's face spoke of sadness.

We came across a small house. You could tell elderly people used to live there by what remained of the decorations: crucifixes, stained portraits of Jesús and María—some of the portraits varied, some looked very pastoral complemented by their drenched and weathered water stains—and broken ornate porcelain dolls with their old and simple embroidery, probably dressed by those forgotten and disappeared viejitos.

The river had eaten away most of the surroundings, but the little house latched on to the main road desperate to keep its place in this world. We climbed the concrete stairs that were tacked outside. They lead to the roof. There, we walked to the ledge of that roof and sat on its edge and watched the river flow and flow, the sound hummed, and it soothed. The outlook was desolate, the river was so gorged you could not make out where water ended and land began. But we were safe on that roof because it was sound and sturdy and the river only ate away at one side of the house allowing us to have the water flow. It gave us a chance to catch some fish, so we cast our lines and waited for something to pull on them. And we waited there in silence for some time. We feared that night would come to us and leave us stranded because it would get so dark there would be no way of knowing where to go.

Banto was the first to catch something. But it wasn't a fish. A boot got stuck on his hook and he pulled it up. It was an expensive boot, a Dr. Martens, and it was a dark ruby red. I laughed at him and he giggled and placed it next to him and we waited and waited again.

Banto caught something again. But it wasn't a fish. A blazer caked with so much mud. The blazer looked nice, like something you'd buy at Nordstrom in the Mall of San Juan. I told him to keep it because he could probably wear it once it was cleaned. It might not fit him, but I didn't want to make him feel bad, so I just let him have that moment. And we waited and waited again.

I finally hooked something. But it wasn't a fish. A wig,

discolored from all the elements of the river. Banto jokingly encouraged me to try it on, but I threw the wig at him and we laughed. I told him he should keep it and clean it and we could have an entire outfit by the end of the night. And we laughed for the first time together, not at each other's expense, but at the world around us and how together and alone we were.

I stared out into the mesmerizing river hoping for those fish the mongers told me about, maybe I should go for a swim and try catching them the old way, maybe it was only a shrimp that could catch the fish, I didn't know, so I waited with Banto on that roof until the sun started setting slowly behind the dusty haze in the sky, and I stared into that brown river as long as I could, hoping we'd see something alive in that murky water because as loud as it was and as much as it moved, it felt dead to us. We waited and finally saw something, caught between the logs of fallen trees upstream, two heads were bobbing in and out of the river, the bodies surfaced from time to time. You could tell their clothes were nice once, Banto and I saw it and we couldn't stop looking, so we stayed there until the sun dipped farther into the known horizon, and I didn't look away from the fidgeting bodies until I noticed Banto turn away.

MORIVIVÍ

We grew tired of the promises. In the years leading up to her destruction, we held protests in front of the AEE with signs and slogans that predicted how their monopoly would unravel. Their wonderfully layered building grew over those years of protests. Its exterior embossed with fine lettering nestled along la Ponce de León. Electricity was leveraged and that left us with a delicate and neglected power grid. We grew tired of the schemes and fought it the only way we knew how. Yet in spite of all that, the building rose and rose as much as the electric bill, protruding from the concrete like a stubborn weed.

We weren't the first generation to hold major protests on this island; a history as old as colonialism. Some dated back to el Grito or the Ponce Massacre in hopes for independence. We had professors from la IUPI remind us of our legacy and genealogy of resistance. They'd tell us, even if we sold ourselves to an idea, to commonwealth, even if propaganda silenced the majority of our people and they now bought into the lie of the new empire, we were rooted in revolution in spite of subjugation, of the seventies at la IUPI and Antonia Martínez Lagares. How she could've been any of us, how she was too young to die. We owed it to her, Lolita Lebrón, Luisa Capetillo, our mothers. We dreamed in revolution within the gates of our alma mater.

We noticed a monopoly of politics and politicians and things of special interests and we grew angrier as we continued to elect the same families into government. We protested and protested because we believed, even if just to honor those who came before us and those after. We clamored with cacerolas dented in their metal frame from too much use and marched to La Fortaleza or el Capitolio or right at the gates of la IUPI, posters painted in black and words written, screaming ¡No a la JUNTA! or IUPI Without Police or Fix Our Power Grid.

We got to mind that it was the fault of our leaders. As they yelled en el Capitolio and fed us the usual spin every four years, we wanted them to fall. How they tried concealing years of waste and corruption by paving roads with new asphalt during election years. And we hated that many forgot how cheap and deserted things became. We felt strong in adopting no colors; no red, blue, or green. We loved because there is no greater love than that for your home.

We had grandmothers and mothers that reminded us in their daily and subtle actions what it meant to fight back, how they pruned trinitarias and never winced when the shrub and thorns cut into their skin and made them bleed. Their beautiful gardens lined with lemon trees and mangos. All of this in that concrete city.

We had mothers that worked as lawyers en el tribunal de Hato Rey and others that never slept because they were nurses and doctors en Pavía and some in Condado en El Presby. We worked when we could, sometimes near la IUPI en Vidy's, on Thursday nights when students poured into drink and dream about a future that long passed them.

We called Santurce home, but we often made it out to Florencia since it was a small town near Loíza along el Río Grande. That's where we got the best food: chillo, dorado, pulpo, fritura. We'd take breaks from our studying en la IUPI and ride to La Posita and swim until the sun set, then walk to Florencia to dance and drink. Florencia's where we loved. Where we found heart.

But when the calamity came, we stayed in silence as everything around us fell apart in more ways than any Calderón, Fortuño, Acevedo Vilá, the Rossellós, or Barceló could accomplish. And there was no order. And there was no clean water, or hot plates of food, or medicine to cure illness. Simple expectations from the old government were not just unmet, they were distorted. We grew angrier with the promises.

We heard about Urayoán's plan to create a new order. It started with resources taken from the old government. It started with diesel and gasoline, but I knew there was something more to it, perhaps something only he knew the answer to. As time passed, we felt it was the only way to regain some level of control. Many would think it strange to try building something out of nothing, but desperation makes you do interesting and strange things. It makes you believe in interesting and strange things.

"It cannot work. How will you distribute the resources to the other towns?" I remember us later asking him.

"The other towns are not my problem," he'd say. "If they want salvation, they must come to Urayoán."

AT DAWN, DAMARIS and me made the lines in front of the Walmart, breaking the curfew mandated by the old government, but there weren't enough cops to tell us what to do or to control things if those in wait got violent. This is when we noticed the people in red. They began appearing in front of every gas station. They began patrolling the entrances of Walmart,

Costco, and all the Amigos and Pueblos that had food and re-sources. Some of them passed out handwritten pamphlets of a *paraíso prometido*, a place called Memoria, where there was food, water, gasoline, diesel, and order. The pamphlets did not have directions or a name. They simply stated on their crum-bled edges, *follow the reds*. It seemed like bait. At first, those who were given pamphlets ignored them and threw them to the ground.

There was an older man in front of the line at Walmart. He was slender with thinning hair. He wore a tan guayabera and dark olive slacks. He was waiting as we all were for the store to open and sell rations. The line must've been over a mile long and we were afraid we'd miss the rations for that day because we counted many ahead of us.

The people in red drifted from the back of the line to the front, passing the pamphlets along and the old man grabbed one of the pamphlets and spat on it.

"Llévate esto de aquí. What we need is water now. Not later. Now," he said. "We need clean water and food and light."

"But that is what is promised. That is what is here," said the person in red pointing to the pamphlet.

"Here? There is no *here*. Toda la isla esta jodía. There is no *here*. Stop messing with us," the man said. "We need water now. Not later, now!" He dropped the pamphlet on the ground and crossed his arms. He turned away from the people in red with a stubbornness we admired.

THE WALMART HADN'T opened its doors. We grew tired as we waited, trying to keep our composure despite the frustration.

An intercom went off at the front door announcing a cutoff,

only the first one hundred in line would be able to get canisters of bottled water. But there was enough rice and cans of beans for everyone else. It stated there was a portable oasis in the center of town. The center of town was five miles away and we had been waiting since dawn. It must've been three or four in the afternoon.

"We need clean water!" many around us started shouting.

"We need clean water now!" they continued.

A group of tall young boys behind us got very angry and jumped out of line. They marched to the front and pushed the old man out of the line. He started yelling at them.

"Get out of my spot. ¡Coño! I've been here waiting since last night. You have to wait too!" he yelled at the group, but the boys didn't move and everyone watching didn't chime in to help.

"Búscate otro sitio, mamabicho. We are getting in no matter what. Go somewhere else and wait for your water," one of the boys said to the old man.

We wanted to help but we were too tired from the heat.

"Get out of my spot!" The old man kept pleading. We noticed the group of boys had silver pistols holstered at their waists.

"Cabrón, don't get ahead of yourself," one of the boys said and pushed the old man back. The old man wasn't backing off and returned a shove. People around them started stepping away.

"Dale, viejo, let's do it then," the boy said to the old man and the two of them stepped at each other, raised their fists, and swung. The old man threw a few jabs at the stomach, but the boy sidestepped and swung a stiff punch behind his ear and the old man stiffened up and stood erect before falling over like a petrified tree. He lay on the floor and didn't move. We grew uneasy. People around wanted to fight too, if only to let it all out.

WE WERE YOUNG women, Damaris and me. I liked carrying a large knife in my jean pocket because that is what I was taught growing up. I wasn't afraid to swipe at anyone. But there were moments when just thinking about fighting made both Damaris and me sad, because we knew we were all in the same place, scared about tomorrow or the darkness of night.

WE WEREN'T SURE if Urayoán's plan could work. Word got around that he had stolen some of the diesel and gasoline and was going to hide it underground in his new society. We continued seeing pamphlets passed around Florencia in the coming weeks, a new society that claimed it was the center of all things, at the center of the island. The pamphlets were scribbled with bold letterings and markings and some were written in illegible writing, but rumors started circulating and that was more powerful.

Some suspected Urayoán hid the diesel in the mountain town of Utuado because he was convinced it was the center of the world. The ideal spot to start a colony or society or whatever he'd call it. His Memoria. A place reachable only to those who looked for it.

ONE DAY, DAMARIS and I stood at a Gulf station again, waiting on the gasoline to come from the old government. But the trucks never came. That's when the people clad in red showed up. They walked up to the diesel and gasoline pumps and stood guard holding large bats. They wore red bomber jackets and torn red jeans and black surgical masks. The police didn't bother challenging them. They too made the lines hoping to get what little fuel came in from the docks and harbor.

"They say those men work for Urayoán. They say those men are going to bring Urayoán's gasoline and diesel and sell it here because the trucks from the old government are not coming, they are being used for the governor and his people. They don't want to waste it on us," an older woman in front of us said.

"He's stealing it all the same," I said to her.

"So? At least he's doing something about it. Those other pendejos let most of it sit at the harbor. Pa' colmo now I hear truck drivers are on strike. At least his priority is us," she said.

Damaris and me eyed her and we grew suspicious. We didn't say anything for a while as we observed those in red create flanks guarding the gasoline pumps.

"Those aren't men, Mori. They're boys," Damaris finally said.

"Boys?" I said. I looked at those in red and saw their delicate cheeks. They had soft brown eyes and their masks couldn't distract you enough if you looked closer.

"It doesn't make sense," I said.

"What?"

"That they are here. That Urayoán is using his stolen trucks here. That those *boys* would be working for him."

"Yes, it does, Mori. No one else is coming. This is how he's doing it. To get people to follow. No other way about it."

"Wasn't he going to the center? Don't see why he'd waste it here. Seems like a detour to me."

"Look around, Mori."

There were so many people waiting for gasoline and diesel.

They sat in chairs or in their parked cars for miles hoping to get something. They didn't care how long they had to wait, just being there must've made them feel like they were working toward something rather than waiting at home.

"It's how you start these things. You bring in pamphlets no one will look at. As time passes, people will get desperate. That's how you do it, Mori. That's how you build trust."

"Hard recruiting for his little commune? In Memoria?"

"He won't have to. All he'll do is wait. They'll start coming."

We grew frustrated again. Everyone around us didn't budge from their spots. It reeked of desperation yet who could blame us. We took pains the way most do when confronted with disaster. It was a process of numbing and delay. We couldn't allow ourselves to feel beyond what was immediately in front of us, and we knew as a collective that things would never go back to how they were. The old government no longer functioned, and everything was now a total collapse. It became less about their inactivity and unpreparedness and more about how they rationed resources to line their own interests. The only difference was now they didn't bother hiding it and used funds to stuff their pockets.

A part of me couldn't help feeling gratitude that things no longer worked for the old guard. The weight of the calamity forced us to survive, reconsider, and remember. We knew that all incidents and conversations were now marked by this moment, everything prefaced with the *after she hit* effect.

I got tired of waiting and stepped out of the line. I stomped over to one of the boys in red. He tried holding his hand out as I approached and signaled me to get back in line and wait my turn. He was tall but his face was as soft as a child with trimmed delicate eyebrows and eyes framed by long lashes.

"Where is Urayoán?" I asked.

"Return to the line. The fuel will be arriving soon," he responded.

"Where is Urayoán?" I repeated.

"Nena, if you don't return to the line—"

"What are you going to do, cabrón? Hmm," I pushed up against him. I wasn't afraid. Not of his bat or his black mask or his imposing posture. He looked over me and tightened his grip on the bat.

"Nena, get . . . get back in line . . . or I'll—"

"I ain't afraid of you, cabrón."

I took out my knife and brought it up to his chin. He scrunched his face trying to avoid the sharp edge.

"Where is he?" I asked.

"Mori!" Damaris shouted. "¡Ya! Get back here."

"Listen . . . listen to your friend."

"Pendejo." I gave him a shallow cut on his neck and a thin trail of blood let out. His eyes swelled with tears. He wasn't tough or big or grand. He was just a child holding a bat.

WE WAITED IN the sun wondering why the truck hadn't arrived. I grew restless but Damaris remained patient. The air was still thick from a stink of wet leaves, as though water was clogged and rotting in every corner of the island. It didn't matter that it hadn't rained since the calamity. All the standing water refused to evaporate.

My mind drifted to the past, to childhood. Waiting there made you reflect because after enough time passed, there weren't sufficient words and conversations to distract, and you were left with yourself. I thought of the time Damaris and me drifted from barrio to barrio collecting profits for a neighborhood protection organization. This was after Damaris's mother was killed by her boyfriend. I took to looking after her. She carried a patience I never could. I spit fire every chance I got, but Damaris was always there, snuffing my flames. There was something unspoken about her soft exterior and I felt it my responsibility to act on what she didn't allow herself to show or feel. So, I did it for her. We collected money for ourselves and no one questioned the intent because everyone knew what happened to poor Damaris and her mother. It was guilt perhaps that drove their giving. And after we collected enough money, we used it to buy knives and a cot. She stayed in my house and there we grew together. We thought about radical freedom and bought into all the protests. It didn't matter how young we were. To us, it felt like the only thing we could do so that's what we did.

Near my grandparents' home, just off el puente La Virgencita in Toa Baja, there was a small farm owned by la familia Otero. They owned horses and some livestock. An abandoned and rusted silo stood at its center and large mango trees hugged the concrete house. Their house was modest and square, the second floor had the rooms and an exterior staircase led to the first floor that served as an open garage. In the background you could see the ridge of la cordillera, the mountains dividing the island North to South. Before the calamity, it was a green that shifted in color as the rains came and went. At night, their dark shadows outlined the sky and on them were lights dotting its surface.

But after the calamity, you saw only brown. You could see through to the rock of the mountain, and the horizon looked as though it was set ablaze with fire. After the storm surge receded, we went in search of my grandparents. We walked along the broken road and made it to the Otero farm. No one was there. They must've evacuated. What they left behind, however, is still there. Bodies of horses washed on top of roofs and beneath those roofs were so many dead livestock, roosters, hens, baby chicks, cows, and large pigs, all stained dirty with mud, bloated from water.

We came across a brown mare washed up against a large tree stump, her mane twisted and knotted. Damaris poked the horse with a wooden stick, and I stared at its glass eyes.

"What do you think they felt as they died?" she asked.

"Nothing." I responded.

"Nothing? They felt something, Mori."

"Pain, I guess. As though there was nowhere to go. It must've been slow. The water rising and rising, and they were forced to swallow it . . . Look at the eyes." I poked at the open eye of the brown horse. "What do you see?"

"I don't know," she said.

"Look closer," I said.

"Sadness . . ."

"They speak of sadness," I answered.

THE TRUCKS ARRIVED closer to dusk. They were spray-painted in black. Boys in red were latched on to each of its sides with short rifles. When the truck came to a stop, the boys on the truck jumped off and ran to the back in a disorganized formation. They waited there like cheap soldiers. And Urayoán, dressed in a black blazer and dark jeans, stepped out from the driver's seat. He carried a presence that initially struck fear. I wanted to go up to him then and there, but Damaris held on to me and told me to let it be. Now wasn't the time.

URAYOÁN

Off the coast of Ceiba, looking past the long deserted Naval station, past the anchored rusted spires of the docked Paragon drilling rig, you see waterspouts dancing there all nice and pretty. They will be forgotten by nightfall, but not me. I intend to exist in more than one lifetime, and you will record me—*Urayoán*—all bold and beautiful for memories eternal. Forget many of us. But me? You will remember my name.

I'll tell you where I thought of it. How this whole party mixes and matches. There are no more things deeper than language since it is true connection to memory. So says the Tower of Babel. To erase old memory and plant new memory is every attempt of conquest. I am conquered twice, by Spanish and American empires. Now I am given voice the way Lazarus is given life, chosen by committee, loved by puppets desperate to announce my vision. Which is why I link Bayfish to a hagseed. That's what I call him. It is a proper name, born from the seed to a hag of two empires.

Hagseed is not one of us. I found him swimming alone where heroin addicts beg for change and the lights turn from red to green. The overpass exits la Piñero and the sharp turn to la Muñoz Rivera is dangerous, and still, you see peddlers trying for those quarters. Hagseed was more of the developed type and hung around the traffic light entering Universidad, dipping and bobbing between cars, waiting to be ignored. But I didn't. I didn't ignore him because he looked like a shrimp.

He needed a home and that's what I gave him. I trust him but not much because you should never trust the things you find.

The boys in red, though. They are my pets. Homeless children for one. Also, the sons of mental anarchists, the crazy types that hear voices, the ones you used to find in the old Mepsi Center. They follow my lead and that's what I like. The color red is just display and performance because red is the color of passion. I collected many for my illustrious plan and vision.

I can live without the fat one. Banto and all his pendejá, Banto el goldiflón, his crying and wailing because his fat mom fed him so. And how his tetas jiggle whenever he walks and all he does is complain the world don't love him much. He sticks by Hagseed and Hagseed protects him like gasoline. One day I will gut Banto and feed him to my saints and martyrs and we'll feast on pernil for a week. Cheo and the mongers, if Hagseed knew what happen to the rest of his little posse of fishmen, he'd curl up like the shrimp he is, whittle, and cry. That bit of news won't be something you catch in the papers. Lots of people swimming in deep waters in Toa Baja and lots of people infected with sickness. Memoria will be glorious, and I will build it larger than Babylon, with gleaming red gates!

I snuck into Palo Seco after la monstrua turned everything black. That was the first place I inspected because that power plant is the key to the metro area of San Juan and beyond. It may get that nice ocean breeze because it's located on the edge of Toa Baja and I knew—because of my genius—that if it went down and caught fire, the old government would never get on a schedule to fix things. I brought a red with me to check the power connections and saw that the entire island is rot. Not just a little rot, something mishandled or forgotten. A rot like bone corruption, punctured so deep inside it spreads. My wretched old government thought to look toward Whitefish. They should have known, but I thank them for their dealings. Now I see what we need.

This red I take asks me, "By some miracle, are we going to see the island, and everything light up again?" And I told him, "Patience," with emphasis. All new governments need a center, and I knew the center is literal. Mountains deep and ignored where I'll provide commerce, safety, the reds, gasoline, home. All in beautiful Memoria. After that basic necessity, we can fix everything else with me and my leadership.

Then I inspected the goods they hid. I went alone on this. To check the docks where that FEMA stashed some of that aid. I found the layouts for where they performed drop-offs, maps dotting locations, these helicopter operations that tried to send to the center of our island water and supplies. So few destinations for aid drop-offs, it was laughable to see their effort. The old government was full trickster in their dealings. Again, I thank them for it because I see what we need. I internalize the maps that had the final destinations where the gasoline and diesel trucks were headed. Like I said, I trust the reds. They my pets. But the only one who knows exactly how many trucks and where to catch them is me. No one else. Me and the reds went at it during the cover of the stars. I seen old government patrol and police try to protect the gasoline trucks as they drove in the darkness, but that didn't scare the reds and me. The old government said they wanted people to sleep early for their safety and all I did was chuckle because they were bringing all them trucks to me and there'd be no witnesses.

We started on el expreso José de Diego in front of Plaza Río

Hondo, just after the two rivers meet the bridge. I—because of my genius—stole some big Mack trucks, the type that transfer sand from place to place, and the reds parked them right across the highway. Then for spectacle, we set the sides of the bridge ablaze. All this to scare the police of course. When they saw this, they halted, their patrullas stopping with the fuel trucks, and when they got out with their big rifles drawn, the reds in the trucks went full force into the police and made them asphalt. They made a mess, but it wasn't something you could see clearly until morning when the guts and limbs were detached and sheared. It was a plan that worked flawlessly. The bridge was a star glowing against a deep blackness and all my island was peaceful in the flames.

We took the gasoline trucks. We repeated this at different checkpoints throughout that night. It was all timing, which is why I only trust the reds. The perfect heist is all timing. One specific place, near Dorado and the Krispy Kreme. The spot was just near the welcome sea horse statue below the on-ramp. I told them that as soon as they saw that blue and yellow light up the night that they prepare our Mack trucks. They worried they wouldn't see them, but I told them to look at the long bridge, that it would be the only blue light they saw in all the night. It worked perfectly without a mess. The reds said when the police saw them, they simply got out of their patrulla and started walking back to San Juan in the deep darkness. It's the fear fire can put in you because the reds knew fire and burned the sides where grass and shrub grew.

Another place I sent the reds is near Arecibo just as you get close to el Coliseo Petaca. This spot was harder because the highway is ascending from a divided mountain, the expected police lights would come up on them too late for action. I told the reds to scout the top of the two short mountains and wait as lookout. This was tricky because I knew they'd have to fight with their anticipation. So, I gave them fireworks and just as they saw the police lights and fuel trucks begin ascending the hill, they set off the fireworks. You can imagine seeing the vastness of night lit up all splendid in green and blue.

And it worked! The reds got to the police fast, but they had to get messy. See, the thing is this, that spot is the gateway to the west side of our island. At least the fast gateway. By reports, la número dos was half blown away by la monstrua, the highway was the only transitable way west for car and truck. The police knew this and wanted to do things noble and steady so they fought as long as they could. But my pets are good at these sorts of things and they put hurt on those old government people. And I felt no sadness or remorse. It is up to Urayoán— because of his genius—to change fortunes so that's what I do.

When I arrived at the Gulf station, it was for demonstration. I arrived with my truck sprayed in black to match the night. I got out and stood at the top of the truck and told them, "We are here for deliverance. We are not here to tell you to come with us to a safe place, but to a place where there is power, and I along with my constituents will make sure everyone has enough to get the food and water needed. But this place is not for everyone. While we guarantee safety, those in our new society have to listen to me and my council."

They looked over at me there proposing a new life as if I were a leper and lunatic. I had the resources they needed, and they still didn't respect me, so I used the reds to show them. "Look here if you do not believe me, I will turn this station to light with the portable generator." And I got the reds to fill it with fuel. The generator buzzed and groaned before lighting the whole Gulf, and the people there waiting with their disappointment started to pay attention. To listen to me. I told them, "That is your choice to come and go. I will give you all a free fill of fuel. It is a token of the progress we will make in this new place the reds and me are building." But those greedy people only scurried to fill their canisters, their rickety cars, and they went off without looking back to listen to me or my propositions. That's when I got angry and removed my blazer because I meant business. I saw these old men and they had with them four canisters, filling them as quickly as possible. I told the reds to leave me to it and I got to them as they were filling and asked them if they needed help. "I can help carry those for you if you want." I said this with a grin, and I opened my arms wide. "We are just getting what we need to survive. There are many of us at the nursing home and some of us are getting sick in the heat." They said this all meekly to try and win me over, so I played along with them. I went over and patted one of the old ones on the back as he bent over filling his canister. He wore a white undershirt that was yellow from all the washing and age. He had dark sundrenched skin and his eyes were the color of amber. I simply pet him as he bent over. His old friend furrowed his brow and looked at me confused. "How many of these do you need again?" I asked this with concern. "This should get us by for another two weeks. We have some patients that need their machines on and the fans to work because it gets so hot in that home. You understand," he said this to me as if I were some sort of old politician or pastor, so I decided it best if I continued to play with him and I shot him a sympathetic and concerned look. I even nodded my head in approval. "Thank you," he repeated again and again. I walked with him a little bit as he struggled to carry the two filled canisters. Him and his short old friend were stumbling and walking all slow and I was following, repeatedly asking if they needed any help. "Oye, all you need to do is ask and me and my reds will help carry that for you to your place," I said this as I tailed them down away from the Gulf station. I whistled for two of my reds to come with me and the rest to stay at the Gulf handing out the free samples. "It's ok, we don't need your help. Gracias por el diesel. We should be able to make it back just fine," they told us, but we kept follow-ing them and one of my reds started to whistle and chirp like pitirre do and he was chirping away and away as we followed close to the oldies. "Look, let us carry those for you. It's the least you can let us do. We like to finish our jobs, tú sabes. We all cordial, we give you the free sample so it should be easy enough," I yelled this to them somewhat mocking them and I noticed they started to get a little annoyed by my reds chirp-ing chirping. "We get it, you the boss around here. You gave this to us so thank you. Now, let us get back to our home and that'll be that," he started scolding me. Me! The one with the idea to start things new—because of my genius. And I laughed loudly and so did my reds and that's when I shot my pets the look and they started walking faster and faster and were now walking right next to the oldies as they struggled to carry their little canisters filled with the diesel that I generously gifted out. That's when the oldies stopped in their tracks and put their canisters down and they started with that tone that I don't like. "Okay! ¿Qué carajo quieren? What do you all want? Money? We don't have money so you're wasting your time," he told me with a scowl as if he had not greedily taken from me. "Just a simple thank you works for me and for you to allow us to help finish the job," that's what I responded to him. I told him this in a sort of off way because the game was coming to an end. My red that was chirping knew this and stopped his little song. We all stopped there, quiet in that corridor of dead trees. The Gulf station was far, and it was dark now. "The forest plays tricks on you as it comes back to life. You know with all the noise darkness makes," I told them breaking the silence. The night started to get busy again with critters. It was a slow progression but something I think we all appreciated. "Please, we don't want anything. Just to get back to our homes and get the generators started. It's only a short walk now. Please, let us go back in peace," he told me this again. But then the game was over. He looked at me sad, his eyes weepy. I turned around and looked at the reds and they looked at me sharp and eager and that's when they rammed into the oldies and knocked them to the ground. They threw a few mean hits into their faces and the thuds resonated in the air like horse hooves on asphalt. The men cried on the floor lifting their hands above their eyes, trying to shield their faces. I like to think they could no longer look at me all satisfied. I took one of the canisters from them and opened it and poured it over them and they coughed and bled on that dark street. "Please, por favor, please," he told me this again and again and I gave him one last sinister look before I started walking off. I shot a whistle at my pets to grab the rest of the canisters and then my good and loyal reds stayed behind and lit matches and started a bonfire.

BANTO

Me and Bayfish are together again trying to find Ura. After she hit and weeks passed, Ura's plan to steal gasoline and diesel trucks worked. We picked up some dried beans and canned salmon from the colmado in the center of Florencia. It was the only store open and it was running low on supplies. Gabo was the owner and warned us that he too would be leaving to the refugio near San Juan. Said it was impossible to stay any longer. Said they were giving out free rations of food.

Bayfish suspected something foul at work and that made him mope. I wanted to find this new city Ura planned to build in the center of all things. He called it Memoria. That's his wording not mine. Our old Florencia was becoming impossible to sustain and the people that stayed were growing weaker.

"It's time to leave this place, Bayfish."

"And where do we go then? You tell me, Banto. You tell me."

"Find Ura. He's expecting us. That's all we can do now."

"Good idea," he said sarcastically, pacing in his shack under the bridge. The door was open. I sat outside hearing the river cascade, watching the changos pick at the garbage stream below. I carried with me a backpack filled with all the things we fished out weeks ago, the boot, blazer, and wig. I washed all three of them against the dirty water and dried them for some time before packing them in my backpack.

"I'm sure the reds know where to find him," I finally said.

"Then go ask, cabrón."

I paused and let him cool for a second.

"Ura's broods continue to recruit more and more these days," I said.

"Yeah," he responded, rummaging through his detached refrigerator for some pickles.

"I imagine if his broods are successful, this little city of his will go on functioning and the old government won't have much to say about it."

"Yeah," he said again, spreading the salmon on a plastic blue plate.

"Did you catch what Ojeda said on the radio last night?"

"Nah."

"He was going on and on about the curfew and how the old government is warning people not to go out to the streets at night. Said they continue to steal gasoline and diesel trucks. Of course, he condemned it. Said those responsible were hurting the recovery effort."

"So, he didn't get the memo."

"About?"

"Ura's little party in the mountain. Him and his ideas about what a new island civilization should look like."

"Nope. Not sure Ojeda did." I let out a chuckle. "He kept saying that the old government has all these resources, but the truck drivers are not reporting to work. And the cops have also disappeared."

"It's because they're exhausted, Banto. There aren't enough and those who show up are not taking time off. Think about it."

"Okay, Okay."

I stood up and walked over to him. Bayfish ate the salmon he prepped on his dilapidated table. He slurped on the can and took pickles and sucked on them before swallowing.

"You remember Randy? El chamaquito that plays the trumpet. From Candelaria," I said. Bayfish shook his head and kept pulling out pickles. "You know, the exterminator. He quit studying en Turabo and is a dominguero for the National Guard."

"Sure, sure."

"Ran into him at Gabo's shop. He was wearing his camo. Said things are really bad in the center of the island. He also said Humacao was wiped off the map. Said he's never seen anything like it and the lines to enter places like Walmart or Pueblo son kilométricas. He said the trees on the mountains look like they were all sawed in half. Pescao, a complete de-forestation or like some atomic bomb. Imagine it."

"Then why doesn't he do something about it?"

"That's the thing, Bayfish. He tells me they can't. They waiting on orders from the big ups and still haven't received them. Says they ready but are not being told where to go."

"Go to the center. Doesn't seem too difficult."

"You know that's not how it works, pescao."

"Well, maybe that's why Cheo is the way he is. You know Cheo used to work for the National Guard?"

"No, I didn't."

"Yup. He said they shipped him off to Georgia for Basic and after he got back, he just stopped showing up. They wrote him up as AWOL."

"Why didn't they go after him then? Los federales?"

"Who says they didn't? Who says they still not looking for his ass? As soon as he turned eighteen, he enlisted. And just as quickly he disappeared."

"Makes sense why he lives off the grid."

"The mongers are all like that. They all ex-soldiers or some sort of military."

"Bayfish . . ."

I wasn't sure how I'd break the news to him about Jorge and the others. About Toa Baja and parts of Bayamón.

"Dímelo."

"Toa Baja was completely underwater. Most of it. And parts of Bayamón too. You said the mongers went that way before she came."

"Yeah, but that's most of the towns on the island anyway—"

"Bayfish—"

"¡Ya, cabrón!"

He slammed his fist onto the table, and it shook. He hunched over his pickles. I was disappointed in Bayfish. Since the last fishing outing, he was particularly caustic, often snapping at me. When he wasn't, he'd choose to ignore me entirely so as to not lash out. He clung on to his shack now because it reminded him of something that no longer existed, the time of the old Florencia that was now shredded to bits. I grabbed my backpack and made to leave.

Bayfish finished his meal and we both headed over to la plaza de Florencia. He knew where to make contact with one of the reds and track down Ura. I felt obligated to get to Ura. I wasn't happy about it and news traveled fast through the reds about how Ura was running things somewhere in the center of all things. I was scared because I knew Ura's patience was thin, he played with people and I was afraid if I got caught up deeper with him, he'd start really going hard on me. Bayfish brushed off these concerns the way he always did. His loyalty toward Ura was a thing of wonder and while I understood, it crossed me.

The reds were in la plaza tossing stones and rubble from

a fallen light post. They snickered and ran around with their oversized red bomber jackets. Not all of them were tall. Some couldn't have been more than eleven years old. Whenever the reds convened, there was always a leader or captain or whatever Ura named them. The designated leaders wore blue string tied around their bicep. I hated interacting with them because the broods never communicated clearly. They'd stare at you unsure what you were asking and seemed to relish playing dumb because it threw people off.

They ran up and down the fallen concrete posts and continued to throw stones and rubble at each other and yelled loudly and if you squinted, you forgot that Florencia was abandoned. They occupied so much space in their wild freedom.

When we asked them about Ura, all they did was giggle and run off. They jumped from tree to fallen tree. Bayfish yelled at them. Told them who he was and his affiliation with Ura. All the reds did was pause, then pretend to hide behind debris and escombros and yell out, "Ura, Ura, Ura!" Stupid and childish kids playing the streets. They tossed large stones and rubble at us and ran into an abandoned building.

"Should we go after them?" I asked.

"Nah. They'll be back."

Bayfish scanned me and flicked my backpack as if noticing for the first time.

"And this? Planning a permanent move?"

"Check this out."

I teased the wig out from my bag. It was cleaner and dry. Its original color was probably a bright blonde but after all the mud and dirty water it had a brown tinge to it. I shook it and then put it on my head and made this long goofy face.

"Fo, Banto. That thing stinks."

"It's not so bad . . ." I took it off for a moment and sniffed it and coughed.

"You put it on," I tried shoving it in Bayfish's face and he swatted it away laughing.

I put it on again and forgot the smell. I couldn't smell it when worn, so I left it there. I then pulled out the blazer I had fished out, shook it in the air, and put it on. It was a little snug on my chubby back, but it fit just enough for me to move around comfortably. I flipped my blonde wig hair back and posed for Bayfish.

"Gonna wear the one boot too, Mr. Pegleg?"

"Nah, that's not my style." I popped the collar of the blazer and threw him a wink. "How's the overall look?"

"Cabrón, you look like La Comay," he said.

"Qué bochinche," I said with Comay's inflection. We cackled and laughed and waited on the reds to tell us where to find Ura.

CHEO

The plan that Bayfish left for me was simple yet I have better ideas. I don't pack heavy, but I make myself lists to leave a mark on this earth in case of sudden death. It's poetry, I think. I want to write eternal lines for me to remember when I am adrift in the deep sea of aging. So I write in a small composition notebook I keep to myself, in my back pocket, where I carry some spare bait sometimes because you never know when you might need it. And even though the other mongers used to jest, I tell them it's poetry and that's what keeps us alive.

- When leaving for something different, there is excitement, at least initially, for a new world.
- Cristóbal Colón is not my father and leaders old and new create the same old new pains.
- Urayoán loves fire.
- I worry in order to set the rules for a new place a sacrifice is needed because everything new is borne from tears.
- You lose connection to the island and you learn how things used to be before everyone lived virtual.
- I live in the rose and in the sea.
- Floating globes that service connection orbit towns and many people in cars cling desperate to old reception towers.
- Paper cash only lasts in temporary space and it all burns.
- I live in the rose and in the sea.

- A beast grew inside leaders and hearts, to cover bodies in graves is a new part of the everyday.
- Only when.
- Stock runs low I dream to drift on a sea but only if it leads me back home.
- Urayoán loves fire.
- I live in the rose and in the sea.

People laugh but this list is sent from the angels themselves and it speaks to me. Most everyone looks to the radio or tries to get a signal on their phones but not me. This poetry speaks to me and I'm less alone here with it by my side.

MORIVIVÍ

We saw people acting as birds fly today.

It was midday but the sky was overcast, and it felt like late afternoon. Most days feel like late afternoon. After waiting at the Gulf for diesel, Urayoán disappeared. We decided to look for food in the old city they used to call Hato Rey. We journeyed toward the Banco Popular and all the insurance skyscrapers once booming with life. This was before the calamity. The streets were now abandoned, and the office edifices had blown windows. There were white tents spread throughout La Milla de Oro. Palm trees and thin hedgerows that used to line the avenues were uprooted or left alone and grown wild. The Fine Arts cinema with its grand entrance and escalator was looted and shards of broken glass littered the floor. There were no cars, in all their multicolor, clogging the roads. The McDonald's and CVS no longer bustled with transit, the Burger King the same. We thought to stop in the Econo on Roosevelt. Damaris had a friend who worked there restocking the produce and receiving grocery shipments. But as we crossed Roosevelt Avenue, we saw nothing down the road, a quiet mess and I knew it wasn't worth seeing Econo ransacked. I wanted to venture deeper into Hato Rey and check on some people we knew who lived in Floral Park, a small, tight cluster of run-down houses in the center of all the concrete and tall buildings. Damaris must've felt this, so she shook her head and insisted we keep pressing forward, closer to the center and to the people.

We walked and walked and if you stopped for a moment, you could hear ghosts busy at work. Those echoes left behind after so much noise, vibrations, and sound filled us both. Ghosts of people occupied with their business jobs. Ghosts of men dressed in sleek pants and tight dress shirts, many fat from eating too much fast food. Ghosts of women in office attire and the sharp click of high heels as they walked. If you stopped for a moment and closed your eyes, you could hear laughter or yelling. The humming of cars trembling idly at the stoplight, steaming under the violent afternoon sun. We stopped to hear these ghosts because Damaris was tired, and the memory must've been soothing to her.

La Milla de Oro was transformed into a shantytown surrounded by rows and rows of white tents, some with FEMA insignias, and that made Damaris angry. She still fumes about how the old government and FEMA dispersed emergency funds, such things as strange and foreign companies like Whitefish coming to our island taking advantage of disaster proclaiming a solution to the failed power grid. Emergency funds disappeared into unknown pockets, proposals made to Amazon for the building of their second campus at Roosevelt "Rosey" Roads Naval Station were ignored even after the secretary of commerce sold hard the idea of *paradise*. Instead, the old government kept thousands of bottles of drinking water and aid at Rosey. As our people disappeared in sight and death, the old government continued attempting to sell us to the highest bidder, all for progress and posterity. To this day we're told the water and aid sit at Rosey rotting away. We'd grown used to the constant misallocation of monies from the old government, where contracts were handed out, funds designated, then disappeared while the proposed projects were never realized. We'd grown used to this and even though we raised our voices and growled, we remained static. Continued reports detailed the old government was conveniently misplacing and losing many trucks filled with more aid. At first we thought it was all Urayoán, but after news broke that mayors and the governor were in on these disappearances, Urayoán started looking more and more like a solution rather than a problem. We grew tired of all the promises. We started thinking more about the reds and Urayoán's new town or city or Memoria, whatever it's called. It sounded more appealing as time went on.

We continued with our hands linked. Homeless or abandoned people camped on the floor or made lines into the white tents. Officials dressed in vests and hard hats gave out scraps for food. I was sick of the waiting. Places like Florencia and everything isolated and rural were neglected and Damaris was crying more these days. The tents with their FEMA wordings signaled a false attempt that something was being done, but it made no difference to Damaris and me. I took my knife and carved into one of the tents. I cut around the word FEMA and ripped the black letters from the white tarp. I threw it on the ground and spat on it and Damaris smiled for the first time in weeks. Her long curly hair was disheveled but her face, even stained and dirty, was beautiful. I wondered if it was time to find the reds and go to Memoria.

We kept hearing popping echo in the air and could see afar something falling from the broken windows.

I stopped one of those officers dressed in a vest and a hard hat.

"Why aren't you helping with the older people?" I asked. I was angry. I held Damaris's hand as I kept repeating this to the officer. "Why isn't anyone doing anything to stop that noise? People throwing things from those windows."

I pointed to the buildings above and the officer ignored it.

"If you want food, get in line like everyone else," the officer responded and pointed to the trail of people waiting to be fed. I grew impatient so I tugged Damaris and we moved passed them and kept walking. I didn't want us to stay there in that camp because everything felt lifeless. I feared that if I left Damaris there, she'd waste away in abandonment.

The only means of finding Memoria was through the reds. They were spread throughout each major town and didn't always listen when you asked them questions. They had a reputation of running off like scared cats.

"Can we rest, Mori? Please. I'm tired," Damaris said.

"We need to keep moving just a little more. I don't want us to stay here. You'll get sick if you stay here."

"I'm tired, Mori."

"I know."

WE SAW PEOPLE acting as birds fall today.

Damaris wasn't sure if they spread their wings evenly, but I knew they wanted to reach the sun. Pops like gunfire echoed in the long avenues and the exposed metal frames from some of the empty office buildings trembled. I covered Damaris's ears. I knew the people dressed as birds were failing to spread their wings evenly and Damaris was so tired. Her eyes gray and dark from little sleep. Her hands weak and fidgeting.

As we walked through the camp we wondered if this was the end. If this was how things would be from now on. Everything we grew up loving, now an afterthought. We remembered all the old songs playing on La Mega, the little money we had we'd spend shopping or cooling off from the heat in Plaza, getting dizzy and throwing up after riding la caja de muertos in La Feria, las fiestas patronales, el festival de las máscaras in Hatillo, all of it.

We waited in a dilapidated bus stop hoping the old transport would appear and take us away, anywhere. Then we saw her. An old woman with short white hair. We saw her in the American International Plaza building. The building used to house UBS or AIG or something of the sort but now it wasted there with its blue windows blown and shattered.

She was standing next to the edge of that exposed office. She must've worn a long white dress. I like to imagine her face, wrinkled with wisdom and anger and frustration. Her eyes heavyset and her skin blotched with an uneven tan. Her thinning but full head of hair was platinum cut just under her ears.

She was angelic, the old woman. She carried herself to the ledge and she looked so peaceful. Damaris noticed her and could only wave. Then I waved and we were both down there, below her, waving. Not an agitated or desperate *hello* but something like mourning, a remembrance. And the old woman waved back. She presented herself to the air and she wanted to glide out into that openness. So, she did. She let herself fall. At first it seemed like she would never rise but Damaris and I kept waving as she fell forward and we saw her rise. Her long and torn dress flickered and opened, and she fluttered over us like a pitirre.

"Isn't she beautiful?" Damaris finally said. She held my hand as I hugged her.

"Yes . . . yes."

BAYFISH

It was just before dawn and we sat on two stumps in la plaza Florencia waiting on a convoy headed toward Utuado. The reds plotted and snuck us onto a Red Cross aid and relief unit. Said the unit was looking for volunteers and they got us on the list. They were supposed to pick us up. All we needed to do was act the part. According to the reds, in order to find Ura and his lost city, we needed to make it up the cordillera, deep into Utuado. They were cryptic about it, no other details offered other than ride with the Red Cross until they stop. Then get out and climb the mountain where the sun sets. It was hard to believe them reds and all the games. But we had no other choice. Banto and I went along with it out of faith that Ura expected us.

We were sitting, waiting. The sun crept out of the horizon when the pickup came up the road. The driver whistled and waved us over.

"You two. Camino a Utuado?" He asked.

"Yeah," I responded.

"Jump on back. Careful when moving some of the bags. The mangos and plantains fall out easily."

"Dale, okay."

Banto and I climbed the tail and sat down between these large brown sacks of food. The pickup drove on. There were two other men in the bed of the truck and trailing our unit were a couple other pickups. We drove for some time in silence without introductions. I chalk it up to the setting. It was the first time I saw Puertorro with this sort of fast detachment. I walked through Florencia, so the gravity of the disaster was slow-consuming. I had time to digest what I saw. Sitting there on the bed of that truck, I was thrown every image. All of it captured in brevity and then transitioned into another and another and another.

The pickups eventually pulled onto el Expreso Las Américas headed west. Billboards that used to impose their products and shining lights were contorted and barely hanging upright. The large steel utility poles leaned over and some lay shattered over the expressway, the black wires strewn all over.

"Nice wig," one of the men said. He puckered his lips in the direction of Banto. "Matches his eyes."

"He's an idiot," I answered and let out a chuckle.

"First time up?" he asked.

"Yeah."

"Be prepared. This is nothing. Compared to what you'll soon see. My guess is we'll have to either walk at some point or help clear the road. Regardless, it's a good thing you two joined. They are hurting up there and any help is welcomed," the man said.

He was wearing a black fedora and had wavy long hair. His face was delicate and his black plastic glasses were bridged at the edge of his large nose.

"Doctor," I said, pointing at him. Not so much a question but rather a sure demand.

"Nah, profesor. Catedrático de la IUPI. Estudios latinoamericanos," he said, leaning back against one of the brown sacks. "He's the doctor."

He elbowed the man seated next to him. The doctor was fast asleep and merely grunted when the professor nudged him.

"This one's had a long night. Before this we were in Humacao . . ."

"Humacao? How's that holding up?"

"It's not. There's nothing left. Most of downtown was destroyed by the surge. The water is still camped at the center plaza."

"And the people?"

"Those who evacuated have done well enough. But there are still some people trapped in their houses . . . saw many SOS signs on roofs. But you know how it is. Ever since the old government was destroyed, everyone's pretty much fending for themselves. Those still around, that is." He paused and let out a sigh. "This one case, it'll leave you feeling rotten. An elderly couple didn't want to abandon their home. Kept saying they needed to be with their lovebirds. They had cages filled with them. When we pulled up on our boat, they didn't want to leave unless we took the birds." He coughed before continuing. "El doctor here had to get all psychological. Spent an hour talking to them." He paused and adjusted himself.

"Did they end up leaving?" I asked.

"We tried. Tried to get as many out as we could on our little boat rafts. And it was only when they saw the cages loaded on the boats that they agreed to get on . . . those birds were dead. All of them. Cages filled with soaked feathers. But those two didn't care. Or they didn't realize because of grief. I don't know. But we took what we could and got them out."

"At least they got out."

"Exactly. At least they got out." He looked down at his lap. "We're spread thin. Aid still hasn't made it far out."

"Aid hasn't made it anywhere," I snapped back as a reflex.

"True . . . I suppose. Aid hasn't done much. Those helping are trying. That's all anyone can do."

I shook my head and looked over at Banto. His eyes were shut but his hand was hanging outside of the truck riding the air. I didn't want to talk anymore. Kept hearing the reds in my head, chanting to be careful or we'd end up stranded on the highway.

It was afternoon by the time we turned south from Arecibo on PR-10. The long stretch of highway slowly scales the mountain and open fields greet you when you begin ascending. Banto had fallen asleep a couple of times on my shoulder but I didn't wake him. El profesor and el doctor spent most of the trip quiet. El profesor wrote in a small leather-bound notebook and el doctor sighed and spent the hours scanning the horizon.

"Writing poetry?" I asked el profesor. I noticed the line breaks in the notebook and assumed as much.

"Just notes. Thoughts and ideas, tú sabes. To remember."

"Nobody will forget this, mano."

"You'd be surprised what people are capable of forgetting."

"Well, I won't forget this."

"It's always possible. We fragment trauma and often compartmentalize it. For survival, tú sabes. It helps us move on—"

"I won't forget this!" I repeated.

"Okay, jefe. Okay."

He brushed it off and went back to his scribbles. Banto let out a snort so loud he woke for a second before falling back into his deep beauty sleep. It bothered me that this profesor assumed as much about me and my memory and it bothered me that Banto was fast asleep and didn't come to my defense. How peaceful he looked, and all I felt was a budding anger. How could anyone dare assume we'd forget all this?

We drove and drove and the landscape was uniform in its beige. I didn't see a single car for miles. It was just us, the convoy, driving up, slowly ascending. The highway didn't have many trees lining it. At least not yet. As the highway rose, the road thinned and the remains of trees and garbage started to increase until it was just one lane of road, which we kept on for some time as the convoy dodged metal, wood, and power cables.

We kept at it until the convoy suddenly stopped.

"Banto. Cabrón, wake up. We stopped," I said shaking him. He stretched and cracked his back before coming around.

"We'll be back moving soon," el profesor said.

"What's the holdup then?" Banto asked.

"Don't know. Oye, Luisito, ¿qué pasó?" El profesor leaned over the back of the truck and asked the driver.

I tried looking over our pickup's cab. I climbed over the bags of food and clothes. The road was blocked by large window frames and piles of dead trees. Sheet metal also lined the way. But all the debris seemed placed deliberately, how the frames spread on the asphalt taking up as much space as possible, how the sheet metal stood erect like a small wall and the logs of dead trees were stacked neatly upon each other.

Just ahead I saw small flame pyres and shadows dancing. When their silhouettes met the brightness of the flames, I noticed the figures were reds. They moved around the flames in a dembow sway. And above us, a handful of reds overlooked the highway from some abandoned two-story buildings, and they called out in high-pitched yells, "URA, URA, URA!"

"¿Qué carajo está pasando?" el doctor said.

"Oye, let us through. We are moving with help toward Utuado," the driver yelled out.

I motioned to Banto that we needed to move out and disappear into the forest. That is what the reds told us before we left. To disappear once the convoy stopped. I was afraid. Something told me to grab Banto and run out into the darkness of the dead trees.

I took Banto by the hand and stumbled over the tail of the pickup. Banto didn't ask questions and flopped over and fell to the ground, his knees hit the floor and got cut by the road and he let out a cry laced in frustration. He struggled to get up, so I helped him. He was heavy and his gut poked out from underneath his black T-shirt. His black blazer was stained with red dirt.

"Cabrón, move it. Stop fucking around. We need to get going now," I said.

"I'm trying, pescao."

BANTO AND I ran for some time without a sense of direction. We pushed up a steep hill and used the rocks for support. We kept pushing and rising until he couldn't anymore.

"Ya, pescao! Ya. I can't," he said. He puffed and wheezed. He bent over, hands on his knees, and slid the wig off his head. His blazer was soaked in sweat.

"Cabrón, we need to keep moving. Take off all that shit and you'll feel better."

"Ya! I need a break."

He spit on the floor and shook the wig and wiped his forehead clean before placing it back on his head. I walked over and patted his back.

"Let's take five then."

Everything around us looked the same. The forest was brown and consistent in its stillness and even though I could make out a shimmer of the pyres burning below, I couldn't see much else between the rows of hollow trees.

After some time passed, we kept walking deeper into the density of the forest, the crickets buzzing and the branches snapping underneath. I wondered where to go. I doubted the reds and questioned if I had made the right decision listening to Ura and all his sermons. I knew that if I had decided to stay back in Florencia, Banto would've stayed too. And I thought about Cheo and wondered if he was going to try making it up here so far from everything he knew. So deep into this mountain and away from all the water and coastline. Ura didn't say much else after he told us how he would use the gasoline trucks. He depended so much on the reds I started questioning why he insisted on us joining him to begin with.

We continued to walk slowly up the mountain slope, and off at a distance I heard the sound of a river. It was nice to hear because it reminded you to keep moving. That life continued and we should too.

"Look, pescao! Look!" Banto said. "This must be it! This must be it!"

He pointed to rows of trees marked with red paint. Each marking seemed to form a jagged trail and led farther into the forest and closer to the sound of the river.

"The markings must lead to Ura," Banto said. He seemed happy to come across them. But I wasn't. I felt a sense of deep regret when we found those red markings. I wondered what happened to el doctor and el profesor and what the reds did to them. Banto sounded like a child in that moment, filled with stupid optimism because he was no longer lost or drifting through the dead forest, but I wanted to stay adrift. Banto smiled and smiled and led the way. He slapped each painted bark as we passed in a victorious salutation. *He arrived. We made it.*

CHEO

First, I needed to prepare for the long walk. I heard rumors of people taking convoys, dirt bikes, and other things to Memoria, but I liked the walk. I wanted to see things slow rather than in the distortion of speed. I might have been older than most of those people headed to Urayoán's Memoria, but I knew I had the endurance and feet. Weeks passed since María. Or maybe months? After a certain point we all stopped counting because it didn't matter, every day blurred into each other and it was all the same.

I stopped by Gabo's colmado en la plaza de Florencia because I wanted to get some canned salmon to take with me for the journey. But it was closed. The windows shut and the door boarded with plywood. All along the edges of the canal that led to the river there sprouted wild sugarcane. It made for a quick energy boost. I hastily harvested some of it by striking my machete into the overgrown stalks and cut them into small portable pieces.

As I readied to leave, I felt I was saying goodbye to everything, whether with purpose or by chance, I knew I'd never see Florencia again. Never wait in my hammock after the day's catch with the mongers or never feel the soft heat from the late sun hit against all that rusted metal around us. The old refrigerator was still powered because the Rivera family that lived near it were doing their best to keep it going, to keep it alive as long as they could. They used their generator and fed it diesel every two days. They shut it off at night so as not to waste much. But I admired them for it. They held on to the routine because I guess there was nothing else to hold on to.

I was bringing to Memoria a backpack filled with slacks and clean guayaberas I had not used since before she came and destroyed everything. Maybe there'd never be an occasion to wear such neat clothing. I figured I was thinking optimistically for the future. I also packed many notebooks with me to record my history and write that perfect poem by list, of course. The stanza that I kept thinking about grew from my last list. It was progress.

> The rose is a beast
> in the quiet sea
> if I were there
> to encounter it.

I didn't like the *encounter* part of it because it sounded like I wanted to go out swimming inside her looking for some rose. Maybe the rose is the sea, and the sea is a beast? I prefer listing because it gives everything an order to follow nicely. When I'm pressed for time and need more details, I collect them in my notebooks. On the way to Urayoán I thought I'd collect many stories.

> I live in the rose and in the sea.
> And those sounds are comforting to me
> even when the beast eats away the shore
> my life ~~remembers fire and~~ dark
> so live in the rose and in the sea.

I wanted to be like the great and forgotten poet, Julia de Burgos. She was forgotten but I wanted to reclaim her verse. I liked the one, "Mi símbolo de rosas," where she rhymes and marries the idea of echoes and longing throughout the poem. I sensed this was why I wrestled with the rose and the beast in my head. She liked to echo symbols with the ocean, and I saw why she talked of waves and morning nostalgia. I read "Mi símbolo de rosas" over and over because I knew it should help with my riddle of the rose and beast. The *dreams* the great Julia was referring to are echoes in the morning, when we hear nothing but the day chatter slowly being born into the world. And on these islands, they meet the water and salt and sand and finally have conversations with all that drifted and died centuries ago, I thought. Julia searched for a symbol and maybe that's why she called it "Mi símbolo de rosas" because in the end that one was about hope in the morning, like all days bring in hope.

> *Roses don't belong*
> *in the Caribbean*
> *no more than*
> *roses belong*
> *in the Caribbean.*
> *Rise like the rose*
> *with the sun*
> *and shadows laugh*
> *after nights where*
> *dreams without wings*
> *fail to leap.*

Rose + rise is like a risen? So, the rose I was fighting with could be more than the flower and perhaps it was rising like the sun. Julia referred to shadows like shadows of dreams realized in a night without wings. And I saw why she said that shadows laugh. It must be laughter that will solve my rose and beast riddle. I often don't know how to inject humor in my lines. I had Banto tell me once I write with a suit on and he called me something like obtuse and we fought that time because I was very drunk and angry. I pulled a knife on him and it wasn't until Bayfish intervened that we all spontaneously broke into laughter because in my wrestling drunkenness, I peed myself.

I used to show the mongers these abandoned poems and my drafted lines too. They always laughed. They laughed but their jokes came from history and heart, so it never bothered me much.

But I was alone, and the mongers were gone, and I was all that remained. I saw the reds in congregation on my way out of Florencia. They jumped around and circled me yelling, "URA, URA, URA!" like crazy cangrejos. I wanted them to see words on the page because I believed in their weight. I wanted them to see how I still found rhythm in them even after she hit. When I showed the reds these lines they laughed. They laughed at me. Threw heavy stones with dirt still on them. They mocked me and it felt like a void opened in the earth where currents drifted and gyred and a trench as deep as the Sargasso Sea pulled at me. I felt myself shrink small, small, saw a wave pull me into its tiding, and the deepest trench off the north coast of Puerto Rico became my home. Until I was forgotten.

MORIVIVÍ

We got the location of Memoria. Damaris didn't like how, but I told her I wasn't going to play anymore games with the reds. I simply took my knife and cornered one that loitered around la plaza central de Florencia. Damaris yelled at me to let it be, but I tugged the little shit by his hair. He must've been ten years old. He tried kicking me in my stomach and that's when I pulled the knife and gave him a small incision on his calf and that shut him up. He tried crying his way out from my grip. I knew it was manipulation, so I yanked harder until he gave me the information and pleaded to be set free.

He told me to follow PR-10 south from Arecibo and walk up the mountain when the road ends, said the reds lead the way. I dropped him on his ass with a strong thrust and he fell, then crawled to a stagger before running off. Damaris shook her head while I chuckled.

"What did he say?" Damaris asked.

"It's near Utuado."

"Not surprising."

"Until we see what's there. Might all be a bad joke."

"Better than staying here."

I agreed with her.

We found some abandoned two-stroke dirt bikes. Boys used to drive them around Florencia on weekends treading rubber on the sidewalks. They'd boom through empty street corners pronouncing their existence. On most days, it was obnoxious, a fear that if they weren't loud enough, perhaps they'd be forgotten. Now, it was a sound we missed terribly.

I helped Damaris with her kick because she seemed tired. I kept nudging her along trying to feed her some of my strength. The bikes muffled after a few attempts until they sparked to life and let out a high-pitched growl. I looked at Damaris as she clasped on the steer.

"Will you manage?" I shouted.

She looked away and nodded.

"You sure?"

"Yes!" she yelled. She pushed me softly and rode off.

I got on my bike, kicked, and followed her up onto the highway and we set out.

We rode those bikes and saw everything around us. It seemed like an impossibility. That the entire island was still decrepit and unable to sustain life. As we rode down the highway, the debris and escombros near Plaza Las Américas were scattered all over. The mall was abandoned and even though we saw some cars parked in the lot, there was an absence of movement below. The main entrance to Plaza was barred with hurricane shutters, the large metal insignia which replicated the three shipping masts and sails from La Niña, Pinta, and Santa María lay scattered across the deserted parking lot. Billboards made out of strong steel, advertising insurance companies and Big Macs, snapped at their center and hung over like towels on a drying rack. We rode on the overpass. The old San Juan landfill that long reached capacity and was converted into a golf range struck the color amber. The large INDULAC lettering that used to dress the top of the landfill was destroyed too.

Nature adapts without forgiveness. I say this because there is nothing like our tropical forests rebuilding on their own. As we rode on, I noticed the resistance from the scattered forests, between all the concrete and steel. In the way a flamboyán, even when fallen, can still adjust by sprouting erratic shoots, so long as the roots remain attached to soil. I don't think land really changes, at least not in the ways we expect. It's not the land but us. That's what I want to believe. The land adapts to something suitable. Some may call it a change but it's a new reality. I began to feel that it wasn't change that was constant, it was adaptation. Maybe a kind of change. But it always felt to me that change was an epiphany and the island had none. The island adapted, and those of us who remained merely learned. I think that's what Urayoán wanted. I hoped that's what it was.

There is a mosque tucked away on the face of one of the mountainsides in the valley where Vega Alta and Vega Baja meet. It is painted a leaden blue wavering against the dull contrast of its surroundings. The highway descends as you pass the automated toll plaza. We flipped off the camera as we rode by because we overheard the old government was still trying to collect tariffs for road use.

I thought about God. About what prayer sounds like after the calamity. If it was about resolve before the amen, the many times I thought of my catechism, my baptism, my ritual, my inheritance. I thought about the mosque and its difference, yet I took comfort that cry in all prayers feel the same. The intent is the same.

We rode on and on, the sound from our bikes pelted the air. Since leaving San Juan we didn't see a single moving car. We didn't see any parked on the emergency lanes, none trekking aimlessly, looking for a sense of normal. It was just Damaris and me and that was enough. I wanted to keep that going, perhaps continue riding until the highway ended and we hit Hatillo and there we'd continue on la número dos and speed through the dead traffic lights and ride out west until land ended at the corner of Rincón.

After a couple of hours, we finally reached the intersection with PR-10. We turned south and headed toward Utuado. We knew that outside of Utuado there was nothing, spare PR-10. It was isolated, which was why Urayoán choosing this area started to make sense.

It must've been another hour of evading escombros and debris until the road narrowed. It began to get crowded with more debris the longer we remained in transit ascending up into the mountain ridge. I kept hearing the red's voice reminding me to stop once the narrow became impassable. That we would know when we needed to climb.

We saw some abandoned pickup trucks blocking the road. They were charred, hollow, and blackened. It seemed deliberate. Damaris stopped her bike and powered it off. She walked over and picked through the remains. I did the same and we both rummaged through the burned skeletons of those pickups, tossing singed laminates aside, clearing plastic containers, zinc rooftops blown far from the town center, piles of ash collected from the fire.

"Who do you think did this?" I asked.

"Who else?" she responded.

"The markings, Damaris." I said as I pointed to large red arrows painted on the side of the road in the direction of the dead forest. "That's it."

"We should make sure to look through this mess first. Might find something useful."

"Okay."

I poked around the back of the trucks and noticed a note-book on the bed. I jumped onto the truck bed, avoiding some of the holes on the metal frame and tugged the notebook loose. I couldn't make out any of the writing.

"Look at this, Damaris."

I tossed the notebook to her and she leafed through the black and brown pages and then let it drop to her feet.

"Nothing here," she said in a dismissive way.

"Take it."

"Why?"

"It belonged to someone."

"So?"

"Damaris, please."

She picked it back up. I kept rummaging in the bed of the pickup and noticed an emptied sack. It was worn and aged. I eyed it for a moment and when I made to put it down, I noticed something yellow and white glinting among all the charred plastic and metal. There were these small nuggets that looked like yellowed pearls lined in a jagged row. I looked closer and poked at them until it struck me. A row of teeth fissured from a shattered skull. I jumped back then climbed down the truck's metal frame and walked over to my dirt bike.

"Damaris," I said to her in a hurried tone. "Damaris, let's move along."

"Something wrong?"

"Nothing . . . we should be close. Should try getting there before we lose the sun."

"Okay," she responded.

She didn't hesitate and for a moment I feared she'd look at the bed of that pickup and see it. But she didn't. She walked back to her dirt bike and we got off the road with the bikes and walked them to the foot of the slope that we needed to climb. We left the bikes there, covering them with some leaves and twigs.

I wondered if I made it up. Should I have looked closer, was it really teeth and a jaw? I convinced myself that it didn't matter. For a moment, it made me angry again, accepting all of it as our new reality. Oh, how we lived.

We saw the trees marked in red paint and Damaris and me both knew that it led to Urayoán and Memoria, so we followed each tree and we climbed slowly up the steep slope. I looked up to the crowns of the dead trees. Some were sprouting new green at the tips. The sky above was hazy and overcast but for some reason it felt closer to normal and that made me smile. I tried getting Damaris to notice but she didn't care and brushed it off. I tugged at the sweater tied around her waist, but she swatted me away and pointed up in the direction of the path we walked, as if to tell me to concentrate on it, to not waste time.

A lot of time passed as we continued. I noticed the sun setting through the trees. The slant of light cutting less and less before us. We kept climbing and followed the red marks until they suddenly stopped.

"What happened?" Damaris asked. "Did we take a wrong turn?"

"No. They stopped."

I rushed back to the last red marking and scanned to see if I saw a different path, but nothing appeared.

"Are you sure, Mori? Maybe we turned the wrong way."

"No, Damaris. We followed the red paint and climbed. That's what the red said to me."

"Are you sure he didn't say anything else—"

"Yes, Damaris! ¡Coño!"

I punched the bark of a tree and wanted to yell. It felt like we were stranded.

"There has to be another way. Something we missed below."

"There is no other way, nena. That little shit said what he said."

"Then let's go back to the pickups," Damaris made to walk back down the slope, but I ran up to her and grabbed her.

"No. Keep going forward. Maybe we need to get to the very top."

"I'm walking back, Mori. Not going to keep climbing. I'm tired."

"That's hours back."

"So?"

"We'll never make it before nightfall. It's too late now. We'll get turned around. Then we're really fucked."

"I don't care."

"Damaris, just listen to me. Let's keep—"

"No!" She pushed me hard. "I'm walking back down. This was a stupid idea."

"Damaris, please. Let's just try and see what's at the top. If there's nothing, we'll go back."

"You can do that. I'm not going to keep climbing."

"I'm not going at it alone."

"And I'm not going to keep climbing. I'm tired. Tired of chasing a ghost."

I started to feel an urge to yell as loud as I could because I knew there was nowhere else to go. I didn't want us to split up. We could go anywhere or wait until everything around us dried up and died but I couldn't leave her alone. I wouldn't.

I wanted to cry in that moment, and I started feeling hatred and anger. That this was us, that this was it.

I waited there as I watched Damaris slowly trod back. I heard a whistle in the distance and called out to Damaris.

"Did you hear that?" I said.

"Ya, Mori," Damaris responded as she continued making her way down. Then the whistle grew louder, and she paused, and we locked eyes before looking around us, scanning the dead forest in a collected paranoia. The whistling grew in sequence and pitch. It echoed from each corner, from each hollow tree, even the crowns above rustled, branches shuddering against one another, bark creaking with the passing wind. It wasn't an organized pitch. That's what distressed us, the unevenness.

I ran up to Damaris and we leaned close to each other for comfort as the whistling continued, volume increasing until a chant echoed "Ura, Ura, Ura." We saw the reds poke their heads from behind the rows of trees. They wore red bomber jackets and torn red jeans; their faces covered with black surgical masks.

I took out my knife because I grew tired of the games. I started shouting out, "Come at us or shut the fuck up!" I yelled and cursed until my voice dried up and Damaris tugged at me. We waited for some time until the reds drifted behind each of their trees. They disappeared in the background.

The sun had almost set. A thin fog layered the mountain. I started to feel like we'd never arrive to Memoria, wondered if such a place even existed. I knew Damaris's exhaustion weighed on her. We waited to see if the reds reappeared and showed us a path, but nothing came.

"Forget it, Mori. Forget it." Damaris fell to the ground and slumped her head over her knees. I fell down with her. I don't know what we were waiting for. A defeat overcame us. One that wouldn't be quenched even if Memoria grew right there underneath our feet. It was a defeat found when you've moved past exhaustion and transition into static. White noise. We simply existed and breathed while awaiting the inevitable. I heard it in how Damaris inhaled. I felt it in the way she sometimes pinched the skin on my hands.

I didn't want us to waste away there, so I finally stood up and even though Damaris initially resisted, she too rose, and we turned to make our way down until we heard the shuffling of feet and the strike of wooden spoons against a metal pot. We turned and looked up at the top of the slope and a shadow appeared. The last rays of sun cut through the rows of trees and the shadow grew larger emitting a mountain spectre, a crystal halo pulsing around its head. The figure kept glowing against the sun's last rays, fog, and light. The trees greeted the shadow in a militarized salute and an ethereal figure glided down the slope, the branches and twigs snapping underneath each step until the shadow revealed an ugly face, a brown and deep face with cracked skin and facial hair as disheveled as the wavy hair on his head. It was Urayoán and he walked as if he were God's begotten son sent to save our island, hands outstretched expecting welcome.

BANTO

ayfish and I travel close. That's something we've always done. The red markings on tree bark may lead us to Memoria, but I remember cucubanos when I see me and Bayfish trekking through forests. These small bugs shined and flickered at dusk, little portable stars you repeatedly caught and set free and watched dance, never in desperation, but more grateful whenever let go.

Bayfish was still a seedling in our pack. Ura picked him out and fed him and nursed him back to something human. He took him out of struggle and brought him to Florencia and that's where we met. Mamá said it was all right to have him over when he needed a place to stay. Bayfish was still used to drifting and it was hard at first, latching an anchor to his feet so he wouldn't go wandering looking for water or food.

When Mamá went to work, she spent most of her time there almost as a way to escape the troubles found at home, the troubles with me. And when I told her how I was leaving school and never going back, she slapped me across my face so hard, I thought I'd never feel my chubby cheeks again. But that's where it ended. That was the extent of her anger toward my decision. She was gentle in her short-lived anger. I think she forgot on purpose; a thing you do when there's conviction. Ura had a reputation around Florencia because of some good deed he did way back when. Though Mamá never went into details about it, she and others repeated Ura saved children from drowning during the time of a great flood. I was told he predicted the deluge, a Savior apparent. That seemed to be enough for him to have the streets. Once that happened, there was very little he couldn't get away with.

Mamá saw how Ura and his brood spent their days and knew I found a home with them. Even though Ura led the way in making my life miserable, there was protection in that. *Better him than some stranger,* I thought. I'm sure she thought the same. When Bayfish came into the picture it seemed to distract everyone. I think Mamá figured there was someone else looking out for me so she was absolved of responsibility.

In Florencia there used to be this hill we called La Diabla. It overlooked Ura's spot and behind Ura's place, as backdrop, you saw all of Florencia. That's where Bayfish and I used to go. As the sun set, the clearing below was pristine with its high grass and sugarcane husks that clattered against one another in symphony. Bayfish got so pensive up there with the cane music and cucubanos. He told me how one day he wanted to do something important with his life. I assured him that it was about getting control of what you can.

"But this place is limiting, Banto. I see in the news this and that, about people leaving Puerto Rico and making something bigger of their lives across the sea."

"I don't care about none of that. I want to be here and that's what matters. Home, I guess." I paused for a moment. "This is home."

"Home," he repeated.

I ripped out some grass and dirt next to me. I tossed it into the air for dramatic effect.

"I want to live, hurt, and rot here in this soil."

"Even if things get desperate?"

VELORIO

"Even if I have to cry from pain and hunger every night."
"That's brave of you, cabrón. Look at you all tough."

WHEN IT GOT dark, we marched down to Ura's old house. It was dirty, an old stripping mill used for sugarcane. Long abandoned, the smoke spire was rusted and ready to crumble. Ura liked to put his clothes to dry on the large metal diffuser and if it was a sunny day, the bronzed contraption boiled, quickly drying up the damp cloth.

There was a small hangar with large barn doors next to the house and that's where some of the reds slept. Ura long collected the reds. He let them live there in that large empty house on the conditions that they never fought among each other. They were so grateful, young, and stupid that it rarely happened. It was a commune or compound of sorts. A lost orphanage and Ura the matron supreme. I suppose he always had it in him to build spaces that he controlled.

Over time, Ura grew a temper. An anger budding into sinister conflict mostly directed at the old government. He started quoting the Bible more, looked at Revelation as testament to an end of times. Talked about anarchy. I used to joke with him that he sounded like Rubén Berríos and all those types. He lashed out saying he didn't care for any party or any color. Said everything should be set on fire. He kept on about welfare or electricity or how we didn't have a nation. That was his biggest thing: nation. And so, all that seemed to build over the years and all he needed was an excuse to unravel.

Ura claimed himself prophetic. It started with him believing he predicted the mass migration of people out of our island.

I challenged him by blaming Wall Street. He ignored me. He countered by saying *control* would soon be the answer our politicians needed for the crippling debt. When la Junta was announced, he proclaimed another correct prophesy. I told him Uncle Sam's congress had their own interests, told him that's not what PROMESA or the Fiscal Control Board aimed to do.

"Is that what you meant by control, Ura?" I mocked him.

He chuckled at me and said it was the beginning of things to come.

A part of me wanted to be like him. At least carry some of that confidence. It was as if he knew María was always going to come and end things, turn our island completely dark, strip us of governance, electricity, and people, as if her evil was necessary, how she meant all of it to happen, if only for Ura to fulfill his own ambition. I wondered if he compensated for some past he never had control over. Ura never liked speaking about his history. Only Bayfish knew his story. He made the mistake of slipping some of that info to me once. It was in passing.

I was talking with him about my old friend, Dayanara. She was as pretty as her namesake Miss Universe, eyes an emerald green, pale skin with jet black hair. In all the years I'd known her, she had trouble finding happiness. I figured she was chronically depressed. She confided in me that she was having trouble at home. Her padrastro was abusing her. At first, I thought abuse meant punches and cuts. She simply shook her head and said nothing more. I wanted to get her help, to go to the police. Told her she could spend nights with me and Mamá for safekeeping. But she insisted she could or would handle it.

She killed herself. Took a rope, found the biggest ceiba, and let herself drop. When I heard the news, I didn't cry. I was in denial. Even went to her house after school like I usually did expecting her to run out and hug me. I mentioned it to Bayfish months after and he said it sounded the same as Ura's mom.

"Wait, what sounds like that?" I said.

"The suicide."

SOME OF THE reds played with a basketball in the next room. Ura was painting this large map of Puerto Rico on his wall. He loved to paint and that's one way he entertained the reds. He used those massive walls and a rickety ladder to spread the borders of our island to each corner of the room. He painted. He kept tracing circles on the map's center.

"Planning a coup, I see . . . Ura, is that your target? Are you going to recruit all the jíbaros and march out onto the streets on horseback?" I asked him and laughed. He got angry and threw one of his wet brushes at me and it stained my belly with red paint.

"Cállate, gordo mamabicho," he yelled.

Bayfish grabbed an old shirt from the floor and gave it to me to wipe away the stain.

"What's the plan with this?" Bayfish asked, walking up to him and leaving me behind near the entrance of the room.

"You know how these islands are constructed at their bones. Geography tells us the center where them mountain ranges is is where there's power. I never get why we hang out near the water. We could do so much more in the center, away from estos políticos corruptos."

"Don't get lost in all that, Ura," Bayfish said.

"Cállate, Bayfish. I never get lost. The day's coming. I'm marching my path. All of you cabrones will follow. You'll see," he snapped.

"Just be happy we get to eat and stay dry from the rain. Be grateful we are alive. That's what I do," I yelled from where I stood. Still pathetically dabbing at my belly.

"Banto's right, Ura. I worry you getting into it too much."

"The time will come, and you *all* will follow," he said and let out a laugh. "A true calamity will sweep this island. It'll force everything to change. It is written. It is written in the words."

"No te entiendo, cabrón. What are you getting at?" Bayfish asked.

"You'll see," he repeated almost to himself. "You'll see."

He climbed a couple of steps down the ladder.

"Oye, goldiflón. Come here," he said, turning his attention to me. He waved me over. I was still dabbing away at my belly.

"We headed out, Ura—"

"Come here, come here."

I slowly walked over to him with my shoulders slumped. Ura there on his ladder surveying the room. I tried not to look at him too directly so as not to provoke him into action. I stood below and looked at him the way scolded dogs do. He picked up the half-used paila of red paint and poured it over my head and shook it until there was nothing left.

"¡Cómete esto, mamabicho!" he yelled out and threw the empty paila across the room. Some of the reds heard the clatter and rushed in and when they saw me standing there slicked in red paint, they laughed, pointed, and jumped up and down.

"¡Cabrón!" Bayfish yelled and hit the ladder. Ura slid down the last few steps and shoved Bayfish so hard he fell to the floor.

"Stay out of it, huelebicho."

"You going to cry now, goldiflón?" he said. He stuck his face in front of me and pretended to cry. "Go ahead, cry. Cry, cry, cry."

I tried wiping away the paint from my eyes but more dripped from my head and ran down the front of my face. I was glad for the paint because I did cry. I cried and I imagined how dumb it must've all looked, me drenched in thick red paint crying. The reds danced and yelled out "URA, URA, URA!" in a chorus. I wanted to run out of there, but I knew that unless Ura gave the order and Bayfish escorted me out as a sort of protection, I might have provoked Ura and his brood to do more.

"Huelebicho. Goldiflón. Don't tell me when and how to feel," he said. "Get out of here, maricones."

BAYFISH AND I eventually left. We walked again through the bamboo forest headed toward Florencia. I continued to sob. I tried to hold it in, but the more I tried, the more it came out. I felt so fat and pathetic smeared in red. Walking in the darkness trailing Bayfish the way abandoned dogs trail strangers. He didn't look back as we cut through the bamboos. I'm sure he tried finding words that could ease my sadness. But all that came out was, "Sorry about that, mano. Sorry he did that to you." He repeated it every ten minutes or so until we eventually reached the forks and la plaza de Florencia.

I didn't want to walk anymore, and I just fell onto one of the metal benches that lined the roadside. La plaza was quiet, and all the shops were closed.

"Come with me, Banto."

"I don't want to go anywhere," I said between breathes.

"Come, mano," he said. He grabbed my hand and forced me up. I didn't want to go anywhere but he insisted and pulled me along and we made it to the bridge near the river and Bayfish dragged me along past his shack and we followed the low canal that led to the chinchorros and reached the pier where the mongers usually shipped out and he walked me along the river until we reached a sand bed. The water smelled thick of salt and I could see broken plastic, rotting wooden chairs, and old tires half-buried in that sand. I'm sure the river was filthy, but Bayfish took off his shirt. Scaly hair covered his stomach and back, and his long and scarred neck was reflected by the crescent moon above. He gently pushed me in front of him and made me walk with him into the water.

"Look, Banto, look," he said, pointing to the cucubanos flickering over the dirty river. They danced atop the water. There weren't many of them, but they lit up if only for seconds, their soft lights shining.

"It's nice, right?" he said.

I didn't say anything back. All I could do was shake my head, watch, wait until those tiny lights over the river flickered, faded, and fell into the water and died.

URAYOÁN

They say red is colored fire and I like it that way, to see things ablaze with horror. That's why I asked the reds for a grand gate. Memoria will splinter this earth into two great divided halves and on one side you'll see a big and bright gate that remembers. Like those times I read about in dusty pages, when people like me—prophets, leaders, geniuses—cut into the bleeding and our followers died fighting. When I talk about our history, I will say that we tried to be free from masters and owners. That's enough for me.

I want my gate to commemorate me and all my ideas. It's tiled red to make our visitors' spines bleed. That's what my pets did. They stole from different ferreterías red tiles, cinder blocks, and bags of mix to create the gates Memoria deserves. It didn't take long either. Fact, no one was paying attention up there. With la monstrua, what happened, and what was lost in the disaster they didn't keep much account. Things easily slipped because of people's absent recordkeeping so that sped things up for me and Memoria.

They say Utuado is made up of spirits. Its pride is native. There is a ceremonial park used long ago by ancestors in order to celebrate and exalt greatness to something like God. That interests me because there are traces of that in my blood. Some try to deny the origin of us and our roots, even say that's where our passivity comes from. All lies! I see no way you have a Columbus type bring his disease and death and no blood is spilled. My name is **Urayoán** like the warrior that in legend ordered the killing of Diego de Salcedo. My origin is that of the warrior that drowned all the conquistador's phony immortal mirage. My name begets leader, cacique of Memoria. My name begets declaration for beginnings.

This Utuado town near my Memoria wasn't going to get in the way because the old government abandoned it just like everything else. Like all good cacique's old and new I had my pets that worked for me and kept the order. I debated for weeks what was the root of anger and malice in the old system and I thought in brilliance, *Age! Age! Age!* They tried to feed us age as wisdom yet that's how bad habits perpetuate and how pain is passed on from one generation to the next. I don't want Memoria to inherit that mess, so I was very cautious about ancients trying to sneak into my wonder. If you can believe, some did show, they followed the trails laid by the reds and when they appeared, they tried to impose their thoughts on how to build my red gate, and that's when I knew I didn't need that kind of wisdom.

It's night and dark and just off highway PR-10 that leads to Utuado there are rocky paths that crawl out like spider legs. People carved them into the soil so they could get to the caves. But I loathe the time they tried turning profit from land. They built fences and gatekeepers and charged people to explore nature. They charged! Memoria is not to build profit but to escape from the old and start anew. It's not about cuarto for me. It's about perception.

I remember when I was also the age of the reds, I visited Cueva Ventana without a gatekeeper. It was still part of the land without markers or signs, found only if you knew where to look. But one day, when I was older, I returned to Cueva Ventana and there was a man with others putting up fences and kiosks, and when I asked him what he do, he said, "We are setting up an entrance and will be handing out safety helmets. We put in work to make the entrance into the cave easier, a wooded staircase and a strong rope for support." He said this and first I stared at him like it was a joke and tried to walk by him, me and my pets tried, and he put his arm up all rigid and flashy as a stop sign. He was inflated from frequent gym visits, but that didn't scare me. Because it's about the mind, not how physically strong you get. I said to him, "Let me by, me and my brothers have been coming here since we were little at no cost." He didn't listen and tried his power and tone on me, "It's going to cost you five dollars plus the helmet rental to get to the cave. Please get in line and wait your turn." That was what really set me off and I got so violent I kicked up dirt from the ground at his feet. "No one asked you to build your nonsense here and now you charge five dollars for something that is nature and free. Who gives you the right?" I said this angrily and some of my reds held me back a little. "We charge because we've invested resources for people to have a smooth experience and enjoy the view," he said, and I repeated back, "Who gave you the right?" and he responded all smart and smirking, "Our investment gives us the right." I couldn't believe the confidence. I stood there with my fist clenched as my pets tugged on them. They knew too many people would witness. If I hurt him bad enough, I'd be taken away, they'd be left without a cacique. What made me glow with rage was seeing all the arrivants, they parked their big fancy cars along the emergency lanes of PR-10, some parked near the gas station and along the side grass. They didn't question the charge. Paid all happy, grabbing a helmet. I thought if enough people fought back, the cave would be returned back clean and free.

But no one fought the man there with his gatekeeping pad writing down inventory or something or collecting the cash. I was red with anger. "This is a public cave, a part of the earth," I said this as my last attempt for him to drink reason, but he threw it back at me wearing the same satisfied caripelao look, "The cave may be public but the land where the cave sits is not. It is owned by a man who just bought the acreage from the previous owner. If you are not going to pay the fee, then you have to leave." He said this looking at his pad. Didn't even meet my eyes. I wanted to take a stone and bash his skull open. Was just about to when the reds, all three of them, dragged me away before I started a riot.

WE DROVE THE stolen fuel trucks through the rocky and crater roads slow and slow. My older reds who drive followed my truck until we reached the large clearing the size of three baseball diamonds. The roads rose slowly connecting to the clearing, almost like a perfect tabletop nestled there in the middle of all the tall piercing mountains. This is how Memoria is stationed. The crater roads are impossible to travel and somehow the fuel trucks traverse without incident, evidence that it is anointed by God. I prophesied to succeed! We took the trucks and drove them near the edge of the clearing where the forest started and the steep slope down began. Where there is the thickness and wild of the trees, the land drops deep. In order to reach us you have to climb, and that's what I like most about Memoria. The only other way to enter is through the surrounding forest of the clearing but the slope is so steep you see anyone coming. Since el Río Caonillas is within distance to the clearing, to Memoria, it serves a perfect pattern, a perfect center with waterlines to the two large lakes nearby.

My plan was easy. I made my pets dig large pits into the ground, they stole some crawlers and excavators from Utuado and pushed the dirt around until there was enough for the trucks to mostly submerge. We buried the trucks leaving a hose attached to syphon the gasoline and diesel. Even if the old government comes looking, they'll never find them.

Memoria will need shacks and outposts for my reds to live, survey, and keep the entrance secure and regulated. But the gate is what I wanted created to perfection. So that's what we did. I also wanted the paths that lead to Memoria marked. Trees with red paint because in the end, that's what my Memoria is meant to be, a haven where order and food and law is found and that's constitution. And the reds brought the red paint, and they went dancing down the steep slopes dotting every so tree with a smudge of bright red.

As time passed, we soon ran out of supplies. The reds told me they needed more cement mix for my grand gate. The remedy was paying a visit to Utuado. We sneaked with the cover of stars into a town drowned in water. Most of la plaza central near the church was abandoned and the local shops were dressed in a layer of mud and soot. Me and the reds followed the streets in silence and, just where the hill descended from the center, we saw a line with people napping. The line stretched and turned the block, but I knew they were waiting for gasoline and diesel. "Give the young people the pamphlets," I said this to the reds. They always carried a batch with them, so my pets went on ahead scouting for the young to join Memoria.

We followed the narrow streets block by block until the town opened up and there was the ferretería. It hid in this empty parking lot. You could see the skeletons of a chain-link fence, the chains warped loose and free. The building was like a hangar and toward the back were these large wooden barn doors where they loaded timber to contractors and that's where the cement mix was. Since the reds and me didn't have a car yet, we went into the building to sift through the long inventory aisles for a couple of wheelbarrows. Later we'd steal cars and pickups but now was the time for feet and wheel-barrows.

It was dark and I used the flashlight to shine the bags of mix as the reds loaded them onto the barrows. I marveled at their music, how each lift was like a choreographed dancer, and that made me a proud cacique. We loaded and loaded and also snared wire and rope to take advantage while we were there, when there was a flash in blue strobe. The police from the old government were parked outside and that's the fear I didn't want because then there was a potential for violence. "Ura, should we fire a few rounds at them?" a red asked me, and I told him, "Patience." I turned the flashlight off waiting to see the next move. I saw from the open door the blue strobe probing the darkness and I knew they could see us there in the hangar, so I signaled the reds to make toward the exit with the barrows. They moved in desperation and ducked into the main building back to the entrance of la ferretería and I saw the officers get out of their patrullas and stand there with their lights scanning the building, the doorframe, and the parking lot. I readied my pistol.

But the officers just went back into their patrullas and drove out of the lot and rushed back into town. I turned to the hangar and I could breathe better knowing it didn't call for violence since it makes for a sleepless night. I turned my light on and scanned the aisles to see my pets, but they were nowhere in sight. I sounded my whistle, which usually caught them running back in order. Nothing. I kept whistling but then my rage was growing and I yelled out, "¡Oye, cabrones!" and heard just the soft buzzing of insects. I walked out to the entrance and scanned the parking lot again and saw nothing. Then I saw a light born on the horizon and it looked like a fire growing and growing. The fire started filling the night and I saw that the reds had set cars on fire where the line of people waited. They ran back up the road to me hunched and crouched and chanted, "Ura, Ura, Ura."

They grabbed the barrows and they wheeled them out of the hangar, and we hurried back through the narrow streets of Utuado. We came up on la plaza central and the church and saw everyone frozen. The people that were in the line for gasoline watched the flames dance and spark. Everyone floated around the lit cars like moths, even the officers too. We stood there with the people from the line and we all were looking at fire and flames.

I noticed the church more because the plaza was now lit up nicely and I noticed its age, the yellow paint on its walls faded by the sun. The two short bell towers like eroded stumps of wood. The rusted iron gate at the side that led to a small garden was open and it all looked pathetic. I stayed looking at the church until I noticed something on the top. A fat girl and she was holding on to something. She was seated there staring, wearing some dark flowery thing, and it was a person next to her but the person looked limp and soggy.

I whistled to the reds and pointed at the church. We took

the barrows with us and we made it to the open gate, and I told them to go. I waited outside with our supplies and then I heard a red soft yell, "Ura, Ura, Ura." I walked into the small garden made up of trinitarias and amapola shrubs giving it this messy color mix. The garden cleared a thin and weeded path to the ladder. I made my way up the ladder and climbed and climbed until I reached the rooftop and stood. I could see all of Utuado from there, the dark outline of mountains as backdrop, the cars that the reds set on fire below. The people standing around doing nothing. "Ura!" the red said and hurried me from my view. I smelled something rancid and terrible, so I covered my nose. The reds were all covering their faces with their hands pointing at the fat girl. She was in a trance looking out into the horizon, hugging a rotting corpse. She was big and strong but looked vulnerable. I made as if to move her, but she didn't falter. The reds poked the thing next to her and held back vomit. "No more Energy. No more Energy," she started saying. "No more. No more." She called gasoline and power this. It was instant music to my ears.

I touched the fat girl on the shoulder then I snapped my fingers in front of her, but she still didn't move. "You got a name?" I asked this and heard nothing. "Let us help you," I found myself saying and I signaled the reds to grab the corpse and they refused at first, but I shot them the mean look. They grabbed the green and rotting body from the fat girl and suddenly she sparked to life. She gripped the corpse harder and started repeating, "No No No," in a hoarse and exhausted cry, not loud or angry, but defeated. "Come with us, nena. We have a place to stay," I said and surprised myself with my sudden generosity. "Marisol, Marisol," she started to repeat as she clung to the dead thing. "She's coming too," I tell her and started helping her up to her feet and the reds took the body and lugged it down the ladder and placed it into a barrow. "Mari . . . Mari . . . Mari," she started repeating again as I helped her down the ladder. It was something strange that came into me, to take her in, but I had a feeling it was important, so I followed my gut—my brilliance, my genius.

So the reds went on ahead, pushing along the barrows filled with rope and wire and mix and one carrying a dead rotting thing. We walked away from that church and the blazing cars back into the cover of darkness and snuck through the narrow streets until we reached the impossible paths that led to Memoria. When we arrived, I told the reds to set a cot up for the girl and her dead thing and they first refused but I shot them that stare again and they quickly acted accordingly, setting a cot far, far from most things in Memoria for the fat girl. I walked her over to the cot and she sat there without moving and I could tell she had not slept for a long, long while, so I patted her on the back and told her, "Get some sleep, now. You're in Memoria. We here to take care of things. Sleep." I said this and all she kept repeating was, "Marisol, Mari, Marisol." And I reminded her she was there too. We lay the dead thing next to her and that's when I saw her really grow heavy and slump and fall into her cot and I knew she was diving into her dreams. The smell of the dead corpse was thick and heavy, so the reds and me backed away and walked to our corner of the clearing where our cots and the Energy trucks were. "What are we doing with that thing, Ura?" a red asked me, and I responded, "We'll figure it out later," with uncertainty, and the reds knew this and that's why they kept pressing. "The smell will get very bad. Worse than it is now," my pet said, as if I didn't think that too, so I snapped back with a short burst of anger, "I know! Go to sleep. We'll plan soon."

That night I had this beautiful nightmare. I saw Memoria in a fire and all the reds chose not to run but stay and rejoice as the fire grew angrier. Then the dryness of the surrounding forest caught the blaze too and the yellow and orange wave spread into the darkness and you saw it crawl to every corner of the island burning and smoking, the membranes of our home seared into our memories, and that made me wake up in a sweat and curse. I turned and looked into the darkness, to Memoria, and looked at all the potential and it frightened me how easily everything could catch and sear and then turn to ash.

TWO

CHEO

I knew Vega Baja like the hairs on my feet. I used to work part-time en Tortuguero BBQ before landing in Florencia with the mongers. I walked and walked. It would be days until I reached Memoria, but I knew someone dear that still lived in Vega Baja, so I figured it fine to stop and visit my old friend.

Doña Julia lived in a nursing home, one of those medical places that care for the sick and aging. It had two floors and a wheelchair ramp that led to the second-floor entrance. A verandah wrapped around the entire house. The house was painted an orange peel color and the roof and windows were white. The house was located on la número dos so it wasn't hard to find and during my lunch breaks working at Tortuguero BBQ, I'd bring some ensalada de pulpo to Doña Julia and I liked to joke with her that someday they would remember her like her namesake, the great Julia de Burgos, and she liked that a lot because I knew she felt abandoned. Which is why I needed to see her. But this time I only brought her my company, no pulpo.

The house was quiet and so was the road. Weeks had passed since she hit our island, but nothing had changed. I thought I'd see the streets busy with congestion or lines trying to enter the Amigo grocer, but it all sat in silence and it made me feel uneasy. Those who remained searched desperately for resources. Immediately after she hit, this was clear as sunlight. But now it seemed like a desert, like nothing had ever existed. I thought about more lines for my poetry, things I picked along the way and wrote in my notebooks.

Brown as the ferns may be, I see the green color returning at
  the tips.
The heat from the sun is hotter when green disappears, and
  I bathe in sweat.

I also came across life again; caimans trotting the streets, pigeons hanging on electric wires, mosquitoes, caculos. Even saw a mongoose rifling along the side of the road. The sound of songbirds returned too. Somewhat at least. Their songs were different, which added to my anxiety.

I missed the ocean since leaving Florencia, so I took a short detour on my way to Vega Baja. Yesterday I trekked along Playa Cerro Gordo. I wanted to see the coast again because even the river back in Florencia didn't open the way the ocean does. I stumbled through the sand with my notebook in hand and watched as the brown waves hit the beach and swept my toes. I came up with these observations.

- The currents drift in different patterns since she hit.
- I see no blue or green reflected in the ocean's horizon.
- It all looks like a muddy river that lifted sand and sediment.
- More garbage than usual. Plastic of sorts and refrigerators rusted on the wet sand.
- Glass Bacardí bottles washed up, some with rum still in them.
- If I squint and look into that horizon, I see these large metal barges floating.
- I predict they carry something we could've used weeks ago but now what does it matter.
- There is less beach sand and the brown guck is angrier as it eats away at the land.

· I miss the foaming spit of the water before she came because now it's all thick and still.

Today, standing in front of Doña Julia's nursing home, I wondered if she remembered the way the tide enters and recedes, in all its comings and goings. She longed for all that was, I know I did too. I knock on the front door a few times waiting for someone to answer and let me in, but no one came. I looked through the sun-stained windows but couldn't make anything through the cloudiness. Then a young woman dressed in floral scrubs came around the verandah. Young and pretty, skin coconut and hair a dark brown.

"I'm trying to see someone. Is it possible to go in?" I said to her.

"Come to the back. Let's use the back door," she responded, and I walked with her around the verandah.

At the back of the house there was a double screen door and she opened and held it for me as I walked inside. There were hospital beds in disorganized rows. But what frightened me the most was how quiet everything was. I didn't hear the sound of a generator. I worried about the heat and the elderly.

"Who you here for?" the nurse asked.

"Julia."

"Doña Julia? She's right over there," she said, pointing toward the far end of the room.

"And the power? Do you have a generator for the machines?"

"We don't turn it on often. We can't. There's not enough diesel to fuel it. The Puma down the street closed about a week ago. Said they stopped receiving trucks," she said and turned back to a spreadsheet or crossword puzzle or something. "Así es la cosa."

I walked over to Doña Julia's bed. The room seemed divided in two. The front of the house near the entrance was curtained off and these large crates stacked atop each other formed a makeshift wall. I saw through the thin curtain silhouettes of unutilized dialysis machines.

I dragged an empty chair and tucked it near Doña Julia. I rubbed her hands delicately and smiled.

"Julia. Julia."

"¿Quién es?" she said, waking from a dream, and she squinted trying to make out who I was. "Cheo?"

"Sí, Julia."

"Cheo, ay Dios mío. Cheo," she said, raising her hands and placing them on my shoulders. I leaned in and gave her a soft kiss on the cheek.

"Dios te bendiga. I was passing through and wanted to see how you were."

"Ay, Cheo. I'm okay, gracias a Dios. We are here working through—"

"Do you have water and food, Julia?"

"Ay, mijo, we have what we need for now, gracias," she said and smiled and her eyes spoke of sadness. They didn't want to tell me how she really felt, and I wasn't going to press her.

We spent some time talking about the night María passed, and Julia said she remembered howling and a shaking like an airplane engine had fallen from the sky. She told me about her friends, whom she hadn't seen since that night. She pointed to the front entrance of the house and I knew what she meant. It's funny, how she spoke relaxed my anxiety. Not because of what she was saying, but how she viewed it all as another passing event. Her eyes smiled at me and she pet my hand, all tender.

My eyes watered a little bit every time she pressed her fingers into my palms.

"Do you have water, mijo? Do you have food?" she asked. It saddened me to see her trying to take care of me again like she used to do when I was much younger. Doña Julia saved me from myself when I was young and stupid. She taught high school most of her life. Was my music teacher down at escuela Palos Matos.

"I have enough, Julia. Not enough to shit proper. But I have enough," I said laughing, and she closed her eyes serious mocking.

"Bueno, mijo, I haven't shit proper in more than a decade. So, you tell me."

We laughed together and held each other, her eyes lighting up the world.

We stayed there talking about her history, about her deceased husband, and I could tell she found happiness in recollection. We talked until she started fidgeting as if forgetting where she was in time. She tried getting up from the bed.

"Let's go for a walk," she said to me, and I saw a determination in how she spoke. "Let's go to la Laguna Tortuguero. I haven't seen it in so long. I want to see it again, all overgrown. I want to smell the salt in the air."

"We need to be careful about the caimans then," I responded holding her in place.

"Caimans?"

"Yes, they swim there and are always looking for food."

"Ay, virgen. No. Forget it. Let's stay here."

The nurse gave me a thankful look from across the room. After a few hours passed sharing with Julia, I left. I kept walking and could only write about her. I sketched her image into poetry and tried capturing her in my pages. I might never see her again but at least she was there, written in her beauty. It weakened me to think that lines weren't enough, that my skills were terrible, and I wouldn't capture her as she always was to me. But I tried what I could and in that moment, it was enough.

Tonight, Doña Julia is sleeping to the sounds of monsters.
In her last days she remembers his name,
which is ~~a lot~~ like mine. Cheo Gabriel, a husband for thirty
    years,
his name, Cheo, is mine.
Except he has left her and is a rose and a beast.

Tonight, Doña Julia sang to me under her large white quilt,
stained yellow from ~~her day's~~ sweating.
She could barely lift the quilt over her mouth,
as she shook her head and repeated, "No, no."
But her eyes smiled back at me.
I nudged her to sing ~~one more time~~, if only just to me,
one more for my long walk ~~down these streets~~.
I wanted to hear her ~~voice timber~~ notes
and stir the silence of the night awake
for the days grew softer even as nature returned ~~to life~~.

Julia performed en Bellas Artes in Caguas,
late in her years, and once in Santurce, ~~an achievement~~
she shied away ~~from,~~ yet I reminded her how impossible
and beautiful that all was. And she nodded her head
    agreeing.

It wasn't in those songs I hear her desire but in how she
presses her small hands onto my coarse palms and traces
    lines,
youth, to the undeniable, echoes of my childlike yelling,
    my own knees stained in blood when I fell while running
    away from her classroom, how she collected me and said
    nothing, nothing was needed, she walked me back to her
    classroom, and comfort and that was always enough.

She still remembers the scent from the wooden stage, how it
    carried
a perfume citrus and aged. How the wooden stage echoed
under the soles of her shoes. The red chairs in the theater,
some half-empty, comfortable, silent, but stationed and
    attendant
like her audience. Julia remembers the resonance in objects,
and her voice shakes a room. She sings and sings
that voice struck with years of laughter and anger and tears.
I still hear her. I cry as Julia carries me. I cry because I
    left her.
To walk alone and catch the echoes of deserted trees,
drifting, drifting, home.

Those are her lines. I thought about so many things and
meant to go back and strike out more excess. I imagined this
should be better. It all should. Maybe what I was concerned
most about was this thing with the naming. I liked Doña Julia
because she carried the name of our great poet, Julia de Burgos.

I remember I read for fun some of that bastard Walcott and
his *Star-Apple Kingdom*. In his epic "The Schooner *Flight*" he said
names are really what history contains, the power history con-

tains. But what always stuck with me in that poem was how he explained the colonial scar, and us colonial and colonized know the pain of language. Language knows the pain of history. He said it through the voice of Shabine. A voice so much like mine, like ours. Doña Julia was like Maria Concepcion in "The Schooner *Flight*" waiting idly as I ventured out into a terrifying expanse. What then would become of me? What then would become of my poetry?

Walcott tells of nation and empire. It's more like he sings it through Shabine as he travels from the edges of Trinidad and Barbados. But then, what do we do with this fucking island? This, my land? What do I do? Is my island a nation taken and given like the final play in a losing game of dominoes? The end in tranque? I'm not sure what Memoria is really. I'm afraid. Afraid that Ura only sees a past and that he too is mimicry.

There were clouds overhead as I returned to my walk. Perhaps they are fat and ready with rain which hasn't fallen since huracán María long deserted us. I imagine it would be convenient for it to rain now because my emotions match. There is a loneliness on the island, and I felt it before. Before all this. When the mongers and me saw less and less people wanting to fish out in the sea. The loneliness is probably felt by everyone. And the clouds hovered low enough for me to touch them, but I didn't want to. I just wanted to walk and maybe cry a little.

I continued my journey west looking for that place Bayfish believed in. As I drifted farther away from Doña Julia and Vega Baja, I felt her closer to me in the poetry. I guess that's what it's for, to carry and keep no matter how distant we drift out to sea.

BAYFISH

The reds built a gate tiled in blazing color. Ura demanded things that didn't make sense to Banto and me and we kept quiet because Ura seesawed between madness and light. It was an ugly and bulky gate with an uneven frame. The cinder blocks were placed rather lopsided and the mix used to empañetar spread out in clunky lumps. The red tile he insisted on was placed scattershot and at times looked more like a bad mosaic. But Ura was satisfied. He looked on as his reds dug up the clearing and transformed Memoria.

At the center of the clearing, Ura wanted ceremony. Said a great fire needed to be built every night and everyone had to attend evening dinners around the glowing flame. It wasn't a ritual yet, but I knew that's what he meant to do. Ura's vision for Memoria was inscribed in a maxim he came up with. He made the reds carve it into the concrete footing of the gate: A PLACE ANNEXED IN HARMONY THROUGH *HIS* LEADERSHIP.

Then there was his own Tower of Babel. He wanted the reds to collect plywood and sheet metal they'd stolen from Utuado to build a dilapidated tower. It was to be his office and that's where he planned to meet with the citizens of Memoria, the reds serving as his secretaries of state. I waited to hear if he had any special roles for Banto and me but he never called on us. He stole some generators and placed them in the forest entrances and that's how Memoria got light. Ura only turned them on at night because he didn't like the noise much. Which is why he stuck them deeper in the forest.

Every person living in Memoria was given a small amount of diesel to do with it as they pleased. Interesting how Ura orbited around the gasoline and diesel as the only essential. I pressed him about water, which seemed necessary, and he lashed out at me.

"Don't question me. My pets and me are planning, Bay-fish."

"I'm only saying we can't survive off diesel, tú sabes."

"No soy pendejo. I know. Give it a break. We are coming up with something."

He started repeating that more often. Said him and his reds had a plan for everything.

The following day, Ura and the reds drove in with an oasis, a truck filled with drinkable water. It reminded me of those small milk trucks. He stepped out of the driver's seat feeling accomplished. Never mind where he stole it from. Banto stumbled up to him in defiance.

"Cabrón, that's for Utuado. You take that from them and what else they going to drink?" he said to him. Ura stroked the scruff on his chin and tried ignoring him, but I knew Banto wasn't going to let up.

"Cabrón. You hear me?"

"Cállate, goldiflón. I'm busy."

"¡Cabrón!"

Banto made to grab Ura's arm but he grabbed Banto by his neck and threw him aside.

"Leave it, goldiflón. Don't go getting noble. You ain't no white knight. You can't even sit on a horse without killing it."

The reds cackled and jumped up and down and Banto turned and left.

"Bayfish!" Ura yelled to me. "Get the containers from the

shed and fill them with water. We going to ration the load. Everyone gets their share."

"Okay, Ura. Okay."

Memoria had many people and more streamed in each day through the Red Gate. Ura got to mind that there'd be an age limit for entry. Said he didn't want old people in his Memoria because they represented old traditions. He used his reds to regulate those who strolled into Memoria. People from afar soon got word that fuel was given out in Memoria, and that's how we developed a system of trade. They needed to bring in valuable goods to get small containers of gasoline or diesel in return. He regulated it hard, when some pleaded with him to stay in Memoria, mostly older folks, he turned them away and said their only use was in trade. Some even tried trading for clean water but Ura used his reds to scare them off.

One of the girls from Utuado, Camila, never spoke up. She hung around next to her cot and hordes of flies buzzed like a thick cloud over her corner of Memoria. Banto developed a liking for her. He spent his days keeping her company. Sometimes they'd just sit there quietly and not say a word to each other. I'd pass by them, hands over my nose, and Banto'd be sitting next to her wearing his stupid blond wig swatting the flies from his face. He said she was ill. She needed *real* help because she hardly ate and spent most of the day talking to the rotting body. Banto played along and spoke to the corpse too. It made Camila happy. It was the only time I saw her animated.

URA WOKE ME early one morning. There was a thick fog hanging over Memoria and you could barely see your fingers. The fog brought in a dampness that soaked every surface.

"We holding an emergency meeting now, Bayfish. Wake goldiflón and meet us in the Tower," he whispered to me.

"About?"

"You'll find out, pendejo. Wake fat-ass up and come to the Tower. Be quick about it."

I rose and forced my way to Banto. I shook him awake. He then proceeded with his ritual. Every morning Banto started the day by putting on the dirty blond wig he found in Florencia. He then squeezed into that blazer. I wanted to tell him that both those things smelled funky, but he seemed happy.

The Tower had three makeshift floors and a rickety steeple the reds fashioned out of logs wrapped in zinc sheets. When you walked in, you could see each level from the front entrance. The most that fit in that space was a small table and some chairs. Ura said he did all his final deliberations on the third floor because it had an opening where he looked out and saw Memoria. He claimed inspiration hit him most with that view.

The chairs were laid out next to a shellacked wooden table. The reds had painted the inside of the Tower a dark green and wrote random words on the walls. Phrases from regguetón songs, Fiel a la Vega, the Bible. In particular, long phrases drawn from Genesis and the creation of man. Quotes from Revelation decorated the sidings as well. It actually looked beautiful, the collage of experiences. And for a makeshift shack, the walls emitted familiarity. They also tacked pictures of Ura, their great and prized leader, in different poses, some were sketched out by the reds and the other photographs were taken of him working on paintings back in Florencia. It all seemed like a shrine, a collector's cave of Ura memorabilia. Or reminders that he was important to them, and by extension, important to us and everyone who now lived in Memoria.

Banto and me sat down and waited. Ura wasn't there and that bothered me.

"What's this about, pescao?" Banto asked. He rubbed his eyes with exhaustion and fiddled with the wig he wore.

"No sé, Banto. Ura wants to speak to us. Must be urgent."

"It better be. Sun's not even out. I wanted to get good sleep. I was thinking of walking to Utuado. Or at least to Caonillas to wash some of my clothes. We should start early since people like playing in the river at noon. You down?"

"Maybe."

"Come on, pescao."

"Maybe," I repeated.

He sighed and placed his hands on his belly. We waited for twenty minutes and finally two reds walked into the Tower. Ura shortly followed. They refused to sit down.

"Pues, cabrones. We need to talk about it," he said.

"It?" Banto said.

"*IT!*" Ura snapped.

"I don't know what *it* is, cabrón."

"The smell. The fat girl and her little corpse. They are smelling up my Memoria. Can't continue having it around. People will start leaving and that'll be that."

The reds circled and paced around us.

"I don't understand, Ura. Why don't you try talking to her? Maybe that's all she needs. To be heard," I said.

"The bitch won't talk. She just stays there staring into nothing and speaks to that thing. Mano, I'll have what she's having porque esa nota está brutal."

"It's her sister, cabrón!" Banto said.

"And?"

"She's hurting. She's hurting really bad."

"She can hurt with it gone."

"She's afraid she'll lose her if you take her body."

"That's not our problem, goldiflón."

"Then why let her in? Hmm? Why let her into Memoria at all?" Banto started getting angry and his voice trembled.

"Careful, goldiflón."

"I'm trying to make sense of it, cabrón. Trying to see what the point is to let her in and then complain about how she's out there grieving."

"I let her in out of the generosity of my heart. Because I am kind," Ura said, placing his hands over his chest mocking Banto.

"You're a piece of shit, that's what you are."

Ura slammed his fist onto the table. He postured up on Banto as if daring him to speak up again. Banto felt as much. I knew he wanted to fight back and hurt Ura the way Ura hurt everything around him, the way he hurt him over the years. But he simmered down.

"I'm getting my pets to take it from her. If she starts to fuss and cry, I expect you two to calm her down and hold her back while they do the work," Ura said.

"And what of her sister? Where are you taking her?" I asked.

"Don't matter. Toss her over a bridge. Stick her in a black garbage bag. Feed her to strays." He paused. "I don't give a fuck. Makes no difference to me."

"It makes a difference to her," Banto said. He stood from his chair and tumbled toward Ura. He was short compared to Ura so it was an ugly mismatch. He threw out his fists in desperation. The reds jumped between them and they restrained Banto. Banto's chubby cheeks were slicked in sweat. He heaved and his wig was thrown out of place.

"You'd be smart to fix that temper. That won't do you no good around here, goldiflón."

I was afraid Ura planned to beat Banto purple. The room grew stuffy in that brief silence. The reds held Banto back, his round belly poking out from underneath his blazer and T-shirt. Ura scratched his scruff without saying anything else. He kept glaring at Banto and I heard Banto start to whimper, expecting the hits.

Ura met Banto's eyes and shook his head and walked out of the Tower. The reds jerked Banto around before letting him go, following Ura out the door.

"Banto."

"Ya, pescao. Ya."

"Banto, you're going to get yourself hurt. You need to keep it in check."

"¡Ya!" He stumbled to his feet and wiped away the sweat from his forehead. He pulled his shirt over his belly. "Who else is going to stand up for her? Stand up to *him*?"

He fixed his wig and left. I waited. I sat in the Tower for some time thinking about Camila. Thinking about Banto. There was an anger in his eyes that morning. Even subdued and whimpering, he had seemed brave. I wanted to jump in and save him or save Camila, but I felt restrained.

It must've been some hours before the yells were heard throughout Memoria. I returned to my cot and tossed an old baseball into the air as I lay there waiting for the morning to pass. The yells were vicious and cruel. Everyone in Memoria stopped their day-to-days and turned attention to Camila's corner. The reds, dressed in black tracksuits, white gloves, and their black surgical masks circled Camila, dodging the objects she threw at them, waiting for her to tire out.

"No! No!" Camila yelled. She was vicious in her replies. She rammed into the reds and tossed them around, but they were relentless. It was like watching angry pitirres ambushing and pecking into a guaraguao, poor Camila, the strong hawk and her talons unable to strike at the red swarm. Banto was sidelined too. He fretted, his hands over his head and his belly rippling as he moved forward almost running. He stopped himself just before reaching them and it was just us two looking at the reds push and poke at her as she grew angry and threw branches and dirt. She kept screaming, "No!" until her voice cracked into hoarse gasps. Ura must've been watching it all from the Tower.

There were too many of them for her to fight off. The spectators eventually turned away and tried to go on as if the madness wasn't happening. The reds sedated her, it took four of them and she heaved and growled into the air. They held her against the dirt with all their weight as another batch of them took Marisol. The body was mutated and transformed something hideous and cruel. It reeked with every shift. The decomposition had destroyed any resemblance to her human form, the worms and maggots falling from her limbs sickened me.

"No! Please, no!" Camila cried, her face pressed into the dirt.

"I'm sorry, Banto. I'm sorry," I said to Banto.

That was all I could say. I placed my hand on his shoulder. He didn't say anything back and I felt him lean into me, a subtle and soft touch, I knew what he meant by it.

* * *

VELORIO

THAT NIGHT, THE reds turned on the massive fire at the center of Memoria. Everyone gasped as the center caught flame and burned. They seemed content to be there experiencing light again. Banto sat with all the citizens of our little society. He stared into the dancing flames, absent of time and place. I knew he wanted warmth and the comfort of bodies because he felt so distant from everything. Ura wasn't there. The reds danced around the flame, banging on empty metal trash cans and blue plastic barrels making a dembow beat. The sounds echoed and some of the people moved to the rhythm where they sat. Others stood. A few danced with the reds. The fire cracked and burst and I could see every corner of Memoria.

I walked to Camila's cot. She lay there, a curled fetus mumbling to herself. And it scared me. It didn't make me sad or desperate. It was a soft and delicate terror as if waiting to hear a newborn take its first breath. Suspended without support. Maybe I should've said something to her in that moment, but I thought of nothing.

I passed near the Tower noticing the door ajar. I heard Ura's voice so I snuck closer to the wall and listened in.

"What do you want us to do with that body, Ura?" A red said. There must've been two of them in there with him.

"Should we toss it into the fire, Ura? Should we watch it burn?"

I heard steps in the Tower, light movement and the sound of ruffling papers. Then I heard bottles crackle against each other in a cooler.

"No. That thing is too smelly. Burning it will make everyone angry and we don't want that. Don't want her to make a mess of things either. She'll probably set everything ablaze in a fit."

"We'll get rid of the fat girl then."

"Yeah, Ura. We'll get rid of her too."

"No you won't, cabrones."

"Then what, Ura?"

"Then what?"

There was a long pause.

"The refrigerator," Ura said in a whisper.

"Freeze it?"

"Freeze it," Ura said.

"That's far away, Ura. Walking with that disgusting thing through the forest will get us sick. It'll break into parts and limbs if we drag it around in darkness."

"We going to need travel. A car or pickup or something."

"Steal it from the streets, cabrones. Utuado is forgotten. Lots of shit to lift. Take some gas with you, steal a pickup, and take that *thing* and freeze it."

"Now? Ura, it's late——"

"Now! Take it and freeze it with the rest of them."

"Dale, Ura."

"Okay."

The reds tossed some empty beer bottles out the door. One of them walked out of the Tower, took his half-empty bottle, and shattered it against the Red Gate. They cackled and disappeared into the forest. I crouched up next to the slightly open door and peeked through the slit. Ura was seated on the third-floor drinking and painting on an empty wall. From what I could see, it was the central fire of Memoria and he painted sharp strokes for the flames, emphasizing the burning, emphasizing the destruction.

CAMILA

Ura hurt me today. Not the kind that's physical but the kind that hurts your heart. It made me miss home, but I didn't know the way back. Even if I did, there's nothing for me there except darkness and stars. Mari's gone and I don't know where they took her. All I know is that my chest lumped and twisted thinking about Marisol, how she couldn't breathe freely, how I missed our pillow talk. I didn't want her buried and even less with the masses they makeshift fitted underneath, near el Parque Ceremonial of Utuado. I thought it too crowded for Mari and how much she occupied, her grand presence and all. I wanted her to stay above ground as long as her flesh was still living, even if it was green, it was still living. The bugs and insects showed this. Otherwise, they'd stop pestering her body. Insects show what's alive and dead, I never see them hanging around clean metal and dry tile floor.

Mari was fascinated with critters. She used to collect the shells of hollow insects, caculos, crickets, even ants. She liked putting them in this little black matchbox under her bed. It didn't bother me when we were in Memoria and there were clouds of flies, white maggots, and a rancid smell. I knew she'd like those things. We were together and that's all that really mattered.

One time her boyfriend, Ezekiel, visited our house. Mami never found out. Marisol was good at sneaking, hid their gatherings after school or back home. She made me promise not to tell a soul. Ezekiel tended to get handsy in her bedroom and I watched from the chair in the hallway. But if he got aggressive, she quickly rummaged under her bed and pulled out the matchbox and showed him the insects she collected. That seemed to calm him.

Mari turned sixteen a few months before María. The night of her big birthday celebration, Mami invited some friends. That day, Mami didn't know Marisol invited Ezekiel. She would've beaten them both. He showed up mixed in with a couple of Mari's school friends, so it didn't look so obvious. But I knew, even if Mami didn't. Everyone gathered en la marquesina de casa and they sat around in white plastic chairs listening to bachata, Ednita Nazario, or Olga Tañón. But when Mami really wanted us kids to simmer down, she blared boleros. That's the mood-killer Mami enjoyed. It was for the adults, not for us. They'd sing together as we stared at one another with confused eyes trying to find something to entertain us.

Ezekiel waited for Mari outside the bathroom, everyone was distracted en la marquesina. Mari went to pee. He followed quietly behind her. I did too. He waited for her outside the door, she didn't know he was there. He looked around nervously and I could tell he didn't want to be seen. I watched from the kitchen because it had a subtle view there, away from the hallway, but you could see enough. When Mari opened the door, he jumped on her, sucked on her lips, and grabbed her chest. I could tell she was uncomfortable and that's what bothered me. He kissed her neck and tried pulling her into the bathroom and that's when I stomped toward them and made coughing sounds.

"Cami, go back outside," Marisol said. She pushed Ezekiel off her and they stood there in that cramped hallway.

"Mami's going to be mad," I said. That's all that I thought of. Mami pummeling Mari in the face and swatting Ezekiel with the metal broom.

"Cami, vamos. Let's go." She walked away from Ezekiel, touched my shoulder as she passed me, and returned to her party. I stayed there and Ezekiel leaned against the wall. His eyes frustrated and upset. He buried his face in his hands then let out an exaggerated sigh before returning to the party. I heard him mumble something to me as he passed but I was happy he didn't have the nerves to say it clearly.

I wanted to get back at him because I didn't like Ezekiel, I didn't like that he put Mari in danger with Mami. When everyone gathered around and readied to sing cumpleaños, Mami instructed me to cut the cake and give everyone a piece. The cake was one of those big yellow cakes laced with blue and white frosting, which I liked most.

We all sang in the kitchen and Marisol looked so pretty, lit up by smiling faces and a chorus of affection. Her black curly hair falling over her soft shoulders, her round face the texture of a copper statue, and her big eyes squinting in happiness. And Ezekiel loomed over her, in the corner he leaned against the wall as everyone sang. He fixated on Mari with a mean determined look that upset me.

After the singing, everyone moved back out to la marquesina and waited on me to cut the slices, place them onto plastic plates, and hand them out. I quickly ran into Mari's bedroom and grabbed her matchbox with the skeletons of insects. I cut everyone a nice piece, but I cut a bigger piece for Ezekiel. My slices were messy and most crumbled on the plates. I took the little skeletons from the insects, crushed their wings, and kneaded them into Ezekiel's yellow cake crumbs. I picked the lighter colored caculos and plucked out the legs of dried and dead grasshoppers. I pushed their shells into his cake and snickered because I knew he was greedy. I knew he'd stuff his face without first looking down at his slice.

The crowd ate and cheered Marisol, told her how great it was to be a woman. Some recited their own experiences from that age, but I could tell Mari didn't care much. It was just nostalgia, they all recounted because they wanted to return to their own youth. They continued. They clapped and told jokes, yet I waited and waited as Ezekiel chomped away at his cake. He sat hunched over his plate and stuffed big chunks of yellow cake into his cheeks until he checked his lips. His face jerked back when he pulled out a wing from a caculo. It was confusion before realization and the moment it hit him, he stood up and let the plate slip from his lap.

"¡Coño!" he yelled out and everyone froze in confusion.

"¿Qué te pasa, Ezekiel?" Mari asked him.

"The cake . . . it has . . ."

"It has what?" she asked.

We all stayed quiet waiting for him to explain. Ednita's voice rung from the portable speakers. The more time he spent with attention drawn to him, the more he knew he'd be figured out by Mami. I locked eyes with him and smiled, I wanted him to see me. It made him upset. Enough to say, "Never mind," and clean the mess of cake from the driveway. I chuckled a little and continued eating. He walked to the garbage can and threw out the rest and made to leave the party entirely. Mari followed him with her eyes. She knew she could not go after him because Mami would see and put it all together.

It was late at night by the time all of Marisol's friends and Mami's guests left. They kissed and hugged us as if we were all a family. Hugs from strangers are a weird thing. Sometimes they feel more genuine than those from your sister or mother.

After the house emptied, I was charged to clean the mess. Mari went into her bedroom and came out and threw the matchbox at me. She crossed her arms and signaled at it with her pursed lips.

"Eres bien estúpida, Camila."

"What?"

"You know what."

I tried to play dumb and I could tell she wasn't believing me. She knew.

She left me to clean alone and she walked into the dark street and stood next to the garbage cans. She stood under the light post before disappearing into the bamboo forest and I figured she was headed to the river. Alone with the stars.

Mari is maniática like that and that makes me terribly sad to remember how much she hated people but enjoyed the quietness of nature. That's why this Memoria seemed beautiful, away from all the sounds and voices.

I wanted Mari with me forever, to spend the rest of her time lying next to me on the dirt, or by my little cot. But now all I see are nights where strangers circle a big burning flame and they dance and laugh and play music and it's not quiet at all.

BANTO

Ceremony was ritual. Ura mandated every citizen of Memoria need not only attend, but also participate in sermon. He expected everyone to give half-hour decrees by the fire. They served as announcements of gratitude. Toward Memoria, toward the reds, toward him. At first it became repetitive nonsense, the reds performed and spoke of Ura's eternal gifts, his giving soul, and they even acted out short skits as tribute to the *hero*, as they called him. They used props found and harvested from Utuado; disjointed and rusted car doors, blue FEMA tarps they stole from houses that were abandoned over the months, black electric cables from fallen and dead utility posts, even the abandoned electric transformers were put to use. The reds used these things to build Memoria, and whatever was left over they applied to the evening skits. It was the new television. Ura sat in the center of ceremony, he had the reds fashion an old Mercedes car seat and place it smack in the middle. He could oversee everyone, observing and enjoying the entertainment acted out by the reds. As much as it became routine, when the decrees were given by people other than the reds, I heard genuine gratitude and that confused me.

This was every night's ritual. The great fire was built by the reds. There was a designated crew that wore black tracksuits and they'd go off into the dark night to collect the fallen trees, broken logs, brown and aged shrubs. Upon their return they banged on the metal trash cans and they chanted "Ura, Ura, Ura," as they piled the wood and readied the evening events.

Cami hardly moved from her corner. She spent days petrified on her cot after they took her sister. She didn't eat. I walked up to her and sat on the dirt in front of her and she just looked through me. I talked to her about the weather, the forest, the river and how it still roared and rumbled in its crest. I mentioned how Memoria started feeling like home because kids who weren't the reds showed up. Mentioned Moriviví and her friend Damaris. How they came all the way from Florencia, where Bayfish and I were from, and told her I thought they meant good, they were good people. I tried bringing her some cooked goat from dinner, but she'd leave it, let it collect insects, roaches, ants, and poked at it with her big fingers. She even allowed the bugs to crawl onto her, the roaches skating from one finger to the next, the ants marching angrily over the palm of her hand. When I made to toss the plate into the trash, she grumbled deep, so I left it. I spent many nights in her corner of Memoria hoping my presence gave her life. None of it shook her out of that trance. The only words she mumbled were to herself and most of the time she just repeated Marisol's name, sometimes rocking herself to sleep, sometimes pretending Marisol was the rotting plate of food.

I argued with Bayfish that I was not going to give a decree for Ura. And that he should not expect me or Camila to participate. Bayfish said he'd talk to Ura. Said he'd do his best.

"You sure, pescao? You know how he is," I said to Bayfish.

"Yeah. I spoke to him several times in the Tower. Even reminded him about Cami."

THEN ONE NIGHT, it happened. After dinner was served, I rationed out a few tostones and goat meat for Cami. Recently, she had started nibbling on the food I brought her. I was so happy she was coming around. I made it a point to eat in that corner and believed that if she saw me there enough times, eating and smiling, wearing my stupid blond wig and my fancy blazer, that she'd remember what it was like to feel.

I started heading toward her corner when Ura banged on the metal trash can and everyone stopped and looked at him.

"Banto. My dear, Banto. It so happens that tonight is your turn to perform sermon," he said, smirking. The fire crackled and only the insects and coquíes could be heard scoring the night.

"Ura," Bayfish interrupted. He got up from his log. "Ura, cabrón. Let's not."

"Banto! It is your turn to perform sermon. As part of citizenship in this illustrious Memoria, you will give out your decree," Ura said, gesturing toward the center fire then patting his fingers on the metal trash can.

"Ura, I'm going to eat dinner with Cami. Let me go, por favor," I said. I hoped he heard the sincerity in my voice.

"Banto. My dear goldiflón. My dear Banto."

Ura rushed past the logs near the fire. The reds trailed him. They circled around me and Ura swaggered and swayed his way up to my face.

"Banto. Perform sermon. Come on. It'll only take a few minutes of your precious time."

"Ura, cabrón. Let it go. Just get the reds to do another skit y ya," Bayfish said. He stomped over determined to save me. But the reds, they appeared in droves and trickled between Bayfish and Ura. Ura observed it all. It pleased him to see his little broods acting with devotion. Moriviví and Damaris stood in confusion.

"Ura, Cami needs to eat. She doesn't eat unless I'm there."

"You and your girlfriend can have your date after you perform your civic duty, Banto. My sweet goldiflón," he said as he stroked my cheek. I started to tremble a little. The silence didn't help, and the crackling of the fire made my chest bounce.

"Ura, please."

"Perform sermon!" he yelled and everything metal shook with the vibration of his voice.

I didn't want violence. I looked over to Cami's corner and saw she was seated up on her cot paying attention to what was happening. Her silhouette blended into the outline of the forest and her broad shoulders imposed her strength. I wanted to be like that, strong in how I carried myself, quiet but feared.

I toddled over to a log, placed the tray of food, and made my way to the center of ceremony where the flame was hottest and the sound loudest. I knew everyone was watching me, knew Cami was witnessing this, so I tried walking straight by picking my shoulders up. It hurt to straighten them. I coughed then cleared my throat not knowing what to say. To declare gratitude for Memoria and Ura, to preach as though God watched over expecting a stirring message. The silence grew louder as Ura and his reds returned to their seats and glared over me expecting a performance.

"Memoria . . ." I paused. I tried picking through my mind for the correct words that would satisfy. "Memoria is like a song. A song that we used to hear as much as Marc Anthony's 'Preciosa.' It reminds us of a past. A time we collected pan en la panadería. A time we held funerals at home. A time when . . . the goats listened and huddled next to each other and it rained, and we could smile . . . knowing . . . knowing the future is beautiful."

I paused again because I felt it was nonsense. The faces looking back at me, Damaris scratching her neck, Moriviví letting out a yawn she quickly covered with her hand, Bayfish concerned and paranoid, and Ura all satisfied with himself.

"Memoria is—"

"About Ura," one of the reds interrupted. "Ura, Ura, Ura."

They started chanting in a chorus. I fiddled with my wig and fixed my blazer's collar.

"Ura . . . Ura is a gift. He is the one you turn to when things are dark and difficult. He is a song that you hear like songbirds and roosters in the morning. The fog is like Ura, it deepens us. It reminds us we like to feel each other's touch. To be close. For Comfort. A gift like . . . Navidad y los Reyes. The grass left out for the horses because there are no camels en Puertorro. The grass is nice. It has rain and dampness in mornings when—"

"That's terrible," the reds yelled out. They started growing restless. "Ura, Ura, Ura."

"Ura is a gift that we didn't deserve but were given because everyone needs salvation, I think. Everyone is part of this world; the way rivers need oceans. The way rain needs clouds. The way trees need . . . insects—"

A red threw a piece of goat meat at me and started cackling. Then another one picked up a branch and sticks and threw them on the floor in front of me. More of them seemed to enjoy my flinching up there in the center so they started howling and picked up some small rocks and threw them. Some missed me entirely and fell into the fire behind me. Others struck my nose and knocked against my forehead—those stung a little.

I wanted to run out of there but noticed Ura was growing uneasy, then angry. He stood up from his Mercedes seat. I wasn't sure if Ura was angry at what I said or if he was mad at the reds for the disruption, or if he was mad that they weren't throwing enough at me. He began growling and grunting and all of his little broods turned to him and started doing the same, the growling and grunting growing and growing. The fire danced and it made everyone seated in front of me look as though they too moved with every gasp for air.

"Ya, Urayoán, ya," Moriviví said. She dug into her pocket fishing for something, but Damaris yanked her arm out. She looked disappointed at Damaris, but that didn't stop her from running out front and center. She put herself between the soaring rocks, they kept hitting me and her. She quickly grew tired of it. She stomped over to Ura in a rage, the brood realizing the danger.

Bayfish used that moment of distraction to sprint up and grab me by the arm. We hurried out of there, the grunts and growls growing fainter behind us and the light of the fire dimming as we moved closer and closer to the corner of Memoria near the edge of the forest. Bayfish took me far, past the cots, past the fuel trucks, out through the Red Gate and into the dead forest.

We ran without knowing which direction we were headed. I stumbled as I ran, the wig getting heavier as I built up a sweat, the blazer weighing on my back from the humidity. We ran for what seemed like twenty minutes until I heard the river. As we got closer, the sound of the river transformed into a soft humming, a soothing sound. Bayfish stopped and found a large boulder to sit on. In that darkness, the stars dotted the night's black sheet, a small moon accenting the vast canvas. It took me some time to catch my breath. In that moment I felt déjà vu. Bayfish and me often running from something or running somewhere. Most of the time provoked by Ura and his malice.

"You're lucky, Banto. You're lucky she stood up between you two."

"Why? What's he going to do?"

I played tough.

"Banto, you're lucky. We should wait until they all finish eating. Until everyone's asleep."

"I'm tired of hiding and running, Bayfish."

"I know."

I found a small boulder next to him and sat down feeling the moss under my shorts. It was damp and cold against my calves. We both gazed out into the river shrouded by the dead trees, some slowly budding.

Bayfish placed his hand on my shoulder and shook me a little.

"Take that wig off, cabrón. Aren't you hot?"

"Yeah, but it's a part of me. I like how it looks."

"It's got to feel shitty on your soaked hair."

"Yeah . . . but it's not so bad, I guess."

"Whatever suits you, mano."

We kept waiting and it seemed like things froze around us. I got a bit uneasy and jumped off the boulder. I went to the water's edge and threw some on my face, I took the wig off and dipped my whole head into the river cleaning the grime and dirt from my scalp.

"What do you think will happen to Morivivi?" I asked.

"Dunno. I wouldn't cross her."

"You think Ura's afraid too?"

"Nah, but she'd cut him up if he tried anything."

We lingered near that river until the moon seemed to disappear from the night above. Bayfish finally got up and led the way back in the direction to Memoria.

When we reached the Red Gate, there hung an eerie silence, the ghost of the ceremony fire remained, a graying smoke trail lifted from the dead embers, everyone asleep on their cots. The reds weren't in their usual spot surveying the entrance to Memoria and that worried me. I wanted to check in on Morivivi. I signaled to Bayfish and we walked quietly to her corner. I could make out the outline of Damaris on her cot. Morivivi slept beside Damaris. They were ok and that made me feel at peace. I glanced over to Cami's cot. It was very dark in that corner. We went to see if she was fine.

"Coño, where did she go?" I said to Bayfish.

"You think she ran off into the forest?"

We rummaged through the dead shrub and leaves behind her cot and peered into the rows of dark trees but didn't see anything.

"What if she followed us when we left earlier through the Red Gate?" Bayfish said.

"Coño, mano. Coño. We just came from there, pescao."

"Let's go back. Retrace our steps," he said.

His optimism didn't convince me.

"Banto, come on. Let's go back. We'll find her."

"Okay."

We started back to the Red Gate but I noticed a light shining from inside the Tower. I went toward it. Bayfish resisted at first but followed me until we reached the shanty door. I poked my head inside and didn't see Ura. None of his brood either. I noticed someone standing on the third floor. He rummaged through the pamphlets and Ura's paintings then traced his finger against the scribbles on the walls.

"Cheo?" Bayfish said. He lifted himself over my shoulder. "Cheo! Cabrón!"

"Oye, pescao," Cheo said.

Cheo climbed down the tattered steps and hugged Bayfish. I think we felt lifted in that moment, if only for that moment. Seeing Cheo again, his balding head, his aged and light hair. It felt as though a piece of Florencia returned to us.

"I see Banto is still here. Still wearing that dumbass wig," Cheo said. He grinned.

I returned a wry smirk.

"You all right, mijo?" Cheo said.

"We're looking for someone, Cheo. It's a young girl. Super trigueña. Big with a wide back and thick strong arms. She has short hair. Her name's Camila. She must've run off after a big fight between Banto and Ura," Bayfish said.

"A fight? Loco, what's happening around here?"

"Ura. Ura's getting dangerous," I cut in.

I told Cheo about Ura and the ceremony. Told him about Cami, Moriviví, and Damaris. Told him about the diesel, the trading, the regulation of citizens by age. None of it seemed to surprise Cheo. He simply scratched his bald head and let out these intermittent sighs. He lifted his eyebrows from time to time as I told him these things, but nothing changed his demeanor.

"Where is he now?" Cheo said.

"We don't know. He disappears at night sometimes with his brood," I said.

"No sé, mijo. I know you're not going to like this. But I think we should sleep. Wait till morning and then try figuring all this out. It's late. You're tired. I'm tired."

"But Ura, Cheo. What if he—"

"Vamos, Banto. Let's sleep the night and tomorrow we put all this together," he placed his arm over my shoulders and brought me in as we walked out the Tower together. "Pescao, where do I sleep?"

"Sleep on my cot tonight. Tomorrow we'll find Ura and look to see if he has an extra one for you."

"But, Bayfish. Ura's rules. His regulation," I said.

"We worry about that tomorrow. Relájate, mijo," Cheo responded. He brushed off Ura and his rules. But he didn't know what Ura was turning into, or what he always was. I feared for Cheo having trekked so many miles only to be turned away. Yet he emitted none of that fear. He held a cool demeanor and it made me believe, even if just for a second, that things could be alright. Things could turn out okay.

URAYOÁN

No one lashes out at me and gets away with it. That's how I see things. It is cause for violence. I see the faces of my pets, their expectations, I feel the eyes, citizens of Memoria, needing me to assert my will. But I find my anger effective when it's planned rather than in the moment. When that new one, Moriviví, comes to me with her sharp tongue I decide to wait. The reds grow anxious for her punishment. But as I say, some things need patience. After Hagseed and the fat one run out together in the forest, I tell my reds it is meeting time in my beautiful Tower of Babel. I go and wait for the important pets to show. They come in slumped and angry, feeling defeated because they didn't see blood and I whistle loud to bring their attention to me. They refuse to mobilize in their usual discipline, so I shoot them that look they fear with the whistle in higher pitch. But they still drag their feet, staring at me as if I were a drifting ghost. This makes me rage and I slam my fist on the waxed table so hard it cracks and that gets their attention. I tell them we need to first remember that it is not all violence in Memoria. See, our promise to new citizens is that we protect them from that sort of thing. They come running away from bandits and thieves, they come for something like peace, they find safety here in Memoria. I tell them all these things and that's when the reds grow curious and press me.

They ask me why I even let the fat girl stray from Utuado into my beautiful Memoria, why let her in and the stupid dead sister. I tell them we need the bodies—I want Memoria grown. Then they ask why the refrigerator and I tell them that collecting is important because no one is going to pick up after the dead, sticking the bodies in a refrigerator lets loved ones hold on to their memory, we can access corpses, display them to show how we preserve what's important. Through my efforts and my grace, they can hold on to what they wish, though some things are better left forgotten, but I grant favors, it's reason enough for new citizens to believe in Memoria. They come here knowing their beautiful dead are tucked away nice and safe and preserved better than a grave. That satisfies the reds but they're still raging because goldiflón didn't get his beating. I keep reminding them the fat one is important to Hagseed and I promise them a gutting will happen later. I messed with him enough during ceremony and now he knows where he is. In time they understand but it scares me it took repetition until my throat was hoarse for them to see my thinking. After persuading and persuading I finish, and they seem tamed for the night.

Ceremony was over. I started implementing a curfew for my citizens of beautiful Memoria because that allowed for us to keep safe. Some of the people start questioning me, saying that the old government did this curfew thing too. But that's when I really rage, that's when I start listing all Memoria is improving on and creating for their souls. Like with the reds, they need me to repeat and repeat my message. I tell them how they all receive their rations of goat and plátanos, how they have the safety of the forest shielding them from bandits and thieves, I tell them they have the light eternal because my Energy stock gives and gives. I tell them about the trade system that filters outsiders, how my wonderful pets vet the people and those who don't live in beautiful Memoria, can trade for

Energy and that's how we get the stock. All this—because of my genius—is the gratitude I expect and when I say this enough, they start to change just like the reds, they start to believe again that Memoria is as it always has been, a place annexed in harmony through *my* leadership.

This isn't the worst of my frustrations. The next few mornings I see Hagseed return from his honeymoon with the fat one and they bring with them the age I despise. Hagseed comes to find me and takes me aside near the grave of last night's great fire and he says, "Cheo is here, Ura. He came all the way from Florencia." He says this emphasizing distance as though that will win me over. "I see Banto has returned too. Bringing in more than what's needed won't work." I throw this to him just to make him honest, I don't like when people try for tricks with language. It works because now he's scratching his shrimp neck, all scared and ugly, looking for the words to respond. "Cheo can help here. His experience is useful," he returns back to the old man and that's when I know this is more than tricks. "We have rules and Cheo breaks those rules. I don't know what else to tell you, Bayfish." I say this and this drags him down. The usual fog in the morning is now also scared like Hagseed and looking to leave because that's the gift I have, even the clouds think before action when they enter my beautiful Memoria. I decide to test Cheo a bit and make him come to me, and that's when Hagseed and the fat one really start getting on my nerves. The reds, they sense this too because they gather round hoping for violence. I scratch my beard and look at this desperate old man, this Cheo that Hagseed enjoys so much, and I say to him, "What's your purpose here then? Goldiflón and Bayfish must've forgotten to mention, you don't fit our profile. The best I can let you do is trade with me and my reds." I say this knowing I am going to make an exception, just to see the outcome of the experiment. I want to test Cheo, so I wait for his response. "I'll stay out of your way. Out of everyone's way. I can help with what's needed and anything else." He says this and I enjoy the response but for the fun of my pets and me, I need more so I push him a little harder. "Maybe we don't let you trade with us. Maybe we send you back to Utuado and you can survive among the crazy, the mad, the violent, the bandits, and thieves." I am not done. I want to tell him a little more to see how far he will go with me. "Or maybe you are banished, maybe you go back to Florencia. Or maybe you can't step foot on this island again or—" I want to keep at it but goldiflón doesn't let me, I see I get to him before I can break Cheo. "Por favor, Ura. Please. I'm sorry for all that happened. Cheo is good—" and I interject, "I didn't ask if he's good. I'm saying maybe he's not welcome here." He ponders in his stupidity before he responds, "He will help with what he can. Bayfish and me will share our rations and help out too. Please, Ura. Please." He says this and I want to burst out laughing. It is meant for Cheo but the fat one, as expected, is weak. I look over at Cheo. Then Hagseed. Then goldiflón. I look at them and pretend I'm contemplating the secrets of life just to keep the suspense. Cheo is stone, he shows me no emotion. His confidence bothers me. Hagseed is careful in how he makes eyes. And goldiflón is pathetic, as he always is. I wonder what will happen next—if I turn Cheo away, how many tears will stain the dirt, or will there be any at all. But no one is looking. It is just the reds who only want violence. And that's not enough of an audience to impress because tears and violence are better when people can see. I wave them off. I tell Hagseed Cheo can stay, conditionally. I know one day I will make all of Memoria fear and cry. Until then, I let them think it's okay.

MORIVIVÍ

It didn't bother me none after I confronted Urayoán. Damaris was careful at first but after the ceremony, after I looked him straight in his eyes, I felt nothing. There was no terror emitted from those brown and soulless windows, rather I saw a scared boy. He was just like everyone else. Just like me and Damaris and Banto and Bayfish. We were all scared that time would weaken our endurance and that no matter how many Memorias you tried erecting, they'd all fail because we were alone. I'm convinced the only one who has no fear is Camila. How she used to wait and wait not even time forced her into action.

The reds wanted a fight. When I stood up to Urayoán I almost pulled my knife. I told him he should be careful because you never know what nightmares can creep over you during a restless sleep. He rolled his eyes expecting something. It must've comforted him, the thought that his little animals would come to his aid in the event that I struck, but I took that away from him. I left him there and walked with Damaris back to our corner and I knew that the reds were furious about it.

We fell asleep and it was the first time I felt peace. I watched Urayoán toss utensils and plates onto the floor in a fit. He yelled at all the spectators that dinner and ceremony were over. He sent everyone off to bed like a defeated father does a child. He scurried back with his reds into that Tower.

* * *

VELORIO

MEMORIA SEEMED DISTANT, divided between Urayoán's reds and those who complied. Most of the mornings I spent helping newcomers set up their corners and cots. We'd cut some of the fallen logs and set them around sections like cubicle markings in an office space. Other times I'd help gather royal palm leaves and tie them to the ends of cots and metal poles and that gave people the impression of homeliness and comfort.

Damaris did a lot of note taking and sketching. She worked in the composition notebook we found in the burned pickup trucks some time ago. Since the calamity, time no longer mattered, and weeks or months felt like years. Maybe months or years did pass. We weren't keeping record anymore. Damaris wrote down the names of all the people that seemed nice, she itemized the stock, the way the red gasoline and diesel candungos colored the clearing, she sketched the faces of people. When I asked her why, she simply responded, "Who else is going to do it?"

Urayoán spent most of his nights holed up in his Tower, you'd see his face gleaming out from within, the decrepit cutout in the wood made it look as though he was inside a TV set. He'd stand there surveying Memoria and seemed satisfied in knowing all these people borne out of necessity followed. He seemed content in finding ways to keep his reds happy. But over time they got bolder and challenged him.

One afternoon a red was inspecting two men trying to trade for diesel. The men walked through the Red Gate and a pack of reds swarmed by with metal broomsticks. The men brought with them a burlap sack of dried cod. The reds grabbed the cod and started grunting at the men. They circled around them pretending to lunge forward and bite. Urayoán saw this and ran to them. When the men explained, he turned to the reds and demanded the fair exchange, but the reds kept circling, acting like a pack of stray dogs. Urayoán let out so many whistles you'd think he serenaded songbirds. None of it worked, and so he stomped over to the fuel trucks and gave the two men their share and grabbed the burlap sack filled with cod and returned to the Tower. The reds snickered and bellowed. I wasn't the only one to see this. Others working to make their cots and corners feel more like home watched it all unfold. Some shook their heads and others let out soft chuckles.

A FEW NIGHTS passed and Camila hadn't returned. Banto came to Damaris and me and wondered what we should do.

"Cheo and Bayfish say we should wait it out. But I don't trust that. She hasn't been back and it's dangerous out there," Banto said.

"Where do we look?" Damaris asked him.

"I don't know. I don't know."

He paced back and forth putting both his hands over his head, his dirty blond wig tilted.

"Is she from Utuado?" I asked.

"I don't know. I don't know—"

"Look at me, Banto. Easy. Think. Is she from Utuado?" I asked again. I placed my hands on his shoulders. His chubby face was sweating. He scratched his eyes trying hard to think over the question.

"I'll ask around," Damaris interrupted.

She got up and drifted from cot to cot, from corner to corner, asking if they knew about Camila. Banto and me waited for some time until Damaris returned. She was frustrated and slumped back down onto her cot.

"They don't know do they?" I said.

"No one does."

I turned away from Banto and walked back to my cot.

"So, we're doing nothing?"

"Give me a minute, Banto!" I yelled.

I tried to remember Camila. Her eyes and her hands, I tried to remember how she walked and moved, but nothing. I only saw her stranded in her corner traumatized by how they took her sister away. Then it hits me.

"The fucking reds," I said.

Damaris and Banto realized what I meant to do. I got up and picked out my knife from my jean pocket and marched toward the reds. I scanned to see if Urayoán was still holed up in his Tower and saw movement from the open door. I tried to find a red alone and vulnerable, but they were all in swarming packs, running and jesting and howling.

"The generators," Damaris said.

"Yes! They always leave one on patrol."

Banto objected to the idea of confronting a red.

"They'll get angry, Moriviví. They'll call out for help," he said.

"I don't care, Banto. I don't care anymore," I responded. Damaris and me started making our way to the far end of Memoria, opposite the Red Gate and to the far left of the fuel trucks. Urayoán collected a small field of generators he stole over the passing months. Said some he *found* in Utuado. Others, he'd *borrowed* from barrios near Arecibo, from abandoned houses.

The forest was lined with tall grass and reeds. The trees started to have vines again too. Damaris and me cleared a path with our arms and forced ourselves into the long and tangled rows of eucalyptus trees, many of them trying at life again, their leaves pushing in haphazard directions. Most of the green grew only at the tops because many branches hadn't grown back. It reminded me of a forest from *The Lorax*.

We walked down the rows of eucalyptus until we saw the generators. Some were covered with blue FEMA tarps as disguise, others had shrubs and dead leaves over them. Only one red guarded the generators. He sat on a beach chair and wore an oversized baseball cap. He was half asleep, his cap covering his eyes and his hands over his small belly. Damaris and me jumped him. I grabbed him by his bomber jacket and Damaris covered his mouth. He kicked and squirmed until I showed him my knife. I waved it in front of his eyes and asked him about Camila. He struggled to find words and could only shake his head and I grew angry. I made to cut him, and he let out a loud screech.

"Utuado!" he said. "She came from Utuado! We found her there after gathering supplies and Ura got to mind she come to Memoria. That's it. That's all I know."

"Where?" I snapped back.

"The church! The church!" he repeated. "That's all I know. That's all. That's where we found her. I know nothing else, te lo juro."

WE WAITED FOR the cover of nightfall because the darkness allowed us to move freely. Banto said he wanted to tag along so we agreed. Bayfish was hanging with his old friend Cheo. They took trips down to the river and tried catching fish for Memoria. I spent most of the day thinking about the crying red, how fragile he looked, how helpless and pathetic. Damaris spent the day continuing to scratch words into her notebook. She told me she overheard the reds talking with Urayoán in the Tower that afternoon. They whispered that food was running very low. They ran out of goat meat and all the farmers in the surrounding area disappeared. They left their livestock diseased and dying so it wasn't safe to go out killing and harvesting the animals nearby. None of it surprised me. I wondered about Bayfish and Cheo, if their fishing skills would be handy. But it's just the river, there weren't enough fish there to feed all of Memoria. I thought again about the red crying in the forest among all those helpless trees, until Damaris shook me back. She smiled.

"This will all come to an end, Mori."

"It's what comes after that scares me."

"It's what comes after," she repeated.

CAMILA

I went back into the forest because that's where there's peace. I went back into that quiet because there I could hear Mari singing. It took some stumbles, but I let the trees marked in paint lead the way and that's when I came across a familiar road. Even though it was narrowed with garbage and escombros, I knew it would lead me back into Utuado. I passed the burned pickup trucks and climbed the wall of debris. It felt like something only those red monsters would do, garbage set on purpose to block pathways.

Moriviví inspired me. How she ran up to Ura and readied to cut him. I know it's a knife she had in her pocket; I saw her think about it. After Banto and the shrimp went running I figured it was time to move again and that's why I was returning. To where the movement of water and mud took Mari from me.

It was dark and I followed the road, deserted and lonely. When I came up to the short bridge connecting la plaza central, I noticed it was eaten in random places by the water, holes cutting through the concrete and tar. I saw the church there all abandoned. Its quiet and short bell towers surveyed the square. All the shops stayed in silence and only the echo and scratch from my walking steps made sound. I wondered where all the people had gone. I imagined everyone left in rapture as soon as they took Mari. Maybe Mari helped take them up high into the sky.

The narrow streets buffered the soft wind that blew, the river seemed to be less angry and had returned closer to its original size. All the sediment and soil evidence of its banking. The broken and destroyed landscape was a memory I'll keep.

I came to the Shell Energy station and that too was deserted. I saw Mami and me standing in line there under the hot and mean sun. I saw Don Papo or Ezekiel scared about being stupid and lonely. I wanted everything to go back to how it used to be, but I knew it was too late for that and that made me tear up again. I dragged myself up the steep slopes that wind around these stubby mountains, they curve and bend like black rivers. I entered my barrio, a place I used to call home. There were some roosters and chickens roaming. They pecked into the ground at the edges of the road. They must have been finding worms again and that made me smile because it was the first time I saw something alive act closer to normal. The wire fences that divide some of the houses on the hill were overgrown with wild grass, these tall reed-like things, and I heard crickets again. I heard some birdsongs clicking in the trees above and the bamboos also danced and crashed into each other, and it all reminded me of a past.

When I got to my old house, it too was sad. The small fence driveway was chained and la marquesina was dirty with trash and empty candungos. The paint was still wearing the color of leaves, a large yellow stain against the light blue walls. The windows were boarded and there was some writing from people that also felt a need to leave their mark in this world. I guess we all tried for that, so it didn't bother me much.

My front door was open. Not in a wide and welcoming way, you'd only be able to tell if you walked right up to it. I entered and I heard the airplane engine again, the sound from the night María came, how it roared and screeched, and all the walls trembled, even the roof wanted to let go.

Pictures are nice. If you hold on to the frames you feel all the fingerprints that once touched their surface. It's like you're touching the long ago. I picked up some of our family portraits and fell down on the couch where Mami spent so many nights, where she cried quietly, thinking I wasn't listening. Where she obsessed with the transistor radio and the voice of Ojeda. How it calmed her because it reminded her that others hurt too.

I stared at the black-and-white picture Mami had framed of us three. There was Mari, her hand over my shoulder and her long curly hair falling down her back. In the portrait I'm staring at her with flat eyes, but a short smirk. I think of her and how nice she was to me, how she was always there, how pretty she was, and I know she is me so I must grow into something sort of like that. She was a sculpture, in how she stood, the way her clothes fit against her curves. And I'm a rugged square. Mami is strong too, but a sort of fragile strong. Her face is mostly blurry in the picture but even if it weren't, you'd never see her smile. She had this fear of her crooked teeth and that's where I get it. We're standing in front of the house—that's the day Mami landed a nice teaching job in town. It was really cloudy and windy that morning, but you can't tell from a black-and-white picture. That's Mami's effect. She likes black-and-white photos. Says they age better, age eternal. I placed the picture on the table next to the abandoned transistor radio. I wondered if it still had life in it. I didn't want to find out.

The hallway was shorter than I remembered. Maybe it's because of the mud turned to rock coming from Mari's bedroom. That's where I should have left her. That's where I should've left my Marisol. I passed by the bathroom and heard crying from the night we ran in there because we feared we'd fly with the entire house into heaven, and that's where Mami and me prayed once the river came through the window and buried Marisol; it was Mami's denial that kept her speaking to God. And I think that's why Mami eventually gave up and then disappeared.

I walked into Mari's room and I saw her there, eyes shut and dusty with dirt, her hands thrown upward bracing for the hard mud. I went through her drawers again. I combed through the hangers in the closet and smelled her clothes, but they didn't smell like her anymore. They didn't smell like anything. She liked wearing flower print dresses sometimes, she liked wearing black jeans most days.

I wanted to return to that night, to our bathroom, and hold on to Mari, the moment before she decided to go to her bedroom. I wanted to force her back to the grubby tile floor, wedge her beneath the wooden vanity, and tell her that we all need to wait out the storm together.

I walked back to the kitchen and rummaged through the drawers and took out a short cutting knife. It wasn't too sharp, Mami hardly sharpened the knives. Because she never sharpened them, whenever she cooked, she slammed them down hard into the cutting board, the board bruised. I missed Mari. I started to miss Mami. I wanted to see myself, in anger, open, breathing air. I took the knife and slashed into my thick skin. Not deep or mean. But something small and just enough to let out blood. I made marks up my arm, each one burning like bee stings and softly bleeding. I did this and I felt again and the air hitting against my open skin reminded me of my Mari, how bruised and green she looked even days after. I wanted to cry but felt anger. I kept slashing, more frantically, until I got tired and my entire arm burned on fire, the blood collecting neatly in rows along my arm.

I went back to the couch and fell, my bloody arm staining the cloth. I thought about how nothing would change, no matter how much time passed. I fell into a deep sleep. I had one of those dreams where you can walk on air, see the island beneath you, all the green mountains cutting into the sky, the trees a deep and uniformed green, the vines grown wild up their massive bark, ferns sprouting high, water in the humidity of the air, the ground always wet but never drowned. You walk on the air and you see how the green changes the closer you get to the coast, the closer you get to the ocean's blue vastness all looming and beautiful, how the concrete takes over, all the houses crammed next to each other, stacking the landscape until it all turns busy. At night the lights are soft in contrast to the dark mountains, you walk on the air and in suspension, you finally see the closest thing to God: the stars. I slept in my comfort knowing the old house still carried the scent of my past. When I woke up it had rained. I saw the water collected in cracks on the sidewalk, some of it still tip-tapping against metal, the small little pools reflecting the night sky and the stars shinning as they always do. I thought about going out and stepping into the water with my bare feet, so I could feel the cold again, so I could kick the water up and watch it scatter and disappear in the darkness.

I went back to where they found me, the last place Marisol and me rested, on the roof of that church where I saw Utuado melt into sunset and it didn't matter if there was light or dark because God saw it all the same. I would wait there until the horizon ended for me. If someone finds my body, they may see it cut open in some places, slits dry with blood, but they'll see that I was living, opened, waiting, dreaming.

BAYFISH

Memoria was desperate. The things we collected became spoiled and fuel seemed useless if we couldn't find people from outside to trade with. Ura confronted an old farming couple who tried entering Memoria. He wanted to know about their livestock. The old man wore a straw hat, one taken straight from a bad history book of Puerto Rican clichés. He was thin and his white shirt was oversized and stained with dirt. His wife wore a soft-blue T-shirt, also oversized, and stained jeans. They both seemed too weak to move past Memoria, both seemed ready to die here.

"Hombre, you only getting diesel if you give us las vacas," Ura said.

"We can't give them to you because—"

"Enough! Tell me where they are. Tell me and you'll have two candungos filled with diesel. Two. That's double what we normally give out."

"We don't need diesel. We need a place to stay. There's no more food and our cattle are very sick. They can't be slaughtered for food. If you—"

"Tell us where to find them, viejo. We'll judge for ourselves."

"I'm telling you they are sick. If you try eating them, you'll poison everyone here."

Ura got angry again and the reds grew impatient with Ura's seemingly new genteel approach to conflict. They started chanting up again, "Ura, Ura, Ura," and that made Ura nervous. He brushed his hands against his sweaty forehead. His hair had grown out, now shoulder length, and his face was elongated by his scruff for a beard, a dirty uneven patchwork. He looked desperate for a shower. The reds kept up their taunting and Ura started pacing.

"Tell us where your farm is, maricón. Tell us now and I won't let my pets hurt you," he grabbed the old man by his shirt. But the man didn't scare. As though he'd run into young boys like Ura all his life, the pumping of fists and rage as a first line of communication, he looked comforted by this fact.

"Ura, Ura, Ura," the reds chanted. They threw their hands up in the air and swayed them side to side.

Ura finally snapped and punched the old man in his jaw. The man fell to the ground and his wife dropped to his side and shielded him from another one of Ura's blows.

"Ura!" I ran and jumped between them. "If the guy tells you the animals are sick, then let it be. What good will that do? What are you getting from all of this?"

The reds started the jumping and chanting and growling and Ura turned away as if readying another swing.

"Ura, ya," I said again. "Back off." I shoved him backward and he nearly fell over, but the reds held his waist upright.

I knelt down and faced the old man and his wife. I whispered to them, told them to leave, to follow the painted trees down the side of the mountain. That they'd come up against the narrowing of the main highway, where debris and burned pickup trucks piled the road. I told them to trek their way back down and make it to Arecibo. I told them there were probably settlements on the coast. That it was safer there. But they seemed hollow, they knew my advice only meant one thing for them. Their eyes spoke of sadness. Of a helplessness that grew the more I tried consoling them.

Ura waited for me to finish. I stopped talking and gently held
the hands of the old couple in my palms. He whistled at the
reds and they rejoiced. The reds gathered and started chanting
in their usual *Ura Ura Ura*. Spectators around Memoria chose
to ignore it, everyone too weak to get involved. The reds gathered and jumped up and down, their red bomber jackets and
black surgical masks moving with their bodies. They grabbed
and pushed me away from the old couple. They hoisted each
of them over their heads and I watched as they marched into
the quiet forest, the chanting fading and fading until I heard
nothing.

A RAIN SHOWER pelted the mountain and Memoria lost its
mysticism. Citizens began to grow exhausted from getting
drenched, their cots dampened as the rain pitter-pattered
against the zinc steeple of the Tower, against the plates left on
the logs around ceremony. Ura had favorites among the reds,
and they hung out with him in the Tower. Ura watched from
his shelter as his people soaked in water. We looked up from
time to time at the Tower and we'd see him through the cutout window gazing into the horizon.

I helped tie some royal palm leaves over cots and that kept
some dry. But newcomers or those who never got around to
building anything got soaked and looked miserable. We were
afraid the dirt would soon turn to thick mud and become difficult to walk through, water patches began forming all over
and the water drained through the clearing in a red-brown
stream.

Two fuel trucks ran dry days earlier. The reds were instructed to unbury them and replace them with the last two

trucks in stock, they started on the holes but the rain undid all their efforts, the water collected and collected and the dirt moved back atop the buried trucks. It all started to look like a shallow pool carved into the earth.

Banto got to mind that Moriviví and Damaris knew where Cami was and that gave him hope. I encouraged him to go with them, I wanted to stay behind and keep an eye on Ura. Ceremony was becoming more than decrees of gratitude. With his curfew in place, he managed to find more innovative ways of hurting others and those who didn't satisfy him with their declarations were thrown lumps of dirt by the reds. It made people work harder on their speeches and you even heard some rehearsing throughout the day, which pleased Ura in his Tower, to hear the echoes of voices practicing with his name on the tips of their tongues.

Memoria was desperate. Then the rat infestation came. Rodents got into the stock of dried cod and Ura grew furious when he found the fish in the bags gnawed with shit pellets all over. Cheo chuckled when Ura threw the sacks of cod back into the center fire of ceremony. He chuckled loud enough I was sure Ura heard it.

ONE AFTERNOON, A group of young boys started a fuss. They cried in front of the Tower in protest. They cried because they didn't have any more toilet paper to clean their shit. Ura ignored them. He used to take proposals and concerns from citizens of Memoria in the Tower. Over time, he locked himself in there and left the reds to field the complaints or requests. The young boys were orphans, like the reds, like all of us now. For some reason, Ura didn't care to ordain them into his red puppets and left them to fend for themselves.

They walked to the Tower door smelling terribly and the reds grimaced before kicking dirt on them, they kicked until the group of boys were dusted in brown and red soil. Yet the boys continued to plead with Ura. One of them even showed them the stains in his underwear but it didn't have an effect. Ura waved them off and the reds poked them back to their cots with metal broomsticks. Moriviví, Damaris, and Banto shook their heads in unison, not in disbelief, but in reluctant acceptance.

THAT NIGHT, THE three of them went out into the dark forest in search of Camila. Banto had high spirits and he led the charge wearing his usual blond wig and black blazer. I wanted to believe he'd return uplifted and determined, maybe we'd all decide to leave Memoria and head elsewhere, to the beach in Arecibo, back to Florencia. I watched them march away and it filled me with sadness.

The following day, Cheo and me woke to the sound of a car honking its horn. It must've been just after eight or nine. Banto, Moriviví, and Damaris hadn't returned. It was Ura and his reds. He drove into Memoria through the Red Gates on a stolen Camry. Its red paint was discolored, the doors and hood dented in random places, the windshield cracked down the middle. The Camry had a sunroof and Ura poked his skinny, long body through it as the reds steered the car. Ura whistled at the citizens to come around. As people assembled, the Camry stilled. Ura rummaged below the roof and pulled out stacks of Bounty and toilet paper, he tossed them in the air the way basketball players shoot free throws. Everyone clawed up trying to catch some, everyone smiled, grateful because they could now clean their asses.

"Harmony through *my* leadership. Through *my* leadership," Ura shouted. The reds pressed the horn and the Camry reverberated; the honking echoed in the clearing.

"Qué charlatán," Cheo said, shaking his head. "Wonder if he's figured out the food problem yet. Is he going to ride in on a horse giving out free T-shirts next?"

I laughed in agreement. We resigned ourselves to the role of spectators, watching as Ura injected Memoria with a new false sense of hope. I waited to see if the group of boys who pleaded for toilet paper were in the crowd, but they weren't. The group of boys stayed in their corner, seated on their cots, and observed. They didn't even try to get up. I knew they smelled awful. I worried, if they stayed that way, would the reds make them disappear the way they disappeared Marisol, the way they disappeared the old farming couple?

It was a natural impulse. I quickly rummaged through my rations supply. I kept most of my toiletries and papers in a black storage chest. I stuffed everything I thought they might need into an empty canvas bag and walked over to them. I opened the bag in front of them and tried passing each of them some of my rations: soap bars, sticks of Old Spice, a small bottle of Suave shampoo, a four-pack of toilet paper. I tried handing each of them all these things, but they sat dazed. They fixated on the Camry, they fixated on Ura. He made the reds drive slowly around Memoria as people packed around the car waiting to see what he threw out to them; they kept following him until he ran out of stock and disappeared into the car and circled and drove out through the Red Gate. I wished it was only the reds that started the teasing, wished it was only the reds that participated in catching and laughing as Ura threw paper towels. But it was Memoria, strays from Utuado, strays from Florencia, they all followed Ura around the clearing, they chased the Camry around until it sped off down the Red Gate. I got up and returned to my cot leaving the canvas sack with the group of boys.

THE TRIO STILL hadn't returned from Utuado searching for Camila. I worried they might show up at night and the reds would catch them and report them to Ura for violating curfew. Cheo grew impatient with Memoria and Ura. We spent most of our days near Caonillas, sometimes fishing, sometimes washing our dirty clothes, mostly killing time to avoid returning.

"Why don't we just go, pescao? Let's just go. There's nothing here worth keeping."

We sat on a large boulder watching the small schools of chopa swim by Cheo's hook.

"I want to stay, mano. I know it doesn't look impressive—"

"It's not." He fiddled with the rod and adjusted his angle. "If anything, it's going to turn bad fast."

"You don't know that."

"Mijo, anyone who stays there for five minutes knows that."

"Where else do we go then? Hmm. Give me a place and we'll go to it."

"Home. Florencia. We go back to Florencia."

"You speaking of home this, home that. You starting to sound like Banto, mano. Florencia's not home. Not anymore."

"Home is always home—"

"Not to me."

"Whether it looks the same or not, it is what it is. Call it what it is."

"I call it vertedero."

He paused.

"That's sad, mijo. Sad that you feel that way. We build home where we want. Like the mongers. Like you and your shack. Don't you miss your shack? We built that corner, el barrio, the relationships. It took me a long time to see that. In life. It took me a long time to realize that."

"Okay, Cheo. Okay," I said sarcastically. "Not ready to go."

"What are you holding on to here, Bayfish?"

"Nothing."

"Why do all of you believe in this so much?"

"I don't know."

"What is it? Why are you so afraid—"

"I don't know!"

He broke into a short laugh. It was for himself, nothing he wanted to share.

"I'm thinking I'll be going back, mijo. I think I've seen enough here. I miss the ocean. I miss being near the ocean."

I glanced at him briefly. Didn't want him to see my eyes, to see the hurt. He hadn't been in Memoria long and he was already leaving us stranded.

"It's a long walk back, mijo. I'd rather you join me. Rather you and Banto come. Coño bring the crew. We get Morivivi, Damaris, and Camila. We all go back, and we rebuild. We don't need all this crap—"

"How? How do we do that? With what resources?"

"Pescao, it's not always about that."

"It is. Shit, you sounding like Ura . . ."

"I'm sounding like ese cabrón? You're not listening to yourself. All you repeat is resources and resources. For Urayoán it was gas and diesel. For you it's resources."

"Cheo, we need something to get things started up. Shit doesn't fall from the sky and just happen."

"Chico, you're not listening—"

"Then tell me already!"

I stood up and looked down at him. He was small and me standing over him made him look childlike.

"You forgotten where you started? You forgotten what made Florencia home?"

"Ura's the one that found me in Río. Ura's the one who gave me a place to stay that wasn't the streets. Ura—"

"Urayoán uses people, pescao. He collects them and uses them, and when they are no longer useful to him, he gets rid of them."

I felt a little embarrassed.

"Us. The mongers. Banto. We are it . . . Listen, over time, we'll figure things out. It'll be a slow fix. We don't need anything fancy. We'll go and rebuild block by block. Slowly people will return."

"A lot of people died with that *things get better over time* talk. You know that right. I sound like Ura? You sound like the old government."

"Okay, pescao. Okay. Clearly, you not seeing it."

I knew he had given up but something inside me didn't want him to stop trying. Maybe that's what I was looking for. For someone to care and try. For the feeling of abandonment to stop. I saw the desire fade in Cheo's eyes and that made me sad.

"It's dangerous out there, Cheo. By chance if we managed, there's no way to keep safe. There are worse things than Ura and the reds. Even a stroll into Utuado is dangerous," I said almost as consolation, trying to keep him talking. To keep him invested.

"For whom? For whom is the danger? I walked many miles alone. I survived."

"You're lucky, Cheo. Look, Ura and those reds, they offer shelter. Safety. I know him. I know the reds. It's better to know what's coming and what to expect than to be surprised."

"Then you'll never have to surprise yourself. Good or bad. Shelter and safety given out of fear is no home, pescao. It's no home."

"We'll cope. We have to."

"Because there's no other choice—"

"Because we need to . . . like you said, survive."

"Okay, pescao, okay."

Cheo didn't say anything else. He fiddled with his fishing rod and looked at the humming water and watched as it soothed him. We didn't say much else for some time until Cheo got a nibble. He reeled in a large chopa.

"Look! Survival! We going to fry this one!" he said. He pointed to the gray fish and tossed it into the small plastic cooler.

"Cabrón," I responded and smiled.

We managed to catch a tub amount of chopa, tucunares, and red devils. I teased Cheo about the pesky red devils, their small bright orange bodies floundering atop the rest of the catch, it made things temporarily better. The sun dipped farther behind the mountain shadow and the colors set fire to the sky. It was the first time I'd seen everything light up in that way. It was the first time in a long time, and it brought me back to the time Banto and me looked over Florencia from La

Diabla. The only difference was there weren't any cucubanos glowing around us as we walked back to Memoria. Still, I felt us come closer to something familiar.

But returning to Memoria was a sharp wake-up call. We walked through the Red Gate and everyone stared at us. The reds, the citizens. We saw so many young kids hungry. They eyed the plastic cooler and the fishing rods. It's as if they smelled the fish. Cheo and I didn't hesitate and when we got back to our cots, we grilled the chopa and tucunares, their bright green bodies seared until ready. We cut them into tiny squares and gave it all away. We even fried the red devils, pierced them onto branches like a pincho. The gills and fins fried stiff. After we handed out the last bite, he turned to me.

"Oye, pescao, I'm thinking we go back to the river and try catching more for the rest of them."

I was tired and the night was slowly creeping in. I worried about curfew.

"Come on, pescao," he insisted.

"Alright, Cheo. Alright," I responded.

We collected some more bait from Cheo's stash. We changed into some fresh clothes. Cheo put on a black linen long-sleeved shirt and a fresh pair of cargo shorts. I rinsed my neck and chest with a wet towel, and we started back to Caonillas when Ura appeared in front of the Red Gate. He was surrounded by his reds wearing the black surgical masks. I noticed he held under his harm a rolled-up fishing net. As we moved closer to him and his puppets, Ura lifted his finger and pointed at Cheo. And Cheo felt it. He knew in that moment what Ura was going to ask of him and I started to fear he was right. We walked closer and closer under that ugly Red Gate and Ura smirked his smirk and my eyes started to tear up because I knew.

URAYOÁN

Believe in spirits and I'll make you believe in death. It's the spirits that selected me to lead and that's why I do it. Some come from the bodies I refrigerate nice and safe, but more so it's from God. I hear the voices in the night, and they speak on how disorder will come if I don't use force. I thought first with violence but there are better ways to do it. My pets grow angry, angry now that the sack of cod and food perishables have been eaten by rats and roaches. I used to see that kind in Santurce, they're fat with a thick tail and climb over piles just to get their fill. They remind me of the reds, too, their cunning is fierce. I admire such things.

My reds swear the rats need protein though I'm sure they long to eat something that used to be living rather than dead. They think themselves the sharks of land, which is nice because that's what makes them a menacing scare. I saw how the ancient Cheo hangs around Hagseed and then it came to me—always because of my genius—that he needs to fish for us. It's such a simple solution I'm angry at myself for not thinking of it earlier.

I wait until he finishes his little honeymoon with Hagseed. Hagseed seem to like honeymooning often and I joke to think what the fat one would say if he found out he's tossed aside and relegated to number two. Cheo and Hagseed stroll back early evening from that fishing honeymoon expedition and start a feast for all the little ones in Memoria. They happy and grateful and my reds see all this and get impatient. I tell them it's a time for patience. I see my little citizens happier than when I drop gold onto their feet, when I provide, as I always do. Things like Energy, cots, the paper to clean their shit stains, but that's not enough. Not the Energy, not the shelter, not ceremony or rations of goat. I see these things and I start, even for a small second, to think of spirits. They gave me a language of terror and persuasion and now they show me this Hagseed and ancient Cheo turning their affection because of generosity. What about my generosity!? I think about my beautiful Memoria and I start in on the existential and that never leaves me satisfied, I confess. All these mean spirits tripping over me. I see the reds still loyal and obedient yearning for violence. That's how I thought of sending along the ancient on his mission.

Them two are traitors to my genius. Traitors! They start up to the Red Gate ready to provide for the citizens and *my* citizens follow them at their feet. As if they are Moses or Jesús or God proclaiming commandments. They come close and that's when I signal and present the ancient Cheo with an ultimatum. He tells me, "We are going off to fish by the river Caonillas to feed more of the kids." He says this and I start to laugh like thunder and my pets join in chorus. We laughing and smiling because he doesn't know. "You are going off to fish out in the ocean, old one. With this net here you will go out and bring back a feast for Memoria. You will do this because we housed you. You will do this because I say you will." I tell him this with anger and assurance because I know the reds are witnessing and I also see the rest of Memoria watching. I go on and sweeten the deal because I know only Gods give and take and I want to be a hand that channels this. I tell him all of Memoria is going down to Arecibo, down to el Faro and there we will hold ceremony, the lighthouse as spectator, with a great fire that will see to his departure for my noble command. Hagseed tries interjecting with annoyance, "Ura, ya. It's late. There is no need for this. Let us go to the river, let us make a catch. That way tomorrow we will—" he tries to continue but I can't. I don't need the excuse or his desire to change direction. I shut him off and the reds like this, they start the howling and bite into the air, looking mean and menacing, ready to unleash.

My reds are beautiful. They amassed a caravan of pickups, donated generously by the great abandonment. But they don't go to Utuado's center to collect the caravan of pickups. No, they find all the pickups parked quietly in the pier of Lago Dos Bocas. It's a beautiful lake nestled and wedged in a mountainscape within distance of my Memoria; the steeping hillsides usually are forested in a wild green. It always rains in that lake. There used to be restaurants that you quickly reached by ferry. They even tell me there are submerged houses in the lake, not because of la monstrua and her rage, but because they've always been there, since the old government decided on reservoir creationism.

I tell the reds to round up the citizens of Memoria, preparing them for a grand announcement. I go to my Tower and speak for all to hear. I tell them about the ancient Cheo and his generosity. I tell them the fish will flow once he returns from the sea. I tell them we leave to build ceremony and that will send him off with good omens. And they cheer. They cheer a joy bigger than the little fish buffet Hagseed and the ancient tried to buy them with earlier, and that satisfies them. All my people and my pets tumble over the road out of my Memoria, we march and march. A march without beat and rhythm is just walking, so some reds bring with them pots and wooden spoons and they bang into them a smooth, smooth tempo. Everyone is dancing except Hagseed and the ancient, who walk as if in mourning.

I take a seat in the last pickup of our illustrious caravan. My citizens pile onto the backs and the reds drive and drive and the stars are glowing because nothing else shines anymore. I like the night in that light, a dark cave with only dots accenting the ceiling—that lets you see heaven, clear as tears. I don't ride in the front. No, I stand in the bed so I can see the path in front and the trail we leave behind, and it is nice to see things in sharp relief. I watch as the drive descends and the fields open where there used to be farms and in backdrop the shadow of mountains. I watch all this as we drive and think it is necessary, all the fires and ceremony, all the reds and discipline, but that's not how we need live, it's how we build. So many days spent agonizing over our trivial mortality, our end spooks us, it always has. The end makes for desperation but that don't take up my mind anymore since we create a beginning with new memory.

Everything continues in darkness except the shadow of the moon. The reds pull into the short parking in Arecibo. In front I hear the waves, a soft lashing against sand. A concrete canal serves as pier, its access used to be for the island marina even though the marina is now wood beneath the ocean. It is a short, small bay, not like the old capital San Juan, but a half bay and a lighthouse on a slight hill, dead to the right. I see the reds run into the shadows of the night looking for firewood in preparation for a new ceremony. I jump off my pickup and Hagseed wears depression like makeup. His long frown makes me anxious, so I slap him softly on his cheek as I cross him, nothing mean or menacing, a few taps to knock him free. The ancient Cheo is already walking into the tickle of water and I whistle him over and tell him, "Patience." My citizens run up and down the dirty beach, kicking sand into the stars, some splash in the cold ocean and my pets set the logs in the rightful places for ceremony. They pour specks of Energy onto the wood and I whistle everyone to gather round and witness. I start things with a signal and the reds run toward the log pile and ignite the fire. It rumbles larger and larger until the entire beach is brightest. Then I let a special song whistle in the night and my reds know to build the thing that will carry the ancient out into the sea.

Hagseed and the ancient might as well sit on each other's laps for how close they are and that makes me chuckle knowing the raft being built by the reds. Ceremony begins with the pots and spoons and the reds start their tribute and dance. They growl as they've done in the past months letting out short decrees of gratitude. I've never seen so many decrees wished to be heard and it is like all my citizens want to hear their own voices float in the air. They proclaim the grace of Memoria and then they proclaim the grace of the ancient Cheo, how he is sailing off bravely into the darkness to find us all the fish to satisfy our bellies. The thought makes me giggle. I know the raft and net we give the ancient will not hold the angry Atlantic. I think he does, too, yet he doesn't protest, he accepts his fate in that odd way people do after they've lived enough life. The reds form a human chain to the raft, a plank of wood with some logs light enough for bounce. It's all tied together with wire and rope and the reds leave a paddle for the ancient to steer around helplessly in the middle of the Atlantic. The small bay is calm, but I know how ravenous the waters turn once the vastness opens up.

The great pyre burns and burns, and I see how Hagseed comes to me with a sort of aggression. "Ura, we can go fishing in Caonillas, there's no need to send Cheo out to sea. It is dark. That raft won't hold up against the waves." He says this as if it makes a difference when that's what I want: to have him drift endlessly until the ocean pulls him so far out he will disappear and no one will remember he existed. "Ura, por favor. Please. Please let him stay and I promise we will work to make Memoria live—" he continues, and I interject, "Memoria's already alive!" And he continues the pleading, but it plays no effect on my ears. I'm solidified with decision and certainty. I see the ancient standing now in the row and his eyes speak this bright sadness that makes me a little sick, but I let him have that since I know he won't return alive to these shores. "Think of Florencia, pescao. Think of home. Think of everything that we fight for and remember this is it. The sand under your feet, the islet off these shores, the vicious forests that never quiet in stillness. Think these things, pescao, and you will remember home," the ancient says in prophecy as a martyr or apostle or some dying creed and that makes me think how he will be remembered. But I don't let myself go there since the ocean will take care of him. I whistle and have my reds escort him down the row past the great burning. He makes it to the raft and the music is banging and the citizens are cheering and happy with hum and jest. The reds force the fishing net on the ancient and he holds on to it, looking at it like some dear loaf of bread. He caresses it in reflection, his bald head shines with the blazing fire. Everyone now links hands and sways from side to side like the waves kissing the shore. The ancient settles onto the raft and places the net under his feet. He holds on to the paddle since that will be his boatman leading him to death, and I walk up to him in my content. I shake his hand wearing the crossed smirk I like that tells him exactly how this all ends. He tries to pierce me, to press me, without words, his frown all purposeful thinking it will play long-term effects on my beauty sleep. But I—always the clever one—never let the pettiness of glares linger in my mind; I sweep them behind me and tread over them since I know the spirits that gifted me life expect much.

Hagseed runs back to the pickups which is odd. The reds start pushing the raft deeper into the ocean and the ancient prepares his paddle. Then Hagseed appears and runs in splashing, the beach sand like quicksand slowing him as he moves deeper and closer to the raft. I first think he's going to hop onto the raft and they'll both sail into the darkness and disappear. That might have been unexpected and even sad for me because I don't mind Hagseed. I found him and nursed him back to life. I always carry softer spots in my heart for the things I nurture, like a proud father I suppose. Hagseed carries with him this sack and he reaches the raft that is now some space away from shore but still body length accessible in the ocean. Hagseed is a tall shrimp so he can probably walk endlessly into the waves. The ancient leans down and grabs the sack from Hagseed. He seems grateful and I think its food in the sack, or maybe a gun that might ease the passing when things get choppy. But it's none of those things. The ancient pulls notebooks out from the bag and I can't help but laugh since it's desperate, to expect poor old Cheo to be record and book. What stories can be told from his life? What terrors will be left to keep for others to find? That never makes sense so I think it must be a spiritual deliverance, something he thinks God has given him, the gift of record keeping, but I don't see any story he can tell that captures the cries this island feels.

The ancient is drifting and I swear I see his tears. Hagseed leaves him notebooks and a lighter, a portable fire for him to see and from the shore, lit with ceremony and our great Memoria fire, I read the waves, the ancient rites in the rocking, in the choppy water, his raft a tiny candle as it sails forward. It's a tiny brightness in contrast to the black sheet, a cucubano flickering until he suffocates the flame, and he paddles and paddles farther away and I don't see him anymore from our shores.

Hagseed is fallen on the sand, his long neck scarred and ugly. He sits and stares expecting to read the waves the way I do. He watches in hope that maybe the ancient returns soon and even brings in the big catch, tuna and marlins and maybe some tiger sharks for all of Memoria to eat. The reds dance and kick sand and the pots chime and clatter in an offbeat rhythm. My citizens continue their dancing, maybe as a way to guarantee the ancient returns. I whistle again something fierce and the reds begin escorting my citizens back to the trucks. They don't extinguish the great fire. I'll let it suffocate naturally with the rising sun. Everything is set for us to journey back to Memoria, back home. But Hagseed doesn't move. He stays in his sandy chair and watches the darkness in exhaustion. I whistle for him to come but he's being defiant now which is never a good look when there are spectators. I whistle until the reds grow impatient and start honking their horns and they are all honking now in desperation, some even anger. I whistle my fiercest and send the reds to collect frozen Hagseed and three jump out and crawl to him and start their dragging, he fights it at first and he looks like the fat girl when we take the rotting corpse, he fights and kicks the reds so more have to jump into the mess until he drops onto the white sand and is crying an infant's cry, a bawling I never heard or expect. He's crying and hitting the beach with his closed fists and the reds drag him by the feet and he claws at sand repeating, "Leave me here, just leave me." I don't say anything other than signal to move once we have Hagseed secure in a pickup and he's still crying, the tears flowing and the fire burning on the beach, he cries as he's tied to the bed of the truck and then we are off driving in caravan back to Memoria, back home.

CHEO

I'm readied and they ship me out on this vessel, it rocks steady, waves splashing against the logs, my paddle cutting into the saltwater. This island is strange and foreign when you look at it from the ocean, leveled in sight, in that dark outline against the night. There is quiet here, spare the waves. A quiet louder than death after María. Only thoughts can keep me company. And these notes that I write. I'm careful not to use too much of the lighter fluid because I don't know how many nights the Atlantic will give me. I want to save as much as possible if by chance inspiration hits during a restless sleep. The fire still shines, and I see it tiny, a fallen star on a deserted beach shore.

I paddle north but don't need much force since the current is doing most of the dragging. I feel the strangeness grow the longer I drift. It's not a strangeness that discomforts. No. It's almost welcomed. When I finally decide on dreaming, I feel the raft shaking as the waves move faster; the salt splashes against my cheeks and against my bald head and I remember Florencia and the mongers and the pier on the running river and how we shipped out on early mornings down the canals, garbage collecting in small patched gyres, we shipped closer and closer to the mouth of the river until it joined into origin and we steered our boats out into the velvet morning where we cast nets and we'd wait, chatting about the rum and game of dominoes the night before, chatting about Veronica and how close Jorge got to kissing her dry lips, chatting about constipation and hurt. I fall deep into this thinking until I am gone, and the slow growing light welcomes me to morning.

IT IS CLOUDY, much too cloudy in the morning. I still catch the brown and green horizon of my island from where I sit. It is farther away from me, or rather I from it. I think of a list, maybe my last.

- The blueness of the water is only truly blue if there's sun.
- I notice the patches of dark algae get deeper.
- Waves sustain but they don't promise comfort.
- Skin is fragile and blisters fast.
- The sun still hurts even behind graying clouds.
- Graying clouds mean rain and storm and . . .
- The open sea reminds you who you aren't.

I am struggling. Though I doubt anyone will read these pages or lines or verse, I still want to leave my mark with a pen. I keep striking at the phrases that continue to bug me. They go:

I want to give names to oceans still grieving.
Like mothers, they think about their children crying.
I want to describe how beautiful it must be to grieve again.
I want to be honest so that a homecoming does not reappear
on midnight infomercials wedged between static,
I play riddles with the stars at night since there are so many
and no one is keeping record. Not out here.
I lose the games because I can't be the beast
and a rose all in one.

No. That isn't right. Maybe there is too much *want* in this version. And I am still thinking of the rose and the beast. What if I work the rose more and see how it resonates?

~~The beast and a rose are all in one~~.
~~And~~ the beast is . . . ~~the rose~~

No. Again, it isn't right. *Do I give up on the rose?* I am think-ing it is forced crap and doesn't add up. Maybe what is missing is a larger truth. Or rather, a declaration to all my people that have drifted too far away. Away to different settings and thinking about home. They thought about this island and wondered what life would've been like had they somehow stayed.

I've seen my people fly on silver birds. They make habit
to leave, because they must, or they can't,
off to places where water is not clear or warm,
places where the sea isn't spontaneous,
that is to say, she doesn't gather her motions
in each curl of a wave the way it's done near
Ocean Park, or Crash Boat, or Flamenco.

She chooses sargassum to float on salt, plastic, debris.
Not needing cruise liners or caravels
with lights exhausted from travel.
She paints new currents and that is memory.

I want to give names to things grieving,
each dead and dying, some put into cold trucks
after the calamity because the ground doesn't satisfy,

or there aren't enough employees at forensics,
many traveled away on those silver birds.

I want to give names to worn pelicans or gaviotas,
egrets or songbirds, each swollen body after
water persisted in her rage and drowned and drowned,
drowned them all.

For the many syllables that saunter in a trumpet kiss.
For the light glowing at the heads of flashlights searching
grown thickets, left behind to survive.
Noises are what I keep and it's just desert.
I want it to call to me, to write and to say my name.
Cheo. Cheo of Florencia. Of Memory. Of island. Of nation.

I don't like this. The cadence is off in some places, the images forced open or maybe used too many times before. I am only a seafarer with no grand history. But it might be my best attempt . . . No. No. There's more. I turn the pages of my notebook. The waves tumble harder beneath the raft and I hear the rope slowly loosening, I let the fishing net fall beneath me like a black spider web descending into the deep and dark ocean. I flip through the pages and see the lists I wrote down. I see the verse left behind for Doña Julia and I am thankful that I haven't drank water or eaten because I would've cried rereading and reconstructing her beauty, her history. Now, my face is bitten with sores and I wonder and think of my mongers, of Florencia, and Bayfish. I write a few verses with the lists and see how they read.

Leaving is a grieving,
at least that is what I feel

as I watch myself leave
until there is no my island
blocking the horizon.

I remember Cristóbal Colón,
all that is taught of him,
how we've elected to build
statues and name that Plaza de Colón
in Viejo San Juan. There, a concrete facsimile
with a frozen gait, almost lifelike, grips
an unfurled flag with a crucifix finial as crown,
the patterns on rock tapestry indistinguishable.
But I know those patterns speak empire.
Oh, a sort of cheap Christ the Redeemer!
Oh, he must speak like Lazarus in Bethany!

His stone gazes over Teatro Tapia
and its dark wooden patios, arched
like many crescent moons,
serve as shut prisms to nowhere.

Lord, I can't forget the other
ugly copper replica, an obscene giant
planted like a bruised thumb
near the shores of Arecibo.
I think of him and I think of us
and it makes me weep!

It's my father and leaders,
old and new, that create
the same phantom pains.

VELORIO

All, occasions to cry
and I feel no shame.

Are we culprits to our fate
and live by our names?
And that is empire.
And that is violence.

Urayoán believed and I suppose
that is worth something,
not noble or beautiful but it has its worth.
His love for dark fire is that of forgetting,
of our own abandonment.
I worry about what new means
and what rules we etch into law,
if sacrifice is the only way of giving birth.
Should everything new
be born from tears?

Fire, as Urayoán thinks, burns everything,
paper, cash, flesh, it is all temporary.
I live in days where roses are dropped
atop dirt oceans, graves under
Utuado's mountainsides impossible to reach,
impossible to make record, like Memoria.
An angry beast grows inside our hearts,
contaminating bodies in and out of graves,
a new part of the everyday.

Christ! This whole fucking island!
I see it cry for connectivity.

If we fell into survival, we clung to hope
near cell phone towers like schools of fish
wrapped around an orbit, climbing atop cars,
hoping to connect to something,
trying to speak back to you.

It wasn't just you trying to reach us.
We tried to reach you too.
But we've already been grieving
generations of desertion.

I live now in a time of roses let go at sea.
Roses dropped and cradled in waves,
for the thousands of people passed.

I dream and drift on this sea,
but it only leads me back to me,
back to home. I live in the rose
and in the sea. The currents drift
in different patterns. No blue colors
in foaming water reflections,
no green tips speared out of casuarinas,
no familiar horizon.

It all looks as mud,
a land banked by sand
  and sediment.
Even months after.
Even as robles,
palos de tamarindo, guanábana,
eucalyptus, flamboyán, calabash,

VELORIO

all try to inject green back
into the line of the sun.

I want Palo Viejo
or Bacardí now . . .
rum that burns
but soothes,
and as I squint to look back,
just before a new storm stews ahead of me,
I see my island; I see you there
on those shores looking out to me,

a stateless seaman, a mongrel, a mermaid,
a child adrift in that expanse.
I carry you as heavy as I carry home,
as heavy as this pen tries to mark
onto paper all that I am, all my love.
I know the salt and fish will eat this,
that you may never read these lines,
my head is cold and bare, my skin . . .

blistered the same, I'll see the roses
you let fall into these waters,
as remembrance, as memory.
Sing again, in mourning, in celebration,
even if they remain stranded
in the dark and deep,
I poke into these paper sheets
small acts of desperation,
because I, too, sing Borikén.
I, Cheo, write lines in poetry . . .

That is all I can come up with. The water has grown angry. And there is rain falling and falling. I can't see much anymore so I put my notebook and pen in the sack. Then I decide it is time and I sit on the edge of the raft, its rope and wire barely holding together. I take the sack with all that is me inside, and I let it drop into her mouth and it descends slowly down and disappears.

A cloud of flying fish, like silver knives, jet behind my raft. I think, in fear, at least at first, about what will happen to my body. The tiger sharks, hammerheads, are they waiting for me below? Or will my lungs flood with water and take me that way instead. Then a strangeness, a foreignness, serves as my blanket. It won't matter. Either way, I'll drift and all that will be left are words, rhythm, and rhyme.

I lie there and wait, I feel everything around me again, the wood underneath my thin shirt, splintering, the small indents from the falling rain. I wish I could see it all again from a time before. Seeing your island outlined on a horizon heals, from an airplane, from the ocean. It's that harbor in San Juan that heals because it is the sign that you have returned.

I would take the dysfunction and corruption and the pain. I would take all that because it was as much a part of me as celebration and laughter. I was never someone that thought much about homecoming, because I always lived at home. It is only now I see constant gray, clouds like long sheets expanding above, I dream about color again, the iridescent tapestry nature conveys. I don't know if anyone will read this. But I hope they will. Know that I loved. Know this. It is unyielding. My poetry. Our dirge.

THREE

BANTO

U tuado was one of those towns you visited to get away from it all. There was nothing but nature atop mountains, which is why Memoria was so opportune. Two isolations, one leeching off the other. An afterthought it seemed, the way most towns are in the center. Even to those of us who lived on our island, we happened to come across this place for lore, a connectedness to the idea of roots, but was quickly forgotten once the passersby returned to the city coast.

Utuado was beautiful before María came. It will be beautiful after. The streets were thin and drawn together, curved and steep in seemingly impossible angles. With no one frequenting the streets, however, they felt cold. I liked how low-lying clouds sat over the rolling mountains, the way they nestled between the face of buildings, the cooling damp of morning fog, everything wet to the touch. Night masked terrain, but in morning light, these places were most stunning.

Memoria tried for that effect but instead it imposed malevolence that never improved with time, it grew out from the clearing, dressed itself in tall vines, the trees suffocated because they couldn't compete with the rampant overgrowth, the clouds feared to linger, the Tower, the Red Gate, the potholes, the firepit, and Ura's appointed throne. The malevolence.

The night was darkest. We searched for Utuado, just us three moving along the streets, the glow of our flashlights guiding us. Even with crickets and coquíes whistling and chirping, there was no faint murmur from people, or car engines backfiring. No portable generators blaring. Nothing. A disquiet felt deep in our ribs. I wanted to believe everyone slept peacefully in the dark, tucked away safely on the sides of those hills, wanted to believe our island wasn't deserted. It started to feel like Memoria was the only thing alive and breathing.

I scanned the sides of the roads with my light and put a spotlight on the concrete houses and shops as we passed them, each looked ancient and worn. The mountain imposed on the buildings. It kissed their edges in such a way it was a miracle a landslide hadn't gobbled them up like el barrio Mameyes in Ponce many decades ago. Abandoned cars were haphazardly parked, some with doors wide open. It scared me. People leaving as if by rapture. Why would they run off in such desperation? Why would they leave their houses and cars in such a frenzy? I saw red plastic candungos scattered from time to time, as if diesel and gas no longer mattered. I tried calling attention to all of it with my light, tried speaking up but my voice cracked and everyone moved along.

The smell of rotting leaves and standing water still lingered. We walked until we reached a bridge shattered by the river. You could see an attempt to connect each side of the divide, a rickety ladder fell to the foot of the broken bridge, atop plastic debris, fallen trees, branches wedged together by the force of water, and large rocks. Logs purposefully placed along the receded river helped form a connection. A thick rope tied the two sides. If you walked on the logs, it was meant for balance and support.

"We crossing on that?" I said to Damaris and Moriviví. They didn't respond and made it to the edge of the bridge before climbing down the ladder without hesitation.

"Wait. Wait for me," I yelled to them. I fixed my wig and blazer and held my flashlight with my mouth. They didn't slow down, propelling their bodies over the logs using the rope to move faster along the wooden spines. I started climbing down and almost slipped from the ladder. The flashlight loosened between my teeth, I bit down hoping it wouldn't fall into the mess below. I bit down, my heavy breathing causing the plastic to become slippery until the flashlight tumbled from my mouth, hit my belly, then rolled over and fell into the water and branches, the slow current carrying the light downstream, the small light the only thing shining below the river until it disappeared.

"Wait, coño! Wait," I repeated. I couldn't see where the ladder ended so I just hung there on those steps and gripped the wood. I wanted to cry again. I looked at the direction of Damaris and Moriviví.

"Chico, come on," Damaris yelled back. She was more than halfway over and had to return, help me climb all the way down, and walk the tether.

"You need to be more careful, Banto. Now we have one less light."

"Perdón."

I struggled ahead of her as she held her light forward guiding me to the other side. My blazer lifted up with my T-shirt and my entire gut became visible and it embarrassed me, my wig dilapidated and probably smelly too. Moriviví stood above us on the edge of the broken bridge. She helped with lighting as she hurriedly waved us along.

"Wonder where all the people went?" I asked. But again they said nothing. Damaris and me made it to Moriviví and we all took a moment to look back at the severed bridge before walking forward.

"Do you think they got help in time?" I wondered.

"No. No one got help in time. Some are still waiting," Damaris responded.

"How would you know that?"

"You can't be stupid, Banto."

"I'm just saying, there's a rope here for a reason. Someone thought about it. Someone tried helping."

"It's a rope to get out, Banto," Moriviví said.

"Not everyone left, you know. Los viejitos that can't walk or cross the river. What about them? What about those who are sick? They're probably in their homes now. Ura has broods trading for goods. So, someone still lives out here." I paused trying to catch my breath. Damaris and Moriviví walked fast and it winded me. "They can't all have . . . died, you know."

"That's getting out. One way or the other, they got out," Damaris said. She moved faster and I had to break into a soft jog to try to keep up.

"Come on, chica."

"Hurry up, Banto."

"I'm trying."

WE CONTINUED WALKING until we heard a clatter of metal trash cans and music stir the darkness behind us. Damaris glanced at Moriviví and by instinct, they both scurried to the side of the road. I stumbled as they pulled me to the ground, and we crouched behind a short concrete wall, tall overgrown grass tickling my chin. Plastic bottles littered the ground and I accidently stepped on some letting out a loud crunch. Damaris got angry and smacked me over the head and put her finger against her lips. They turned off their flashlights.

If we peered over the wall, we could see the center of town to our right. It was dark down the road. A glowing light emerged from the direction we had walked. The sound of a car started humming. Reguetón vibrated through its speakers and the metal shell of the car trembled. The sound grew closer and closer until the car came over the short hill and within sight. It was a Camry with dents all over and a sunroof. We kept looking and saw Ura's broods driving it. Two of them stood through the sunroof and they yelled into the night, howling and barking. Morivivi shook her head and frowned. She took out her knife from her pocket and gripped it hard.

The Camry stopped just before reaching us, it idled, and the music kept sounding, the frame of the car shaking with every low bass thud, the dembow rising and rising. It made me nervous feeling those vibrations. One of the reds in the passenger seat got out and walked to the trunk of the car and leaned against it. He was a tall one with thin arms. He crossed his hands and leaned back waiting and waiting until more headlights appeared from the small hill behind them. The lights glared over the road and the entire stretch was lit up. I saw Damaris leaning her head against the wall, her eyes shut, her skin stained with dirt and sweat, the hairs on her arms prickled. Morivivi kept at the ready, she crouched in a way that would let her jump up quickly if she needed to, her knife drawn. I could now see all the details of that wall and I studied it as a way to distract myself, saw how the cinder blocks weren't paved and most of the edging was chipped. There were some parts spray-painted black, illegible signatures and messages, and I tried reading them, following the bending of the paint, making out letters but unable to see a message. The grass was uneven, high reeds sprouting in different directions, beard grass combing the edges of the wall, and patches of margaritas silvestres spreading across it, their white and yellow flowering giving color to a hollow landscape. I felt my stomach tighten and let out soft grumbles. Moriviví glared at me and lifted her eyebrows.

"Be still," she whispered.

I couldn't think of anything to say so I tried staying quiet. The music continued. Moriviví peered over the wall to get a clearer look. I did too. I felt I shouldn't. That it was best for me to close my eyes and wait it out, but I couldn't resist and poked over as the reds convened.

The headlights from the arriving vehicle shut off. It was an old and rusted Ford pickup truck. The bed was stacked with metal cages. I tried leaning over just enough to see if I could make out what was inside. Some whimpering could be heard, then soft barks sounded. Each cage was stuffed with a few stray dogs, they must've been collecting them from the streets and houses. The red from the Camry picked up a metal tube shaped like a spear and ran it across the thin cage bars and when the dogs began barking louder, he turned to them and barked back, he growled and yelled and the rest of the brood broke out in laughter.

I felt an uneasiness grow and started sweating, my forehead drenched, the wig growing hotter over my head, my hands clammy.

"We should go," I whispered to Moriviví.

"Be still."

"We need to go. If they find us—"

"Ya, Banto. Ya."

I shuffled in place and the grass around me shook with my movements. I wanted to break out of there and run fast and far. Damaris opened her eyes and tried patting me softly on my forearm, but I kept fidgeting. Mori then grabbed me by the neck and brought me close to her, her knife almost grazing my scalp. She wasn't trying to cut me. She leaned into my ear and it tickled a little as she spoke.

"Take a breath, Banto. Breathe and let it out slowly. We'll leave as soon as they leave."

I listened. I took a few deep breaths and it calmed me for a second. We waited and watched. The reds talked among themselves and pointed to the dogs in the cages. They laughed and yelled over the music until they seemed to finish. They got back into the Camry and pickup truck. They started moving forward. The pickup passed us sluggishly. It didn't have a tailgate so we could see everything on the truck's bed. The cages had many dogs crammed in the space. And next to the cages lay a pile of skinned dog coats. Large butcher knives rattled against one another with the movements of the truck. The skinned coats were spotted with dried blood, different patterns smeared into their thin fibers, white coats, brown coats, black coats, gray coats. I wanted to believe it was all fake, plastic animal pelts you find on the cheap, a toy you'd buy at Capri or something. I stared and saw the dogs; their eyes spoke of sadness. They watched me and I them, some barked, some held their heads low. I felt vomit creep up my throat and swallowed it because I knew I'd make too much noise.

The Camry and pickup descended into town with the noise and music and must've disappeared into a barrio, up one of the mountainsides. I fell to the ground. I took off my wig and my head fell into the palms of my hands.

"We have to keep moving, Banto," Damaris said. "The church is just down the road—"

"They're killing them. The reds, they're killing all of them," I said.

"Yes . . . they are."

"I don't understand. I don't understand."

I started crying again. I missed Florencia. I missed our square and the forks and the canal where Bayfish lived in his shack and the mongers. I didn't understand this place.

"Get up, Banto. Get up," Moriviví said. She bent down and took the wig from my hands and held it. She leaned in and tugged, trying to lift me to my feet. "You get nothing from crying—"

"They're killing them!" I yelled. My nose clogged. I wept because I couldn't think of anything, no words to justify it.

Moriviví dropped the wig at my feet and walked off down the street until she stopped. Damaris stood over me waiting for me to calm down. She waited until I cried it all out of me. It felt like twenty minutes. Or an hour. It made no difference. I got tired and finally it stopped. Nothing was going to change. We needed to find Cami and get back. I was determined to face Ura. I needed to know why he was doing this. I wiped my swollen eyes, got up, and walked ahead of Damaris and Moriviví into the night. They didn't say anything else, didn't even bother turning on their flashlights and instead let the comfort of darkness guide us to la plaza central where the church quietly stood.

Houses and shops lined the narrow streets. Each one of them built tightly to the next, balconies from the old government alcaldía building looked sad in the silence. The old wooden doors from the historic building stained with mud. All the shops were closed, barred with plywood over their windows and doors, mounds of white garbage bags scattered throughout, some torn so you saw their insides, containers of soda crackers, cardboard boxes bent to fit, open cans of beans and empty rice bags. We scanned the roads hoping to see anything alive and moving but it was all abandoned.

At the center of la plaza central stood a large acero statue made of the taíno cacique Don Alonso. The steel was aged and dark. Don Alonso's spine arched backward, the hair frozen and hanging as he lifted something like a cross to the sky, his head in resistant praise. It commemorated the evangelization of the indigenous people, a commemoration and baptism of a reborn body, from an old tradition to an imposed religion. He was there frozen and I couldn't help but think he was us, this island, my people, like we've all been over the centuries, and it made me sad to see, even caciques fail. At the statue's footing, a plaque explained the memorial, and next to the steel-embossed plaque, a piece of wood cut into a square with scribbles in black ink. It read, "Urayoán is cacique, the true and holy, in deliverance for harmony, through *his* leadership." It must've been the reds that placed it there as commemoration. I laughed inside thinking how much Ura also failed, how Memoria was no different than everything that came before.

Damaris and I stood in front of the statue looking at it.

"It's funny isn't it," Damaris said.

"What is?"

"The things we build statues of."

"Idols or gods?"

"Does it matter?" She flipped her hair and bent down toward the makeshift plaque. "Belief is a powerful thing. And it can drive you crazy. If you're desperate enough, anything can look beautiful."

"Why did you come to Memoria? Isn't it the same thing?

You must've thought so or else you and Moriviví wouldn't be here."

"I never said we thought differently, Banto. Never said we were any different."

Moriviví ignored the statue and headed to the church steps. She paused at the top and took it all in. The church was an old Spanish colonial that overlooked la plaza central, a wide wooden door at its center. The two short bell towers topped with small domes.

Damaris and me joined Moriviví up the steps and we pushed the front doors open. It was pitch black inside; the pews scattered in uneven rows. I stayed quiet without moving and I swore I heard the echoes of church hymns, the reciting of padre nuestros, the soft stepping of the monaguillos, they were robed in white and red, they helped lead the holy train, the priest the last in line, ready to sit in front of the altar and deliver his welcome. I felt the warmth from ghosts come over me, a quiet peace reminding me vulnerability breaks even the hardest fool, even if you did not believe or carry faith, in that space, faith carried you.

Damaris and Moriviví shined their flashlights at the ceiling, the soft pink paint seemed chipped in different places, the archways bending uniformly and guiding our sight to the altar. Moriviví fixated her light on the columns near the altar. The porcelain Jesucristo speared and bleeding at the front. She walked slowly down the aisle and noticed a lit candle near the steps leading to the altar gate. We followed Moriviví until she broke out into a short sprint. Behind the column was an outline of a person fallen on the tile floor. It was Camila.

We ran to her. Damaris fell beside her, picked her head off the floor, and placed it gently on her lap.

"Cami. Cami. Vamos, Cami," Damaris said. I leaned in and traced my fingers down her arm. Sharp cuts climbed from her wrist to her shoulder. It was self-inflicted. The blood long dried. So many cuts lined her arm.

"Mori, look," Damaris said, noticing the cuts.

"Camila. Camila, it's Mori and Damaris. Banto is here too. Camila," Moriviví said. She sat next to Damaris and pet Cami's head. The three of them sat there and looked like sisters, protecting and caring for each other. And I stood over them, fat and stupid wearing my blond wig and blazer, unable to say much of anything.

"Is she . . ." I finally said. I was scared.

"She's breathing. She's breathing."

Damaris gave her a couple of delicate shakes until Cami opened her eyes. She looked exhausted. She probably hadn't eaten in days.

I RAN OUT of the church in search of water and food, anything that could help. I ran into the darkness of those narrow streets and heard nothing, saw nothing; the only movement was my body shaking with the flashlight. I left them back at the church hoping to return with something. Anything that could help. I saw a panadería at the edge of town and hobbled toward it, I barely caught my breath and stopped to rest. I took a piece of concrete and thrust it into the window, and it shattered. I kicked the rest of the glass in and climbed through, I cut myself on the elbow with the sharp glass. I rummaged through the stock hoping to find anything, but it was all old, expired, or eaten away by roaches and fungus. I yelled in anger and frustration and kicked one of the metal stools in the store, it rattled and let out a scratching sound against the hard tile floor. There was nothing that I could do, I served no purpose. I jumped back out into the dark and quiet streets and continued running until there was no more street to run on and it was just the edge of the forest, the hollow trees staring right back at me, the way they stared at you in Memoria. The vines had returned, and some moved gently with the soft breeze in the night, the trees like rows of skeletons hugging each other closely. I grit my teeth and kicked the tar on the road again because I served no purpose, I couldn't find anything to help, my fat belly huffing and puffing, the blazer soaked with my sweat, the wig drenched in a strong stink like wet dog. I scanned the dead forest with my flashlight until I realized the obvious, I knew we had no choice. We'd have to return to Ura and his brood and Bayfish and Cheo and all the others that made up Memoria. I'd see the Red Gate again, its dilapidated front, and the Tower just ahead surveying the large clearing, ceremony fires and dembow steps and tributes, decrees and reds chanting and howling. I wanted to run and run and forget this whole fucking island, leave as everyone else had done, but I knew I wouldn't. I knew this was home and I needed to remember Florencia, remember Camila, Damaris, Moriviví, Cheo, Bayfish. If I didn't, then who? Who will remember our names?

BAYFISH

I was tied to the bed of the truck and saw Ura there, his smell of salitre and his stance open. He surveyed the area by turning his head from side to side like the strobe of a lighthouse. As if he was returning victorious, from a battle, to a place I thought was ugly at its core. I was thinking about Cheo. About the mongers and Florencia and Banto. I tried to wiggle myself out from the knots on my wrists, the tight indents cutting off blood, small pinches I felt at the tips of my fingers. I wanted to put my hands over my eyes and cover them from seeing the nothingness that was this island. Seeing how Ura had taken it and bent it to break. I wanted my hands the way rivers need oceans.

The night sky was dull. I wanted to curse.

Cheo was lost, Ura's fire ate at his little raft in the open sea. He was shining the lighter I handed him against the notebooks with all his phrases, letters, and paintings. I slammed the side of my head against the metal bedding until I didn't see it anymore. Until the world turned and splintered and was no longer *after* she raged but a time that didn't exist.

Here, Florencia was being built again by Banto and me and we had cleaned all the rubble and debris from fallen walls, utility posts, broken bridges. We sat across each other clattering dominoes on a Thursday and sipped Don Q straight from the glass bottle. The night was dead and dull. There was electricity for everyone, and it didn't matter if you'd paid the bill or not, the lights wouldn't go out, nor would the water.

Memoria was built into prosperity and the reds had names, they were seated learning about Carlos Romero Barceló and the deceit, of Rosselló's resignation and an independent nation, the history of failed governors. Moriviví and Camila led legislation en el Capitolio or decided to live out their days on the beaches of Crash Boat in Aguadilla. La cordillera was no longer a shell, no longer a ghost in the center ridge of this island. Because Memoria was the center and we'd made peace.

There were cracks in all of this, and I twisted my wrists desperately against each other and flailed on that truck bed until Ura turned and kicked his heavy foot right into my gut and I felt a burning and cough.

"Keep still, Bayfish."

I didn't listen and let the rage crawl up my neck until all I could do was yell. The horror of my voice cracking into the night as the pickup moved. I shook and flailed on the truck bed and continued to yell until I felt my face warm with blood, until my voice snapped, and it became mistuned and uneven. But I kept going and I knew Ura got angrier, he looked down at me, then around not sure what to do. The pickups seemed to slow so I kept yelling until Ura kicked me again under my chin and I felt my jaw dislocate.

He crouched down to me and started to whisper. I felt blood slip from my mouth.

"If you don't shut up, my pets will take you to the semi-trailers en el Parque. To the refrigerator. We'll leave you tied in there with the rest of them all nice and pretty. And there, you'll rot and rot slow slow because it's cold. A slow death that gives you time to think how insignificant you are to this world."

I tried saying something, but my mouth felt sore and it

swelled until it sealed shut. He got up and stood again in position.

"That's right, Bayfish. We'll put you where we've taken everyone that disappears. And no one will look for you. No one will miss you."

I whimpered loudly through my swollen face and I saw it bothered him, but I felt a sadness come over. I started weeping so ugly he couldn't bring himself to strike me again and I saw his shadow looking over me desperate and crying.

MORIVIVÍ

We stumbled with Cami. She was tall and big but between the three of us, taking turns every few minutes, we managed. The stars were dim since the sun was slowly ascending, turning the dark morning into violet.

"Don't worry, Cami. We are on our way," I said to her. She was still absent, her eyes yellow with exhaustion.

Banto held the flashlight and guided us, his short wig smelling, his blazer too tight. But he was here and helping so it didn't bother Damaris and me. I felt her cuts under my palm as I supported her weight and helped her with walking. I felt the dried blood crisp into tiny scabs and I was careful not to squeeze her arm too tight as it hung over my shoulder. Damaris and me looked at each other from time to time and it comforted me to know she was there with me. Banto did the same and we descended down the road until we reached the path that was cratered and rocky and lead to the Red Gate.

We didn't want to return to Memoria but knew that sometimes, in order to learn direction, you have to go backward, even if for a moment. We knew we weren't going to stay and just wanted to make sure Cami rested, drank water, and ate before we headed down the path marked by red paint toward the dirt bikes we hid long ago.

"Mari. Mari. I miss Mari," Camila mumbled as we came within sight of the Red Gate.

"Banto!" I yelled. "Take her with Damaris. I'll go on ahead."

"Mori," Damaris said. She stopped and waited for Banto to replace me. "Urayoán's reds."

"Lo sé, Damaris. I'm going."

Banto and Damaris lifted Camila off the ground and continued walking slowly. I jogged toward the Red Gate with my knife in hand. There was a stillness in the air. There were no reds patrolling the entrance to Memoria. A thin sheet of fog rested over the clearing. I ran through the entrance of the Gate searching for a trap or an ambush, anything to spook us. But no one was there.

I rushed back to Banto and Damaris.

"Where is everyone?" Banto said.

"Come on. Let's get her to my cot," Damaris said. She hesitated to move alone with Cami. Her weight was tiring her out.

"Banto!" she repeated.

"Okay, okay. Perdón."

They set Cami on the cot. She fell on her back with her eyes shut. I rummaged through my knapsack, pulled out a plastic bottle filled with water, and tried feeding her. She resisted at first, spitting it out through her thick dried lips. I stroked her cheek and she made the effort to take small sips. Damaris took out a thin can of sardines. She lifted the tab and jerked the cover open. She fished one out and brushed it up against Cami's lips. Again, she resisted, but after we mumbled encouragement, she bit into the small fish and ate.

We spent some time nursing her until she finished two cans and almost two bottles of water. Then she fell to her side and went to sleep. I watched Banto pace around the entire clearing searching for the reds, searching for Urayoán, searching for Bayfish. He tumbled through some of the high grass near the fuel trucks, he even looked through the burned center logs used for ceremony expecting Urayoán to rise from the ashes, levitating like a small demigod. He stumbled his way to the Tower and surveyed from the cutout window and if you looked quickly without focus you might have mistaken Banto for Urayoán's shadow.

"This place is empty, Moriviví," Banto said, returning to our corner and sitting on the ground next to Cami.

"They'll be back," I said.

"What if they left? Maybe everyone got tired and went back where they came from. You know, back home."

"They'll be back," I repeated. "We should sleep."

THE CARAVAN SHOWED up as the sun reached its highest point overhead. It must've been midafternoon. A train of pickup trucks parked just outside the Red Gate. Memoria's citizens walked down. They were singing. Some banged their pots and pans and they yelled into the air. The reds did their usual dancing and jumping, wearing those tired black surgical masks and ugly red tracksuits. I got up and dusted the dirt out of my hair then held my knife for comfort. Cami still slept but Damaris sat up on her cot. Banto was the first to make it to the incoming crowd. They gathered in the center to perform ceremony. We thought Urayoán was the last to come through the Gate, but behind him followed the reds dragging Bayfish. His ankles and wrists were tied with a thick rope. They dragged him through the dirt and short grass as if he were a heavy sack of potatoes.

Banto ran up to them, but the reds noticed him coming and circled him.

"Ura! Cabrón! What the hell is this?" Banto yelled. Damaris and me sprinted toward them.

"Ura!" Banto repeated. But Urayoán kept walking to his seat at the center of ceremony.

"Vete pal carajo. Cabrones. Mamabicho," he said to the reds. He shoved them aside trying to get to Bayfish but they wouldn't let him. They cornered Banto away from Bayfish as two others went on and dragged Bayfish until they reached the Tower. They left him there. Some of the reds went inside the Tower and the others joined the crowd in ceremony. Urayoán greeted the crowd with his arms outstretched. He shook the hands of his people like a politician campaigning for votes. And they welcomed him. They clambered atop each other and roared in a unified chant, "Ura, Ura, Ura," started by the reds but continued by them all.

Banto wasn't letting up and he pushed against the reds that circled him. But they didn't let him through. One of them snatched the wig from his head, he put it on and mocked Banto, mimicking his belly with his hands and waddling in place. The others broke out into a fit of laughter. Then they all waddled in place, which froze Banto. He stopped trying. The reds kept at it until one of them began spitting on Banto. They howled into the air and more joined in on the spitting and poor Banto didn't fight back. He flinched whenever they got his face. He closed his eyes hoping they wouldn't make the mark.

I expected Banto to grow angrier, but he didn't. He became small. I knew he wanted to cry. He slumped his shoulders forward as the reds surrounded him in a mean dance.

I took out my knife wanting to pierce as many of them in their ribs as I could. Then Urayoán's famous whistle sounded. The reds froze, threw Banto's wig on the dirt, and ran off to ceremony.

"Banto," I said to him. I picked up the wig and shook it before passing it to him. I tried patting him on the shoulder, but he shrugged me off. He took a deep breath and walked off to the Tower, to Bayfish. We followed.

Bayfish was dirty. He was curled on the floor like a cooked shrimp. The scars on his neck red and inflamed, caked in sand and sweat. His shaggy hair knotted at its tips. His face swollen and bruised. I noticed his wrists torn at the skin from all the attempts at freedom. Banto struggled to untie the ropes so I leaned in and cut them with my knife and Bayfish flopped to the floor, his arms and legs splayed out and he kept his gaze up at the clouds in the blue sky, his eyes barely open.

"Oye, pescao. Tell me. Tell me what happened," Banto said. He kneeled over him as if in prayer. But he didn't touch him. I think he feared he'd touch something tender and hurt him.

"Bayfish, what happened?" he asked again.

"I'm going back to Cami. Call me if you need me," Damaris said. I gave her a small gesture and she headed back. She wasn't trying to be rude. I knew she feared for Cami's safety.

Bayfish wanted to say something. He moved his lips, but no words came out. I went and felt around his face and jaw, my fingers gently pressing the bruise under his chin and the gorging lump near his ears. The skin tightened and it felt stiff. It was only then that I remembered Cheo. I remembered the old man. Banto locked eyes with me and we knew.

"Where's Cheo, pescao? Where is he?"

Bayfish kept staring at the clouds, his eyes watered, tears began streaming down his ugly face until he started whimpering and crying again and I knew he had been crying all night because the voice that came out of his mouth was one of desperate resentment, one too weak to give sound but still animated with grief. We stayed there for some time as the laughter and celebration continued at the center of Memoria. Bayfish continued and continued his sobbing until he finally said, "Gone." He kept repeating it the way Cami did with "Marisol." It was the same cry.

Banto grew angry. He watched and waited and the more Bayfish let out whimpers and tears, the more he struggled. He looked different without his wig on, softer in some ways, but sincere in his anger.

There was nothing I could've done to prevent what happened next because I knew Banto had made up his mind. I knew there would be no convincing him. I wanted to do the same, at least in that moment. Banto struggled to his feet. He put his wig on, straightening the disheveled ends by patting them down. He adjusted his black blazer at the cuffs, just a few short bends up his arm. He picked his cargo shorts up above his waist and they protruded with his gut and T-shirt. And he marched over to ceremony. It was the first time he moved with confidence and certainty, his head held higher, his shoulders spread backward.

The reds saw it coming. They saw how he moved, and they simmered down. The noise gradually dying until there was only silence. The citizens seemed to pick up on what was to come so they followed the actions of the reds as they parted a path that lead to Urayoán. Banto so brave. Banto believing more than he'd ever believed before. Urayoán stayed seated, expecting the challenge as if it were some old tribal affair, a war for chiefdom, a battle for a false cacique.

Banto stood before Urayoán letting his anger and courage grow. He clenched his fists. I made my way into the observing crowd. I noticed Damaris looked on from our corner, she petted the forehead of Cami, maybe as a way to sooth her and keep her at peace. I tried squeezing myself closer to Banto and Urayoán but the crowd huddled tightly, a natural circle formed around them both and I was forced into witness. Banto then let out a barbaric yawp and the reds grew excited. They bounced around kicking aside pots and empty boxes and trash out of the way. They made a short but sturdy human rink around Banto and Urayoán. They growled and bit into the air. Some started howling. At first it was just the reds. But the longer they went at it, building and building the suspense and coaxing Urayoán from his throne, the more citizens bought into it. Soon everyone jumped and growled and bit into the air and I too felt my body leap trying to get a view.

Urayoán stretched as he rose from the throne. He cracked his neck and scratched the edges of his beard and combed his fingers through his long damp hair. He was much taller than Banto, at least twice in height. Yet Banto grew because of his conviction. Banto so brave. They stomped toward each other, the reds flogging their hands over their heads and everyone mimicked them until the hands, closed and fisted, resembled a field of reeds on a small open prairie.

Banto readied his stance, spreading his short stubby legs apart, and lifted his two fists just below the line of his eyes. Urayoán let his long arms sag at his sides and he sauntered around Banto, coaxing him to take the first swing. He swayed around poor Banto but Banto didn't give in. He waited as Urayoán continued to orbit around him until Urayoán leaped into the air and delivered the first strike. Banto took the hits as he covered his ears. Urayoán struck and struck without letting up, threw different punches into the head, the fat gut, even tried swiping Banto's legs from under him, but none of it phased our Banto. He waited and absorbed every blow, letting out short heaves as the hits fell.

"Pelea, maricón. Make your move you piece of shit," Urayoán said. He backed off for a few minutes and tried catching his breath. Everyone around raging with that kind of special ecstasy you only get when watching violence performed. A vicarious thrill knowing you aren't the one getting your face split in different patterns, your eyes pulped like a smashed plum.

It was a quick jab. Banto took his first short swing and it missed Urayoán and that's when Urayoán tackled him and threw him on the ground. Banto waited as Urayoán readied his blows and that's when Banto grabbed Urayoán's face and thrust his forehead into his nose. The popping sound resonated throughout the clearing the way a baseball rings against a metal bat. And he fell to the ground and rolled over covering his bleeding nose. It was an unexpected hit, but it knocked Urayoán out cold. And that's when I thought Banto could actually win. He stood over Urayoán and kicked his fat legs into ribs, into the waist, then took the hard edge of his foot and pelted Urayoán on the head and neck and Urayoán flailed on the floor, still covering the bleeding red mess spurting out from his nose. I cheered Banto on and he turned to me and smirked, as though he couldn't believe he put so much hurt on Urayoán so quickly. He turned back to him and started circling Urayoán the way he had done at the beginning. He must've fancied himself a short and fat rendition of Ali, moving those legs of his in crossed patterns, and I felt him so confident in his victory. He continued mocking Urayoán until a red from the crowd extended his foot out and Banto did not see it. He stumbled and fell, and his chubby face landed on the edge of one of the logs. Banto rolled over on the dirt holding his face together the way Urayoán was doing and they both floundered on the floor like stranded fish out of water, hoping for someone to save them from suffocating.

The reds, their loyalty to their cacique unmatched, broke the rink of bodies and helped Urayoán to his feet. They took some dirty towels and cleaned the dark blood smears from Urayoán's open nose. And he collected himself and began laughing at how sloppy Banto looked trying to massage his face. He rammed down on Banto, fell right atop his gut, used it as a seat, and let loose. Every punch reverberating, the sound of bone against bone, Banto looking helpless and dead, his face quickly changing from the color of skin into a salad of red and split flesh. Urayoán went and went, letting out howls that spooked the crowd into silence. I tried breaking the line, tried my best to cut from the ranks but the reds held the circle. I was certain he'd kill him. Banto's body stopped moving, stopped trying to buffer the fists.

Then Bayfish appeared. He threw a metal pot at Urayoán and the pot grazed the side of his face. Bayfish found his voice and yelled, "¡YA!" It shook everything and I thought God himself paused to listen. Bayfish came up to Urayoán and pushed him off Banto. He grabbed Banto by his arms and tried dragging him away, but the reds stood firm, blocking the path, until Urayoán waved them down.

THE SUN HID behind a dense cloud for some time and a shadow swept over Memoria. Then rays cut through, parting the cloud, and each tree that edged the clearing let off sharp spike outlines on the ground. The contrast of pain and dread against a bright sunny day left me feeling detached from myself, as though I floated over Memoria and watched from above how satisfied everyone looked or felt after the spectacle. I wondered how Banto would recover. He didn't have a face. No matter how hard Bayfish took damp towels to it, the blood kept seeping through the open skin. He let out these high-pitched breaths and it made me sad.

We helped remove the black blazer from his body, the wig bloodied, its color stained so that it no longer resembled any shade of blond. I cut his T-shirt off of him with my knife, a way to let his stomach bruises breathe. The skin around his ribs discolored in different patterns, hematoma rings covering every curve along his side.

"He needs a doctor," I said.

"There are none," Bayfish said. He continued dabbing the blood.

"It's internal, if he has anything punctured, he could—"

"Die?" He turned to me and shook his head. "We're all going to die here."

I got up and started making my way back to Damaris and Camila.

THAT NIGHT, THERE was no ceremony. Everyone slept in complete darkness. The clunky spire from the Tower grew as the moon passed, the ghosts from all the yelling heard that afternoon still ringing throughout. Some chatter could be heard from time to time, the reds near the Gate, Urayoán drinking in the Tower, the humming from the critters in the forest. In that full moon, in its white glare, Memoria radiated, and I grew restless.

Damaris slept quietly next to Cami. I couldn't sleep so I sat on my cot and looked over the clearing lost again in thought, the way we reconstruct the past when everything quiets and stops. We linger hoping to make sense of the steps we took, the choices that failed us. I waded through the streams in my mind fishing to discover answers. But all I kept seeing was a great fire burning out in the ocean, all I kept seeing was how our island bent under the tender moonlight and everything shook in the light's timbre. And there were no answers. Just thought.

We made efforts feeding Cami and it got better. She started sitting up to eat and even smiled as she chewed. Bayfish and Banto were in their corner sleeping but Bayfish grew restless too. I could see from our corner how he sat up as the night dragged. He stared in Banto's direction and then he stood up. He paced a bit, slowly petting the scars on his neck. He then walked toward the Gate. I wasn't sure what he was up to. His long shadow cast by the moon's rays reached me. I think I saw him look at me and we stayed locked on each other in that darkness. I imagined a sense of guilt, so heavy it bruises your feet and keeps you stumbling, every step reminding you you're at fault. I didn't want that guilt. I wouldn't carry it. Damaris and me knew we wanted out and we planned to leave Memoria as soon as Cami grew strong enough to carry her own weight. I debated and debated if we'd wait until Banto healed, but I knew there was no going back for him. All I kept thinking about was Cami and with Banto weak, with Bayfish fragile, they'd come after her and hurt her. I promised myself I wouldn't let that happen.

Bayfish continued. The reds at the Gate, even though they noticed him there trekking, they chose to ignore him and continued babbling. So, he walked out and disappeared and that was the last time he'd see Banto, sleeping and forgetting, dreaming and fighting, a mind lingering with a love for a past that no longer existed.

URAYOÁN

Goldiflón is sleeping, still bathed in the blood I ripped from his skin. He looks special and I want to make him a statue atop a mantle, a figure standing erect the way Jesucristo keeps. I think he looks good in that light, how moon decorates everything in a blue and white so I know it's time to set him high and mighty and spirits will welcome this since they speak to me in my dreams.

I see him in all that glory and Hagseed goes strolling in the dark talking to trees somewhere. My pets and I carry stealth in our steps, floating over grass and dirt you never tell we walk those trails. I promise them a gutting and they will receive—because of my genius—my gift. And we march in silence and only the moon lights the way, all the creatures sleep peacefully because that's what I create. I let out soft and delicate whistles and my pets follow, and we stand looking at goldiflón and he's broken perfectly in places I intended. The reds, they seethe in anticipation and I give them the nod they've dreamed about for months, they stick a dirty sock into goldiflón's hole because it's not a mouth anymore given how shattered I made it.

They swift as stars running, again floating over grass you never see or hear our existence. Goldiflón is lonely, no Hagseed to shelter him and keep safe. Nobody to fend off my creatures in the night. They take him and disappear between those wicked trees and we carry him deep, away from spectators. No sound will carry. No one will hear. Goldiflón tries his best to wiggle free from our grip but he's broken, broken in body and soul. He gives up as fish do on land and that satisfies me.

The reds are hungry now, hungry to see me perform. They often sacrifice the dogs and even stray people if the appetite is unbearable. But not tonight, tonight is for cacique. I love all the beauty in a fallen forest, how nothing remembers sound, how apparition is the only company trees keep, how I see the broken and dead logs and isolated leaves sprouting haphazardly. Those leaves forget how the wind feels, how to grow and turn a proper green.

We continue deep and deep until the trees freeze and the water in Caonillas greets our presence, and I bow to her because she is memory, always knowing her origin just like me, cacique of Memoria. The reds like to stash some bones belonging to those dogs they skin and eat, which I never bite into because a good cacique does not eat the scraps and saves taste for just desserts. Like now. Like goldiflón.

He murmurs again and it's just vibration in the night, no words squeeze through his broken teeth. He shakes that mass above his neck, that thing that used to be a head. And I guess a plea for freedom murmurs free. I don't understand why he fights it since I will soon give him freedom. I tell him I made the promise years ago and nothing matters in this world but words. "It is time for you to return to God, goldiflón. It is time we send you off because you are a puppet stuffed and made to guard, that is your use," I say this to him and whimpers are the only sound I hear, no words for poor goldiflón. My pets grow restless as we wait under the full sailing of the moon. My pets are readied to perform, and I start to think how tender the skin is, since blood comes out with an ease like paper cuts into thumbs or birds drifting in wind streams. My reds, how ready they are to see their cacique finally finish the task. This time is for wood sharpened at ends, not guns that don't let you see the brightness leave a body. They hand me a sharpened wood, thin but sturdy like a log. It means I need the thrust and not the cut. I see goldiflón, I see him give up and know he comes to the end of things.

I tell the reds, "Ready the wig and the fat one's blazer since he deserves it in fine clothing." They bring forward the blazer and wiggle him into it, the gut shining bare, no shirt but the blazer. They run to the river and drench the dirty wig and wring it many times, damp and leaking, they force it down on that mass above his neck and he might as well be a scarecrow, that is how I see him. I see the glint in his eyes fading, at least the sliver that is staring back at me. My pets start barking and barking and I hold the spear in my hand and look at the stars and see them wrapped in clouds, see the celestial bodies floating in patterns you never can see when this wretched place used to be a constant bright. I think about my old home, my wonderful sugarcane mill and the way the stalk chimney protruded out from the ground. I think about the barrio, Florencia, the mongers and their fishing, and I think it must be how a person thinks before they go, how goldiflón is thinking right now, a composite in memory, collages meshed to declare an existence, and that makes me sad, for the first time in a long time I feel. How desperate the mind is to grab on to what is available, to remind you that you carried worth but how soon you are a flatline, a drifting gale, a monstrua like María, capable of performance, of death, but how you too will stop drifting. I tell myself I am **Urayoán**, a name bold and beautiful that is remembered for memories eternal.

The reds start howling and I hold on to the spear and it

trembles in my hands, which is all a surprise to me. How easy it is to cave a face in, but to spear a heart, you know it ends. They bark and howl and growl and the night is not quiet, the river tumbling to origin, the crickets evil in their choir, the coquíes forgetting rhythm, the moon daring action, and I growl with the reds and take the sharp end and goldiflón is a beautiful lechón, his hide coarse when the tip first touches it, but as I thrust deep into the gut, he shakes and cries and I hear his voice finally and it is a sad note he plays. I wriggle the spear deeper feeling how it stumbles through organs, how it is not graceful at all in entering, and I shift it upward until there is a large enough hole in goldiflón the reds celebrate. They hold him upright as I continue searching with my spear for the heart, the tear on his gut opening and opening until it's snakes that tumble out and slop in a beautiful embryo onto dirt, a stillborn falling out from a dying mother, the heat of organs steaming and radiant against the white light of the moon. And goldiflón feels it all fall out of him and he no longer fights or struggles, and I feel sadness, I even sense a tear slip from my eye, and I am grateful the darkness hides these things. I let the spear hang inside the body the way a lechón cooks on a spit. I turn away, the reds celebrating and getting on their fours smelling the peach snakes on the ground and touching the fluid they are wrapped in, all more than blood, a sort of mucus that only a body produces.

I take to washing myself in Caonillas, the cold water piercing my hairs, I touch the pebbles under my feet, twist them between my toes, and they tickle. I am naked, and the moon is me and I am it since no one is there with us, we're married and the same. The reds laugh as they still marvel at how things gut with a spear, they tell jokes as what is left of goldiflón rests on the grass and soil, they wait for me to be cleansed and that's what I do, I wash my hair and let it all drift through me, the thick dirty sheet floating behind and under my head and ears. I start to tremble remembering the sounds nature made after la monstrua performed her violent transformation of this island. I tremble because that is natural for the body, things born weeping, to tremble. I think it is the spirit that remembers, and I start to cry now in the river, like the scales fell off my eyes, me floating and looking out to stars in a glowing haze with the moon. I wedge and anchor behind a boulder knowing my pets are cackling at a close distance, and I feel the tears mix in with water from the river, knowing that god is mother and taught me language and tears. I think I hear her, mother, spirits, god, in the ruffling, in the trickle of water against stone, how it is meant to sooth which is why water is origin since we all came in it from our mother and her womb. I hear her. She teaches me to cry, and with my tears I drown the earth.

They know how bodies are forgotten. They know how we care for the dead after she came. I only whistle my sad notes and it is done, the reds carry goldiflón, first dragging the organs but I tell them to tear them loose and they do, struggling since it fights to stay connected to the body, the way the mind fights to stay connected to life, maybe that's what spirits and ghosts are, the mind in energy too stubborn to flatline. My perfect pets carry him over their heads in celebration and take him away. I first think goldiflón is like the fat sister we stored in the great refrigerator, that we keep him there as part of the collection, but goldiflón is a scarecrow, and I remember my rage and it climbs into my stomach and crawls up and up and I am angry because I'm reminded of how much I disliked goldiflón in life, so he doesn't deserve preservation. But what bodies deserve preservation? I think this, then I start to get existential and that frustrates me, so I shift my mind to how beautiful goldi-flón looks with the spear holding him upright, so that's what my pets do and we leave him readied, near the perfect trail, and those stumbling to find things will come up to the famous scarecrow and see the rot change him, collect maggots, flies, cockroaches, ants, and they will flee, if only for smell alone. That is the portrait I paint, and it is perfect in nature, now that I change and transform landscape, the way Memoria is, the way we all are. And so what with it all. It is not about my feelings or my voice but my ability to cry and if they hear me, they will learn from our mistakes.

FOUR

MORIVIVÍ

I am fire and flame. When we woke up, Bayfish was yelling to himself. He threw his cot against the tree bark next to his corner. He shifted through his trunk turning it over. Damaris woke Cami and me.

"Bayfish lost it, Mori. He's been yelling all morning," she said.

"And the reds? And Urayoán?" I asked.

"Nowhere. Everyone's wondering the same thing."

The citizens of Memoria scratched their heads in confusion. The morning was dim. Thick clouds hovered overhead, and it felt cool. The wind nipped our skin.

"Where is he?! Where?!" Bayfish yelled. I ran up to him and Damaris followed me.

"Banto?"

"Where is he?! He didn't just up and leave? He can't even walk!"

I started to put it together, but I didn't want to tell him because I think he knew. The only thing I could offer were words that served as temporary tonic.

"We'll go look for him then. We will all go look for him."

"Where?! Where is he?!"

He fell to the ground, his face still swollen from the other night, his eyes squinting and his long neck sagging as he started to rip grass from the ground. He tore at it in desperation, the blades falling over his lap and the dirt sprinkling over his hands.

"They took him. I know they took him. He couldn't walk. Those bastards took him. Esos cabrones."

WE MOVED THROUGH the thick forest, the long trees hovering over, their thin branches and short leaves revealing an uneven sky. The sun made attempts at shining through the clouds, sometimes lighting up our walk. But most of the time it was overcast. Cami managed her steps cautiously as Damaris hovered near her making sure she didn't overexert herself. Bayfish was different. Bayfish broke into short fits of speed and surveyed ahead and he returned only to scramble ahead of us and return again. He poked his head through the rows of eucalyptus, cut through some of the vines and even searched under broken and fallen logs, at times climbing atop small granite boulders hoping to see Banto from a distance curled and sleeping on a mossy bed, or hiding under a wall of fern leaves. I watched him knowing he wanted to feel control, no matter if it was in vain.

We followed Bayfish's lead until Damaris noticed Cami slowing and that made her angry.

"Are we just going to keep walking?" she yelled from the back. Bayfish didn't let up. He went on until he was far gone. And I let him go. I stopped and waited on Damaris and Cami to catch up.

"He's gone on ahead," I said.

"Sí, claro," she bumped her shoulder against mine pushing past me. I turned to her upset.

"Damaris—"

"No, Mori," she snapped at me. "You said we'd leave this place. You said we'd all leave today."

"Banto disappeared—"

"He's dead. You know that. You know they must've taken him while everyone slept."

She lifted her arms and rested them just over her forehead in frustration. She swept her hair back and rolled it into a knot.

"Mori, let's just go. Let's go now. Cami is sick. She's tired. Let's go—"

"Go where?" I paused. "Where do we go?"

"Anywhere."

"Anywhere?" I mocked her.

"I want to go home. See Mari. I want to see my Marisol," Cami suddenly said. She picked up a branch from the floor and twisted it over itself until it snapped. She turned it between her fingers and used it to poke the rotting leaves on the ground.

I let out a sigh and continued, leaving them behind me until they eventually followed. The line of trees ahead thinned until they opened out in front of Río Caonillas. Bayfish stood at the edge of the river and watched it tumble over the rocks and logs. The river was lined with large pale boulders and rock cliffs that made it glow when the sun hit. If you continued to follow along its path, the river formed a small white canyon known as el Cañón Blanco. Ancient petroglyphs marked some of the white rocks.

When I caught up to him, I saw the trail of blood that led to the water, a dried pool of its dark color smeared over the bed of pebbles. Near the crest, some of the boulders had handprints made from blood, smears swiped over the rock surface.

Bayfish's long neck hung over his shoulder, then leaned into the water and took some into his open palms and threw it over his face. He let out a low scoff. It scared me a little. We both knew who the blood belonged to.

"He was here," Bayfish said.

"You can't be sure," I lied. As a reflex. But I knew.

Bayfish stood and let the water fall through his fingers and started following the river upstream, climbing the white rocks and kicking the fallen branches and twigs from his path. Damaris and Cami didn't say a word and we all followed Bayfish upriver not sure what to expect.

The boulders, few caked with moss, others dirty with dried mud, were exhausting to scale. The river snaked up the mountain in a steep hill. Bayfish wasn't fazed by the hike but Damaris started to lose strength as the rocks mounted and the angle increased. Though she felt the need to protect Cami, it was Cami who lifted her over the large stones and aided her, Cami even raised Damaris over her back and carried her like a backpack until finally the ascension ceased. Bayfish stopped and noticed a corridor of trees leading back into the reviving forest. The trees bent over each other forming a seemingly perfect archway, the crowns were tangled against each other as vines began to remember their form. Even though rays of sunshine tried cutting through the overcast sky, the tangled vines at the top of the trees created a covering, and I felt a negative energy come from that long hall. Black garbage bags stuffed with plastic and food wrappers were placed at the entrance of the path. I wanted to turn back. Damaris grabbed my hand.

"Mori, this doesn't feel right. We should turn back."

Bayfish overheard her but said nothing. He flipped his shaggy hair and entered. We waited a few seconds before following him in.

A smell started billowing. A smell of rot like that of a dead rat's carcass. We walked close together, the three of us, our hands covering our noses. Bayfish continued to lead.

The ground felt moist as we stepped. Our feet kicked up rotting leaves and the weight of our bodies snapped twigs and branches. The trees above rubbed up against each other letting out short creaks as the wind rocked and crooked their spins. Vines slithered around bark like thin snakes. Clouds of gnats hovered over the humid path. We walked through them and they stuck against our sweaty foreheads, some against the edges of our mouths and lips. We pushed forward, swatting and shaking our heads. Bayfish glided across without fretting.

We continued along the path congested with fallen branches until we came across a small rock shelter and it swarmed with flies. They buzzed against each other, their little bodies blotting out the dark inlet. Bayfish didn't care about the flies. He didn't care that they blanketed everything in front of us and just above the shelter, a silhouette, an outline the shape of a cross, crowned the entrance. The flies swarmed the mass over the rock shelter, but we all knew what hid behind their tiny bodies. Cami, like Bayfish, wasn't bothered by their infestation. She walked up to him and they both scaled the short walls up the sides of the shelter as Damaris and me stayed below, watching them stand over us, watching them clear the flies with their presence and they helped reveal Banto. His short hands propped up and tied to a makeshift cross made out of two joined logs. His face still unrecognizable except for the wig. Poor Banto's fat belly was opened and sheared, and things crawled and scattered quickly in and out of the hanging flesh.

Bayfish fell to Banto's feet, the flies moved away for brief seconds. He looked up at Banto as if praying to a porcelain Jesucristo in an empty church. He said nothing. We said nothing. Cami stroked Banto's face and the flies shrouded them both.

* * *

It was Cami who untied Banto's remains from the cross. She shifted his fat body, his limbs resisting at first until she freed him from that attachment. She threw him over her shoulder without wincing, the smell stirred by movement. I felt my stomach twist and I held my reflux back. The cloud of flies followed Cami away through the corridor as she headed back toward Caonillas. Bayfish stayed frozen over the rock shelter.

"Let's go, Bayfish. Let's go back. We'll leave this place. All of it. The four of us," Damaris said to him. She placed her hand on his back, and he said nothing. I felt the anger growing inside him. I started feeling it grow inside me too.

"Vámonos, Bayfish. Come," I said.

"I don't want to go. I don't want to go anywhere."

"Come on. We can't stay here. It'll get dark out and—"

"I don't want to!"

He stood up and jumped off the ledge of the shelter. The moist leaves caused him to slip and he fell on his back and lay there. Some flies lingered. He started to wheeze. I jumped off and landed next to him. Damaris climbed down.

I took him in my arms and rocked him for a bit as he continued wheezing against my chest. He didn't cry. He was too spent for that. His anger spilled over. I rocked him back and forth, waiting for him to settle so we could return back to Memoria.

We made it back to the entrance where Caonillas rumbled. Cami placed Banto's body near the line of water. She lay his head on a small rock. She took some long palm leaves and placed them over the rest of him, covering the hole in the gut, covering the stubby legs. She then took more stones and placed them in outline around Banto. It started to look like a grave and that gave us comfort. That Banto rested near the sound of water, each stone serving as a marker, a place identifiable where no matter what happened to his flesh, the stones evidenced he once existed. I knew that was Cami's intent.

After she finished the arrangement, she stood over him and crossed her chest the way you do at church on Sunday mornings. She then clasped her hands in prayer. That's when I noticed she was crying, the tears falling quietly down her cheeks. Damaris, Bayfish, and I walked up next to her. I placed my hand at the small of Cami's back. We stared quietly, remembering Banto, giving him his final ritual.

"We will find your sister, Cami. We will lay her to rest properly," I said, breaking the silence. Cami leaned against me tucking her head on my shoulder, letting herself feel again, letting herself grieve.

WHEN WE RETURNED to Memoria, the clouds were still thick overhead, pregnant with rain but unwilling to release. The sky darkened and dusk was setting in. Memoria felt still, even though the reds returned and were busy trolling citizens and barking at each other. I told Bayfish and Damaris that we'd wait until it was dark to leave, and they agreed.

Suddenly, Urayoán let out a sharp long whistle from the Tower and the citizens started gathering for ceremony. We waited until almost everyone took a seat on the logs and surrounded the stacks of wood waiting to be set ablaze. We sat near the edge of ceremony for fear that reds would force us into participation.

The reds took the gasoline and doused the center wood with it. They lit the logs and the fire roared to life shooting out sparks and embers. It crackled as the wind hit it, the orange flames erratic in dance until they found a steady rhythm. Urayoán let out a few hard laughs as he mingled with some of the reds.

He stood in front of his throne looking satisfied and content with himself. I felt fury crawl over my skin. I put my hand in my pocket and felt the blade of my knife for comfort.

"My dear friends, my people of Memoria," Urayoán said. "We wait good omens as the seafarer wanders looking for fish. Until that time, we continue ceremony."

He waved the crowd to their feet as a group of reds took to the front of the burning flame and started banging on pots with wooden mallets. They jumped and growled. They readied to perform a skit. My mind wandered. I watched Bayfish, Damaris, and Cami and they stared at the dirt. We were the only ones seated. I thought it might be a good time to leave while everyone was distracted. I nudged Damaris and she nodded in agreement. As we all stood ready to make our way back to our cots and pack, the reds started singing. I looked at the center and in front of the flame a red wore a long eighties hair metal wig. He stuffed rolls of clothes under his shirt making himself look larger and I knew what they were about to do.

The red mimicked Banto. He waddled around with his arms outstretched, then audibly cried. He fell to the ground crying and everyone broke out into laughter. He yelled out, "Mami, Mami, Mami," between his sobs. Some of the reds inspected him as if he were a lost dog. They poked him with branches, they caressed his cheeks, the red mimicking Banto started sobbing louder. A few of them ran up to the crying red and made the motion to fart on his face, the reds in the audience choreographed together and made the sound of the fart and that's when all of Memoria seemed to roar in a happiness I'd never seen.

They did this for some time until a red wearing a large
white robe and a Burger King crown walked in from the back
of the raging flame. He was tall and thin. Underneath the robe
he wore the usual tracksuit regalia. He walked over to the crying red and lifted out from underneath his robe a flimsy stick
sharpened to look like a spear. The reds pretending to fart
turned and lifted red Banto from the ground and they held
him upright and the robed and crowned red took the spear
and made the gesture of stabbing red Banto in his belly. He
exaggerated the thrust and red Banto shrieked and let the ball
of clothes under his shirt unravel and fall. "The fastest way
to lose weight," the crowned red said to the crowd and the
crowd roared with yells and laughter. He bowed and everyone
started clapping. Urayoán jumped from his throne, clapped,
then lifted his fist and everyone greeted him as he paced up
and down the aisle. He shook the hands of the performers and
citizens of Memoria like a victorious politician.

Bayfish slumped over and I felt his exhaustion. I nudged
Damaris and Cami along and tugged Bayfish's arm.

"Vámonos," I whispered to him. "Back to the cots."

WE MADE IT to our corner as ceremony raged on at the center.
The clearing was bright except for the spot where the gasoline
and diesel trucks were buried.

"Come on, Mori," Damaris said. She threw clothes into a
knapsack, but I stared at the trucks. I traced the edges of my
knife with my finger again. Bayfish remained still. I worried
he'd given up.

"Mori!" Damaris repeated.

But I didn't listen. I turned and ran into the edge of the

forest and ran its perimeter, the darkness keeping me safe, the darkness covering my steps. I watched as all of Memoria celebrated their cacique, as they praised their wickedness and I grew in anger and my steps moved faster, hopping over branches, fallen logs, and rocks.

I ran fast until I reached the corner where the fuel was stored. I picked up the diesel hose and poured some into a large red candungo. After it filled, I dropped the open hose and watched as it continued leaking diesel, onto the grass, bleeding into the soil. It kept flowing, a small pool started forming and it swelled. I ran quickly to the other hose that let out gasoline and I filled a small candungo. I twisted the cap and sealed it. I grabbed both the candungos and started back to the line of the forest, spilling the diesel from its candungo until it emptied next to the trees.

Damaris noticed what I planned to do. She ran up to me and Cami followed.

"What are you doing?" she asked.

"Go get your things. We are leaving."

"Mori—"

"Now!"

She saw my determination and resolve. She rushed back to the cots, packed what was left, then tried getting Bayfish to move and come along but I noticed he wouldn't. I stomped over to him and so did Cami.

"We're leaving now. Come on. Bayfish, get up," I said.

"Leave me here. Just leave me and go," he said.

"Come on!" I started getting angry. "This is not the time. We have to go. It's now or never."

"Leave me here," he repeated. I turned and paced back and forth and that's when Cami placed her large hands on his shoulders. She looked right into his eyes, he stared back at her. She smiled and it was the first time I saw her like that. She was beautiful in her grace. She then extended her hand to Bayfish and he took it, he listened.

We walked back to the edge of the forest where the last of the diesel trailed back.

"Do you have a light, Damaris?" I said. I hoped somehow, she carried one with her. But she shook her head. I wanted to yell into the night until Bayfish sunk his hands into his pocket and teased out a Zippo lighter.

From that spot we looked back at Memoria, how all of its citizens danced around the fire, the pots clanging, the spoons lifted, feet kicking up dirt, each person zigzagging among one another, and the fire blazing at the center. They all looked happy together. Free. Yes, free. I started to wonder if Urayoán had succeeded. In that moment, he did. He brought them a levity that hadn't been felt in such a long time, he brought them hope and dangled it in front of them, they ate it from his palm. If you froze all of them there together, they'd always remember it was him. But it didn't matter to me. It didn't change the hurt Cami felt, Banto and his memory, Bayfish and the mongers, Damaris with me.

I flicked the lighter on and slowly crouched, we all watched it and smiled as the fire met the gasoline. How the blue ring of light morphed into that soft orange, the blue and the orange rippling like a wave as it followed the diesel to the trucks. We chose not to run yet. We wanted to see it all ignite. To watch it light up the night sky.

The trail of fire ran parallel to the clearing until it cut into the base of a hollow tree, then followed inconsistently until it met the pool of diesel. A large thunder detonated, a boom as loud and heavy as a turning airline turbine. It reminded me of the night the calamity came, how she tossed full grown trees and uprooted larger heavy ones, dislocating stubborn roots, slamming them against concrete walls, against asphalt.

The fire shrieked in the corner until the hose caught the blaze and the buried trucks grumbled and exploded, dirt and debris flying into the night. And all of Memoria became the brightest spot on our island. Everything changed. The line of trees seemed to bend and aid the flame into the clearing as all started catching fire, everything falling over. Memoria cried and scattered. Its citizens shouted in desperation. We felt comfort as the Tower caught a draft and it too caught flame and stood over Memoria like a lantern shining brightly.

We lingered until Damaris signaled us to head down the slope, the same hill where we first saw Urayoán extending welcome. She picked up the small candungo filled with gasoline and we jogged downhill, Cami waddling behind Damaris as she led the way. I stayed at the back making sure Bayfish didn't collapse or get left behind.

We jogged and jogged into the darkness, the screams disappearing as time ticked away. We jogged and jogged until we hit the base of the long mountainside. It all started to come back to us, the images of us riding our dirt bikes, the trees marked in red paint, Puerto Rico shifting in the stillness of the evening light.

When we got to the dirt bikes, the four of us turned and faced the mountainside. A large smoke plume could be seen streaming upward.

"What do you think will happen to them?" Damaris asked. She didn't address anyone in particular. None of us answered.

We continued walking along the base of the slope searching for the dirt bikes until Bayfish stopped.

"Camila," Bayfish said. "Your sister. Your sister is en el Parque Ceremonial. In Utuado."

Camila frowned. She wasn't sure how to process what he was telling her.

"What are you saying?" Damaris asked.

"How do you know that?" I asked.

"Urayoán. He told me. The reds collected bodies and stashed them in a refrigerated semitrailer. She should be there." He paused. "Along with others."

Bayfish stepped ahead of us.

"Thought you should know," he said.

He kept walking and we followed him until we came across the hidden dirt bikes. But he didn't stop.

"You're not coming with us?" I said.

"No."

"Where will you go then?"

"Home."

"Here then," Damaris said. She pulled out the notebook she had been carrying and writing in, the sketches of Memoria, the sketches of people and their faces. "Take it."

She handed it to Bayfish, and he accepted.

I wanted to keep pressing him to come with us but there was no convincing him. I understood how he felt, how he needed to be alone no matter if it meant trekking like a ghost. I wanted to tell him that we'd miss him or that he always had a place with us. But I didn't. Bayfish disappeared into the darkness and we never saw him again.

We uncovered the dirt bikes. Damaris filled each of them

with gasoline. She strapped her knapsack over her neck. She kicked her bike to life. I told Cami to ride with me and we both got on the other bike. The loud coughing of the motor shook all the hollow trees around us. The short headlights flickered until they beamed, and we set off. We ducked fallen tree logs, clunky rocks, dirt that shot up from the turning wheels. We descended down until the edge of the forest cleared and it was just PR-10 again. We turned south toward Utuado centro, one last time.

We rode onto the emergency lane and snuck by the burned pickup trucks the reds placed there so long ago. We bounced over debris, our bikes shaking from all the garbage beneath. As the direction shifted and the road slightly turned, we saw Memoria lit, ablaze in the grand fire, the line of trees scorched in orange and yellow, the night sky emitting such an iridescence you'd think the stars and moon choreographed and conspired to perform a spectacle, all the light converging in that center, all memory changed with the beautiful flame.

BAYFISH

I am a child like you. Tall and awkward. They say most of my life I have had these scales over my hairy body. It's how the hair sits over the skin, tangled enough it forms layers. I used this to keep warm, which is why I don't like wearing shirts. They make me hot when swimming. I swam a lot back then. That's how we *really* met. Not because of Ura, but because you'd come to my shack in Florencia, under the bridge. You'd insist we go to Ocean Park or La Pocita and hit the water. We caught the last of the day watching people throw Frisbees along the beach, others kicking soccer balls, a few runners splashing through the foam with their dogs. This is memory.

After she came, we tried to rebuild a past. You came to me and told me about Ura's plan. You sat on one of the milk crates and tossed some of my playing cards onto the aged wooden table ready for a quick game. We did this so often it became routine. It became ritual.

"Imagine this place, pescao. Imagine how free we'll feel."

"There'll be no reason to leave. We'll make it what we want. A fresh start."

"I want a pool. A fancy one. Like the infinity type."

"Yeah. Got any architects in mind that'll haul the material all the way up into a forest?"

"No . . . but, you never know."

We laughed because none of it would work out that way and we knew it, but that didn't stop us from dreaming about the possibilities.

I still think about you. The wig you put over your chubby head. The blazer you insisted on wearing, even when the humidity soaked everything, even when it all stunk something awful.

"You think Ura will make us generals of Memoria?"

"It doesn't matter. Titles and bullshit. Coño, I'll be happy with a cot and a corner. Like he promised."

"Not always, pescao. Sometimes it means a lot. Sometimes it shows value."

"You show value. It's not what's named. It's what you are."

"Sometimes we don't have a lot. Especially if we come from nothing, pescao. You understand this better than anyone."

"Exactly. In the end you can take that to your grave, but who's to say when you dead and floating, it'll matter?"

"Now you gone in a different direction. I'm saying—"

"That it matters. Okay, mano. But not always."

"Well . . . I'd like a title."

"Oh yeah? Cabrón, what'd you be?"

"No sé. Something fancy."

"Mr. Infinity pool? Does that work?"

"Fuck you, pescao."

WE WATCHED THE evening news with the mongers down at the pier. They connected a TV to some cheap speakers and all of us collected and listened to Noticentro, how she started growing overnight. How all of a sudden, she'd enter through Humacao or Yabucoa or maybe she'd shift last minute and squeeze between Fajardo and Culebra. But she didn't. No Yukiyú atop El Yunque inhaling and blowing the huracán.

Deborah Martorell told us how intense she had become.

She pointed to her screen outlining the path. And she paused. Almost collecting herself because it seemed like she knew something she wasn't allowed to say. We could see it. No matter how hard she tried to play it cool.

"No va pasar nah. Eso es una tormenta platanera," Jorge joked.

He sipped on his Medalla and stood. We didn't say anything to him because we all knew. We all knew that was *his* way. We all needed to find our own. Jorge tossed the beer can in the trash and walked out leaving us there to obsess over how massive she would become, her piercing eye and perfect rotation. That was the last time I saw Jorge.

I MISS YOU. I miss both of you. I journeyed through the forest keeping close to the expressway. In the darkness. Under the constellation of stars. I walked so far knowing I wanted to return to Florencia. So sure I'd return to my shack and help piece each cinder block back to where it all belonged, rewire all the power and collect the trash in one place. Everything where it rightfully belonged. And I'd wait as the old government sent its resources and helped and everyone would return to normal again. I was so sure. But I didn't.

I stepped closer. Closer. North. Following the expressway, the mountains behind me faded farther and farther until the sun turned everything bright again. The fields of abandoned farms showing under the morning light. The expressway connecting to the interchange, all of it desolate. The color green slowly returning.

I followed it all until I found myself at the beach in Arecibo. The cove where Cheo drifted. The lighthouse still silent and unlit. The ashen bones from the great fire. I walked to the water's edge and took off my shoes. I stepped and felt the cold current rock between my hairs and feet and it all started to change, the bleeding sky, the reflection of clouds in the water, the ripples changing in diameter with the movement of the ocean. I thought about nothing at first because nothing would change. I only felt.

Then it all came back.

I pulled out from my back pocket the folded notebook that Damaris gave me. I fell to the ground letting the sand bend under me, the soft waves soaking through my pants and underwear. The water felt nice.

I am a child, I thought. I leafed through the pages seeing how beautifully Damaris sketched the reds, how she shaded their eyes in dark smears and highlighted their black surgical masks and tracksuits. She brushed the Tower with her fingers, the indents of her prints dabbed along the edges of the page. The Tower looked imposing against the clearing, how she sketched it. She wrote names down, so many names from every person that came through Memoria, a record of citizens, and it was a wonder to me how she collected them all, evidence of an existence. José Gabriel Hernández, Yarizel Guzmán, Adien Medina, Carlos López López, Ninoshka Díaz. All of them, ghosts in a morning fog. All of them like each other, like me. We are all the same in so many ways, they were my people. They *are* my people.

She drew Cheo. He had a round head with the white hairs left on his sides, his friendly cheeks and wrinkles on his forehead. He smirked in that rendition. I kept flipping the pages until the last one had a sketch of all of us. An extraordinary imagination. The six of us grouped together in a caricature.

I do not ever remember us together at the same time. But somehow, Damaris collected us and built us with curves and features, eyes and smiles. We looked happy.

She wrote lines in verse. Poetry maybe. Or notes. I could tell she thought about it for a long time, I felt the hesitation in the words she left behind, how the lines of ink stuttered in different places, after every few words written, how the period mark dragged along the paper. Something stayed with me. I'm sure Cheo would've agreed. The words were struck but I looked through the attempt even if they tried for erasure because we're all poetry in progress.

If we name the guanábana tree a different way,
the green fruit, spiked and ugly in its beauty,
the rot collected with time is nothing more than memory.

I don't have language like they do and don't understand poetry.

But I will say that the attempt reminds me of Memoria.

All of it struggles at something new. And that's beautiful.

I hope you see how beautiful it all was. Or is. I'll give us a title, my friends.

I am a child. Like you,

I am

I am

I am.

URAYOÁN

I am cacique. No matter how the fires and flames crawl over this place, it is written like my name, **Urayoán**—all bold and beautiful for memories eternal. I am keeper of this island and creator of harmony in my beautiful Memoria. Some will try dispelling my importance with their big lies, but I know lies like I know bugalú. I know it the way this land split in half and divided us from north to south. Maybe I am an ocean and that makes me complex. My mother was murdered by the state, and I was murdered by abandonment. But I will not fall into forgetting, I will not drug my puppets until they believe theirs is paradise too. My pets, my people, my Memoria. Complex in the beauty that has been created. My beautiful reds desperate since they don't see fire and flame like I do. They try to scatter in the trees, but they catch ablaze and they screech the way you do when you suffer from a hurting. I see them and the flame consumes everything, the fire I dream in terror is high and mean and it is nothing to me anymore, so I run into the Tower and see all that is beautiful in this life. I see the great flare, I see myself, but I am more than cacique, I want to be more since some hurts go deeper than shallow. In the blaze is a reflection of this island, no longer wretched in uncertainty, but clear like the sky after a heavy rain, how the parrots move in twilight, atop tree crowns, ruffle and tussle, happy again. I watch us all, because I am you and you are me. I think we're all cacique in the flame.

In the beginning, there was a void. I see the emptiness history contains. Then I created. I did so because no one else does. That is love. Necessity. I see abundance disappearing after la monstrua María hit, I see all that stand beautifully, all things in nature that soothe, change. I see the power my actions and my words transmit, my remit, my respite. In the beginning there was memory, old ways and wants. Yes, I need more than prophesy, to tell it more than falsehood, that caciques must live after death. I shall see legend of a storm disappear in the sneak which it came, I shall see how new governments in tall blue and beautiful Fortaleza, in that Old and Ancient City San Juan, reconstruct landscape, transform even. That it is nothing more to them, but voice forgotten and new voice repeating song. Not my song and that is what tears me in the fire. How I see the blaze escalate over my spire, how I look out through the neat cutout and see no more ceremony, see the absence of my waste, absence of my keep. I know it will hurt but I carry strength in my chest and inhale large waiting to feel things collapse over me and I gather in strength knowing how we all need connection to learn about loss and pain and necessity and grief of all things. I wish the ocean learned to speak its terrors to me, the way introductions speak of repressed ideas and meaning. The ocean, how she consumes desire and sets me dreaming, like flame and fire, burning darkness away until you learn to speak our names. She teaches me to cry, and with my tears I drown the earth. She teaches me to cry, and with my tears I drown the earth.

CAMILA

I am eyes ready to see. Finally, I was going to see you again. The last time felt nearly impossible to remember. They accompanied me because, like you, they care about me. The night was still hanging over us, a dark sheet that didn't recede. But it was nice to feel the cool of my mountain again. Things more familiar to me than before.

We rode until we reached a short fall that overlooked the other side of Utuado, and in my line of sight, far, far but still visible, was the burning of Memoria. You'd have liked it like that, lit with the orange and red against dark. The sky was pretty at night with a big fire like that.

The Parque Ceremonial was defaced and Moriviví didn't pay it attention, she parked our dirt bike close to the stones and ceiba. The massive tree with its large roots like curtains and thorns over the bark was not fallen or hurt the way the rest of things looked, almost unaffected by the transformation. The stones however, those mean boys spray-painted all the symbols of our ancestors, chipped away at the caguana with a hammer, misplaced the one with the bird and the one with the sun carved into the rock face, the petroglyphs all part of ugliness. It made me sad.

We walked together, Moriviví so close I felt her arm hair graze the cuts on my skin. Damaris also close. I was between them and it was like I was wearing this tough shell, I no longer had to be afraid of the night, I no longer had to fear desperation or abandonment or hopelessness. The dirt in the center of el parque ceremonial was heavily trodden. Many people left their trails on the ground. It no longer felt spiritual. But with them two next to me, I felt you close to me.

We walked and it ran similar to Memoria, a short clearing surrounded by a line of dead trees. Except the slope cut open and from there you could see the great flame. We walked and walked slow, slow because near the edge where it sloped was the outline of something scary. It was rectangle and rigid and looked unnatural against all the dark uneven jaggedness. Damaris heard the Energy generator still on and that's what it must have been connected to.

I was scared. I didn't know if I was ready to see you, to accept that you were dead, but their presence gave me strength. I inched closer and the buzzing from the generator grew until we stood in front of the rectangular outline. Damaris shined the light of her flashlight against it and the brightness revealed a rusted semitrailer. The side was marked with the word CROWLEY in bold white. I was not sure if I was ready and Morivoví felt this because I started to turn away. She grabbed my hand and held it in hers. Damaris grabbed my hand too and we were linked together.

They looked up into my eyes and they saw me and I saw them both strong. I nodded. I wanted to see you again, even if it meant finding a place to bury you. It was my mistake. It was selfish of me to keep you. I felt I needed you close. Close. Close.

Damaris moved us closer holding on to my hand for as long as she could, until she let go so she could lift the heavy metal latch that held the doors of the semi closed. At first, she struggled with the latch. Morivoví tugged me closer to her and I felt her hair against my arm, and it reminded me of you again.

A clank sounded from the latch. Damaris thrust the two doors open and a waft of cold air drifted out of the darkness. It was cold. We rushed back together and held each other. She shined the light into the darkness. The light grew brighter and brighter in such a close and tight space. We waited until the cold settled out. What we see. What we see. I felt their fingers press into mine and all we could do was cry. We fell down on the dirt and grass and let the flashlight fall too. We sat there, weeping. Our faces spoke of sadness. I am you. I miss you. You are gone. I know. I know.

MARISOL

All Things Are Born in Weeping

Beyond the sea there are many islands and more of us. You can't see us now since so much has been washed away or buried and all that is left is a place talked about as a pearl of the Caribbean. It's like memory and sound, fading the more time presses on. I think of Camila and then I think of Mami singing when the weather turned, and she'd smile while humming "Lamento borincano," trying to forget all that was changing.

See, she sees me in that light and in contrast is when we are most visible. Which is never really about us at all, is it. It is about you. The memories soon forgotten from that place impossible to reach. The trails marked in red paint lead you to rediscover, remember, a Memoria scripted with grave-yards. Memoria held together if only to keep that desire to be complete.

When she took me out from the membrane, I felt cold. It was always cold in that open space. The living do not see it as confinement though that's what it is to me. My comfort is in a frozen river or impossible oceans. And hers is the open air. She wanted me free. I wanted to stay there in my room and be safe where no one could find me even though no one was looking. There, I can forget that my mother tried, and so did my father, and I wouldn't have to remember disappointment. But there are no more parents, no more aged bodies giving wisdom.

I wanted to tell her that it was going to be okay. That she would find me someday, if not in her life then after. Memory can be fraught and evil when it tiptoes close to recollection. Never material and exact. But they took me from her, before I had a chance to leave her with a path clear enough to walk on, they took things as they always did and so they took me away, filed me into a refrigerator with no memory. She needed me and I left her there as empty as this island. And there can be no more words telling about our survival. And there can be no greater ache.

The sea tells us there are more islands and that there are more of us without names. Only memory. It is not us who remember but the water that brings us home and rocks us smoothly. Smooth and soothingly I sang as much as she did when we set our eyes into a broken horizon and wished to forget. That moment was ours.

When she took me from my embryo, she placed me in a deep and dark cave above our town. The sharp stalactites biting down at the lips. The fruit bats rushing out at night and she felt their sloppy formations hit against her dark cheeks. But that is not important. What is, is how desperate she was to stay with me for as long as she could. And I pitied her for it because I was very happy to not worry about my language forced into famine. That I didn't have to live in the periphery of myself.

There are more sentiments here than exist in a lifetime, all of those cries and wails caught in the air and splintered by hearts. There are more lives on this island divided by the millions left stranded overseas, shrieking back home to the sound of static.

When you tried calling your mother over your phone, you heard nothing because all the satellites stopped working for us. So you dialed each number in your register hoping it sparked to life a person on the other side. In that vulnerable space, you soon learned that help was delayed or would never arrive. At the center of knowledge, cities flood under water.

VELORIO

That morning, as the force and pressure and wind hit the shores of Humacao and Yabucoa, every person on this island heard her voice. They rose from their dreams, not under the weight of soft blankets, but with a roar spiteful and heavy as blue cobblestone. It's you that felt so heavy, wanting to escape by riding the wind toward heaven. Instead she served as an anchor, sinking you so deep beneath the waves that it became impossible to hear the wind anymore, uprooting everything you grew up with and turning it brown and beige. You sunk so deep into those depths of water as the monster clamored and raged outside, you heard the lost sailors from our past sink in the rising tide, so far and deep into those sea currents not searching for life but searching for death. A soft blanket covered in bleached coral like bones. A sea foaming with rabia.

I'll tell you about genesis. Memoria runs like a city with a heart, the river pulsing in the exterior serves as a vein carrying memory to its origin. It is said a man caught a mass, a green and scaled creature that looked like a shrimp. Scars crawling up to its neck. The man named it Hagseed and said it belonged in the ocean because shrimp did not live so far upstream, so entrenched in the sewage water that wanted release from its concrete prison. But I've seen this man and he's no different than a fish caught in a massive net, pontificating in desperation without knowing he'd soon run out of life.

There lies the false prophet, Urayoán. He knows how deep and dark caves inlet can be, yet he still looks pitiful in that net, so young and deformed and without a mother. You remember mother telling stories about men like him and how it ends. All you could ask her was if they had their own mother, if they were loved. Yours never answered the question. She deflected, continuing her tale. Said Urayoán built a home among the clearing and trees, a gang greedy to have control over whatever corner it could. She told you to stray away from people desperate for control. In your mind you thought she meant control is wanting a place called home.

In that place, you learned that there was no way Noticentro reported the exact loss of life, that they hid those cadavers deep in large barrels or unaccounted graves, and those same people leaped into a stream where they found life after their death. But none of their names were recorded in any official declaration.

There are more, there are more, there are more. There are more dead things in the water than insects in the air.

There are more, there are more, there are more. There are more elderly in nursing homes exhausted from the heat, dialysis out of reach, their skins spotted and darkened.

There are more stars dotting the night sky because the darkness leaves everything bright.

There are more stories untold by the wind than ears left to hear, and in the hearing, you learn that it was never a lie, never a tale about feeling gloom or sorrow, but about one of abandonment as abandonment was something you'd grown used to.

You see the waterfronts eroded. Far away from Utuado, from our center. Along the coastlines of our major cities, in Ocean Park, they are swallowed by the currents, and residents tired and pleading to officials cry for help, help in restoring the sand. They do not notice how our footprints first indent sand, then our imprints are brushed over by water, the sea-foam cleaning tracks because the tide consumes memory. Like the calamity, the sea reclaims, it transforms. I see it more as desperation, of them wanting to return to a past where they directed the ocean, where they believed they owned land. It's all familiar, that desire to own, it is as old as colonial families.

Casuarinas veil the fenced runway of our international airport. Appropriately, the casuarina isn't from here. It is like the mangosta, the mongoose, brought from far places. Both have embroidered their existence into the Caribbean, both remind me of home.

The casuarina forest in Piñones is etched with a wooden trail, made for strangers, made to see how wood builds over wood. This forest is far from us in Utuado, but everyone knows Piñones the way everyone knows San Juan. The building of these wooden trails is a formal act that allows us to see nature in a controlled closeness. Long palms, tamarind trees, lichen rested above tree bark, fallen coconut peels, the almendra trees collecting abayardes, they move swiftly over the rounded and sandy leaves and bite into flesh if you're not wary. Those casuarinas are as indifferent to these shores as massive cruise liners are to a foreign harbor.

You see how movement is shaken, it stirs a body into terrible trembling, it is how they carried me. In the swaying of flesh and bones, there is resilience.

I cannot save you, Camila, no more than we can control the tide from rising. We have those shores stitched across self-inflicted scars. We hold them close to us the way ringlets keep in standing water. Yet, I know how deeply we care for each other.

I have not missed and longed enough in my lifetime. I have not loved the way hunger creates desire. You see, Camila is me and I am her. We share our memory the way a mother shares the aches of a body that used to nurse children. There is a missing ghost in the space a child takes in utero. And you see me now in a cold shelf, waiting for discovery, extraction, or perhaps something as difficult as rain falling on an already swollen and gorged river. After a calamity, any cloud or wind looking to make declarations is terrifying.

I long for the warmth, the humming of voices, the singing of birds at dusk, and the soft petting from the shell that made you believe in God's love. If we live by the love of beasts, careful not to take in the comforts of acting wild, the pleasures of desperation, how an animal hungers and poaches life to stave off starvation.

We are children, Mami takes Camila and me out to the pier on Crash Boat Beach, at the far edge of our island, so close to Desecheo you believed you could reach it by swimming out to sea. And many drowned daring the waters, many fools fell into the ocean's sleep.

The pier on Crash Boat is worn and made from cheap wood. The dock pilings are busted and sanded down to stubs. Green moss has consumed much of the edges and pelicans perch their breasts on the green waters. Boats are beached on the yellow sand, lined in perfect rows, their colorful hulls displayed like sculpted paintings in a museum.

We go fishing, sit at the pier's edge, and watch the tourists swim nearby. Most of them tread under the decking and swipe at the schools of angelfish that collect below. They yell as though they too are children, discovering what it means to feel the tickling of scales on a ribcage, trying to catch the schools with open hands and watching them jet past.

During the setting hours of the day, after Mami, Camila, and I make our catch, we strip down to our underwear and jump off the pier into the water. The sun is warm, and the water is cold. The sky is colored and bleeding violet, the gaviotas and white egrets fly above us and collect on the pier with the pelicans and fishermen. We are happy floating there, the three of us, Camila smiles at me and splashes water in my face, the salt burning my eyes, but I don't care. Mami floats on her back with her eyes closed, her hands moving slowly, she kicks her feet now and then.

There's a noise unpleasant and cruel, it comes from the shoreline and you hear screaming, people calling out socorro. I turn and look and see shadows jet underneath us and head toward the shore. Underwater planes gliding and crashing into the shallow sand and a white body slopping against the foaming sea. The water turns brown.

"Hija, don't look," Mami says and covers my eyes. I yank her fingers off my face, and she lets me, her hands falling behind my head stay grazing my back underneath the water, we float there trying not to move our feet and hands too hard. I think we should swim to shore but Camila tells us to stay, to not move lest we draw the attention of the tiger sharks. She protects me, she puts her body in front of mine, in front of Mami, and we float behind her, she is our shield and I begin to relax. She is fearless even though she's so young, and it inspires me.

You see the torso of the man ashore. His arms are shredded, his bowels exposed. You see his face, pale as paper and his neck dripping in a mist of his own blood. His small intestine unraveled and strung across the sand. The lower half of his body is missing. People gather and cry for help but everyone knows he cannot be put together, some hold on to the guts, they are red and bleeding and powdered with sand, they hold on to them as if they are surgeons ready to connect the tissue and pulse it back to life. They hold on to the man's head, his hair tangled with sargassum, his eyes beginning to dream again.

We hear sirens sound off at a distance. We hear everyone, everything, but him. The tiger sharks move through the shore, disguised by the dense cloud of uplifted sand and they dance with each other then disappear deeper into the ocean's mouth, the dark cloud of blood trailing their striped bodies out of sight.

I hunger the way tiger sharks do. The way Memoria longs for peace. The way all animals hunger for safety. That even though there is an attempt to create something out of nothing, a place for shelter and love, it is, like all things, corrupted.

I imagine my sister and I growing older in Memoria because we survived María. She survives and I am her.

I see us the way you see us, unaffected on the surface, hardened beneath.

I think that Camila resents our mother and I try to speak to her because we shouldn't hold anger against our parents, they are our parents. I feel she listens to me when I speak to her.

Mami left because she didn't want to die in front of Camila. I understand this. So I tell this to her when she dreams. I also tell her I left because I too did not want to die with witness. The only regret I have is that I wasn't allowed to putrefy next to you. But she is me and she will find me. She will find me the way oceans meet with seas, the way seas die against shores, and how mountains greet the sky. Maybe it's better to say she will join us, and when she does, she will find herself.

Abandonment is something she'd grown used to.
She weeps, "We're not special, are we? Are we, Mari?"
My Camila. You are everything to me. I am always a part of you.

VELORIO

I build for you this chain you can trace back to origin and sound, to stream and river that empties close, closer to oceans. The brown water stirred by a dwelling is an embryo ready to dismember. Sometimes a seafarer reminds you how to speak again and I pray in safe passage that they'll find the routes around the island and cast, shipwrecked on a beach facing the Caribbean Sea. A cove with white sand and seaweed left ashore by straying tides. Some say we are a center that was never truly born. All I know is that my center was Cami, which is at the heart of this island.

I am more than a sight to forget the longer time passes.

I am more, so you can finally see how she carries me. Not in body or mind but a place soon after, one where I meet her, and we are together again without thinking about this or that or anything in between. You are not abandonment. You are beautiful. You are more you are more you are more.

ACKNOWLEDGMENTS

Mil gracias a mi gente de Puerto Rico. Somos creación de nuestra patria. Gracias por enseñarme como cantar, reír, y llorar, pero más por los cuentos que continúan siendo importante. Este libro was built out of a collective. I give utmost thanks to you. This novel is testament.

To our mecca, la IUPI, for taking me in and teaching when others wouldn't. To Dannabang Kuwabong, all the important conversations, care, and wisdom. To Loretta Collins Klobah, you pushed me to strive and dream. To Maritza Stanchich, always fighting for our island. To all the faculty that I was lucky enough to cross paths with en la IUPI. La IUPI es la IUPI. To Río Piedras, calle Manila, and Santa Rita. To Vega Baja, Arecibo, Bayamón, Trujillo Alto, San Juan, all the places that molded me.

To the University of Nebraska for providing a path. To friendship, Shawn Rubenfeld and Cory Willard. To Jonis Agee, for effortlessly believing in me with care and carried enthusiasm in all the times I lost it for myself. To Amelia Montes, continued support that got me through so many cold winters, and for reminding me to eat right, live healthy, continue writing and running because my mind needed love too. To Chigozie Obioma, for opening opportunity and believing in the work. To Kwame Dawes, I wouldn't know where to begin with how much you've done for me, the endless hours you were there to meet and talk it all through, no matter when. I wouldn't have gotten this far without your relentless optimism and perspective.

To early mentors that read words before I felt this would all be real someday. Benjamin Percy, Victor LaValle, Randall Keenan, Margot Livesey.

To Raul Palma, early reader, but more importantly the years of friendship and fellowship and the comfort of your family.

To Claire Jiménez, you read this and believed, reminded me it was necessary, and for showing me how important it is to have a friend of the work.

To Tara Parsons, this wouldn't be real without you and the love for this story. The edits truly made the book better. To everyone at HarperVia and HarperCollins, home and refuge.

To Jin Auh, you understood from day one and made it all happen. To everyone at the Wylie Agency.

To the institutions that helped guide me, the Bread Loaf Writers' Conference, the Sewanee Writers' Conference, the American Council of Learned Societies and Dartmouth College, the MacDowell Fellowship, *Tin House* magazine and Thomas Ross, *McSweeney's*, *Guernica*, and all the other spaces that provided.

To my dearest mother, you've done and do so much. I love you. There are not enough books I can write to repay your sacrifice, raising three boys, loving us. I hope papi is orgulloso from above. To my brothers, so much is possible.

Para mis suegros, Judith Díaz y Nelson "Chago" Santiago, para las cuñadas favoritas, Annette Santiago Díaz y Dyanne Santiago Díaz, para Rolando Ortega, para Dieguito.

And for Jayleen. The only reason this book exists, the only reason I'm still here. Te amo, mi amor. We continue to have Paris.

A NOTE FROM THE COVER DESIGNER

For the cover art I decided to use imagery of palm trees, a classic visual representation of the Caribbean, but have them blowing in the strong winds of the hurricane. The red ink splatter that comes into the page from the left is a visual representation of the reds, who were all over the island and slowly took over, but also depicts the bloodshed in the destruction.

—*Claudia Rubin*